Praise for *Sugar Daddy*

"This book devastated me in the most wonderful way. Beck and Sela are so scorching and real together that I didn't want to let them go. I can't wait to devour the rest of this series!"
—#1 *New York Times* bestselling author MEREDITH WILD

"A totally gripping take on romance and revenge!"
—*New York Times* bestselling author LAUREN BLAKELY

"*Sugar Daddy* is raw, gritty, and exceptionally hot. I couldn't put it down."
—*New York Times* bestselling author MARQUITA VALENTINE

"Wow! Sawyer Bennett steps out of her ice skates and into her Manolos. *Sugar Daddy* is a hot read that only gets better with every page." —*New York Times* bestselling author SUSAN STOKER

"I read it in less than three hours because I am a freak reader when I like something. This book is great!"
—*USA Today* bestselling author MJ FIELDS

"Sawyer Bennett has talent that knows no bounds and this book proves it. From page one to the end I was captivated and enthralled. I can't wait for more!"
—*USA Today* bestselling author CHELSEA CAMARON

"Sawyer Bennett does dark with amazing facility, drawing me in with Sela's story, and holding me there with Beck's. *Sugar Daddy* is compulsively readable, deliciously dirty, and passionately written." —*USA Today* bestselling author CD REISS

"Sawyer Bennett delivers a titillating novel that balances between the desire to seek revenge and the yearning to hold on to love. It's sexy and addicting, and I devoured every last word."
—MEGHAN QUINN, author of *The Randy Romance Novelist*

By Sawyer Bennett

THE COLD FURY HOCKEY SERIES

Alex
Garrett
Zack
Ryker
Hawke
Max (coming soon)

SUGAR BOWL

Sugar Daddy
Sugar Rush
Sugar Free

THE WICKED HORSE SERIES

Wicked Fall
Wicked Lust
Wicked Need
Wicked Ride
Wicked Bond

THE OFF SERIES

Off Sides
Off Limits
Off the Record
Off Course
Off Chance
Off Season
Off Duty

THE LAST CALL SERIES

On the Rocks
Make It a Double
Sugar on the Edge
With a Twist
Shaken, Not Stirred

THE LEGAL AFFAIRS SERIES

Legal Affairs
Confessions of a Litigation God
Friction
Clash
Grind
Yield

STANDALONE TITLES

If I Return
Uncivilized
Love: Uncivilized

Sugar
Free

Sugar Free

A SUGAR BOWL NOVEL

SAWYER BENNETT

LS

LOVESWEPT

NEW YORK

A Loveswept Trade Paperback Original

Published in the United States by Loveswept, an imprint of Random House, a division of Penguin Random House LLC, New York.

Loveswept is a registered trademark and the Loveswept colophon is a trademark of Penguin Random House LLC.

This book contains an excerpt from the forthcoming book *Max* by Sawyer Bennett. This excerpt has been set for this edition only and may not reflect the final content of the forthcoming edition.

ISBN 978-0-399-17860-3
Ebook ISBN 978-1-101-96814-7

Printed in the United States of America on acid-free paper

randomhousebooks.com

1 2 3 4 5 6 7 8 9

Book design by Elizabeth A. D. Eno

Thank you Sue, Gina, and Matt for taking a chance on me and continuing to make me a better author with each book we put out.

Sugar
Free

CHAPTER 1

· ·

Sela

"Oh, Sela. What have you done?"

Beck pulls away from me slightly, his hands holding my upper arms with such gentleness. Those eyes I've come to love swimming with fear. My own eyes fill with wetness again and with one blink, the tears go streaming down my face. I haven't been able to stop crying since . . .

"We need to get her to a hospital," Caroline says.

I immediately shake my head in denial despite the fact I'm covered in JT's blood. Despite the fact he just tried to kill me. "I'm okay."

Beck's hand moves . . . fingers touching the base of my throat so lightly if feels like butterfly wings, which is totally at odds with the panicked tone of his voice. "You've got some bruises."

I shake my head again. "I'm fine."

Then a sob pops out of my mouth, and Beck is pulling me back into his arms to hug me tight. My face presses into his chest, my arms around his waist locking on desperately. I feel slight pressure on my shoulder, followed by a circular motion, and I know it's Caroline offering physical comfort as well. Even with my eyes squeezed shut, the tears continue to leak out.

I have to tell them.

What happened.

What I did.

But I can't seem to open my mouth and make the words form.

As if sensing my inability, Beck releases me and puts his hands to my shoulders. He pushes me back so we can see each other clearly and Caroline's hand falls away. More tears stream down my face, blurring his features. But I know that same look of worry is still there.

"Is JT dead?" Beck asks in a shaky voice.

I can't answer, but merely nod my head.

"Christ," Beck whispers, and I rapidly blink to clear my vision because I need to know if Beck hates me for this.

When he comes into focus, I see he cuts a worried glance at Caroline, but then his eyes come back to me. His hands come up and palm my cheeks. "It's okay, baby. It's going to be okay."

And just like that, the stranglehold on my vocal chords releases. My words pour out in a cascade of desperation, stuttered with tiny sobs. "I didn't mean to. I had no choice. He was going to kill me."

"It's okay," Beck says in a low soothing voice, but I know it's not. "It's okay. You're safe now. I've got you."

"Oh God," I moan piteously, my eyes flicking between his and begging for absolution. "I killed someone."

"Shhhh," Beck says, his hands pressing in on my face to urge me to listen to him. "I need you to tell me what happened so I can figure out how to fix this, okay?"

"You can't fix it," I cry out as I wrench free from him. I look down at the front of my blood-soaked T-shirt and wave my hands at it. "Do you see this? I killed JT. You can't fix that."

"You need to calm down—"

I spin toward the office door, my head dizzy with stress and emotion. "No. I need to go turn myself in—"

Beck grabs my elbow, stopping me dead in my tracks and then pivoting me toward him. "You are not turning yourself in until you tell me what happened."

"I murdered your b-b-business partner," I yell at him, and it's in this moment that I realize I still have some reason about me because I almost said "your brother." I caught myself though, because Caroline's in the room and she has no clue about the relation.

My body shudders as I remember JT telling me he raped Caroline. Knowing that he's Ally's father.

As well as her uncle.

Bile rises in my throat and I swallow against it with unyielding resolve.

"Sela," Beck says slowly but with total command, still keeping my arm firmly in his grasp so I don't try to run again. "Tell me what happened."

My head swivels to the right and I look at Caroline. She has one arm crossed under her breast, the other raised so her fist is pressed up against her mouth in a thinking man's pose. But those eyes . . . same as Beck's . . . are totally filled with fear and worry for me.

I look back to Beck and take a deep breath. "He attacked me—"

"Uh-uh," Beck says with a shake of his head. "Start from the beginning. I assume he contacted you?"

My legs almost give out from underneath me as I realize from that simple question that Beck never once even assumed I initiated contact with JT. He never once considered that I went to JT's place with the intention of murder. He implicitly trusts me and I didn't think it was possible for me to love him more.

I nod. "Left me a voice mail. I listened to it when I got out of class. Said that he had an idea he wanted to run by me that would give both of you want you wanted."

"And you called him back?" Beck asks, his voice with a tinge of ice as he starts to understand the stupid path I put myself onto.

"Yeah," I whisper, my face dropping to look at my feet. "I wanted to hear what he had to say. Hoped I could help make sure things worked out."

"Then what?"

"He asked me to come to his house," I say in a voice so soft I can barely hear it myself. It's a voice of guilt and shame that I would even consider going to that man's house alone.

Beck hears those emotions loud and clear, cursing in disgust. "Goddamn, Sela. You couldn't have been that stupid to go to JT's by yourself. Not after what he did to you."

My head snaps up and my gaze slices to Caroline. I assume Beck must have told her, because he wouldn't have outed me like that. Caroline's head tilts and she gives me a sympathetic smile of sisterhood.

Welcome to the We've Been Raped Club.

Beck's hands come back to my shoulders, and his grip is not gentle or reassuring. His blue eyes no longer swirling with fear but rather looking like pale ice. "I cannot believe you'd fucking do something that stupid."

The real and normal Sela Halstead would have pulled away from Beck and lit into him for calling me that, but I can't. I was so ridiculously stupid.

Caroline takes a step forward and in a censuring voice says, "Beck."

Her message is obvious. Back the fuck off me with the recrimination because I'm fragile right now. But I can't say as I blame him. I totally deserve it. I mean, *What the fuck was I thinking?*

"I'm sorry," I proclaim, my eyes sincerely begging him for his forgiveness.

Beck releases me, pushes the fingers of both hands through his hair, and clasps them at the back of his head, looking down at me as if he doesn't quite know what to do. He's angry and he's worried, and I can't even begin to imagine how he feels about me at this moment.

Caroline steps toward me, her hand coming back to my shoulder in a reassuring squeeze. "Tell us what happened."

I watch as Beck's hands drop from his head and he turns his back on me. He takes two paces and comes up against his desk, palms down onto the edge, where he leans over and bows his head to hear my story.

He doesn't want to look at me, so I turn to face Caroline. Her face so open and ready to understand and accept whatever I tell her. But there's no way I can tell her everything that happened at JT's house.

"Sweet Caroline was a lovely piece that I just couldn't resist, and she put up a much bigger fight than you ever did, which made it all the better for me."

My head swivels to see Beck still hunched over his desk, head hanging low as he listens.

Back to Caroline, who inclines her head and levels me with that look that says, *You and me, sister . . . we've been through the same hell. I've got you right now.*

God, she's got no fucking clue that we truly have been through the same hell.

Raped by the same man.

I take a deep breath and close my eyes briefly, remembering

that moment just after JT told me what he did to Caroline. He'd had the cast on his arm pressing down on my throat and my body was starved for oxygen. He was laying his body on top of me and I was filled with torn panic wondering if he'd rape me again or merely strangle me to death.

Regardless of his plans for me, my arms began to flail from near hysteria and an inherent need to live.

JT looks down at me, eyes leering not with sexual lust but with a crazed hatred. Saliva slips over his bottom lip and hangs in a long string until I feel its slimy touch on my chin. I have worse things to worry about right at this moment, but feeling his fluid on me disgusts me so much I involuntarily try to lift my shoulder to wipe the spittle off me.

My chest heaves, trying to suck in oxygen, but nothing's getting in. Everything around me seems to dim, my periphery going fuzzy and then darkening to gray. I feel so unbelievably weak.

One arm jerks, not intentionally, but sort of haphazardly slaps at JT's face. He laughs at me as it flops uselessly to the side where it hangs over the edge of the desk. My other arm also jerks and slowly starts to lower, coming down to rest softly just above my head. JT continues to stare at me, eyes practically rolling around in deranged glee as he watches me suffocate.

A lazy sense of acceptance swarms me, and I realize I don't hurt anymore. I can't even feel the crush of his cast on my throat, and about the only sensory perception I have is the hard, flat desk underneath me. The back of my head seemingly cradled by the wood, as if it were gently rocking me to sleep. A cold, thin object under my forearm as it lays uselessly above my head.

Wait . . . what is that?

With herculean effort, my brain tells my arm to move . . . to turn slightly . . . grasp for whatever that is, but it doesn't seem to want to cooperate and I realize my brain must be dying.

But then . . . something is in my hand.

And I know immediately what it is.

An image of Beck flashes before me, lying in bed beside me . . . smiling . . . hair all mussy and his eyes warm and loving.

My arm flies off the desk, up and swinging outward, only to come back in a giant arc, where I plunge the end of a letter opener into the bottom side of JT's neck and immediately pull it back in a completely reactionary manner as I'm horrified I just stabbed someone. A spurt of blood hits my neck and I see JT's eyes go from maniacal to shocked in a nanosecond, then they become enraged. I don't think or hesitate, fear driving my actions. I swing the letter opener again, and it hits higher on his neck but still goes deeply.

JT pushes up off me a bit, opens his mouth to say something, and a pool of blood spills out onto my chest. The letter opener is on the same side as his casted arm, so he uses the opposite hand to try to grasp it, but he can't seem to find it. It doesn't matter though, because the first wound is bubbling and spurting blood with every dying heartbeat. His eyes become glazed as I watch him start to fade before my eyes.

His hand tries to grab the letter opener again, but the effort is pitiful and he misses by a mile. Through the haze of pain and death on his face, JT's eyes plead with me to help him, but all I can do is stare in helpless fascination.

I suddenly realize I'm breathing again and have an immediate return of strength and determination fueled by nothing more than pure adrenaline. I bring both my hands up to his chest and shove him off of me. JT makes a gurgling sound as he starts to drown in his own blood, falls to the side, and drops to the floor out of my line of sight.

I immediately scramble and roll to the opposite side, lowering my feet to the floor and keeping the desk in between us. I'm fairly sure he's incapacitated, but I'm not taking any chances. My head sweeps left and right and I finally see my gun lying at the base of a set of bookshelves. I run to it, coughing and wheezing, my throat on fire.

With sure hands, I grab the Walther PPK and swing it immediately back toward the desk, imagining the worst and JT crawling over the top of it toward me.

But I don't see anything.

Carefully, I sidestep my way toward the desk, trying hard not to cough and hack but not succeeding. If he's alive, he'll hear me coming a mile away as my sore throat rebels and demands I ease the pain and scratchiness with repeated barks of hoarse air.

With the gun ready to fire, I hold it out before me with a sure grip, round the side of the desk, and point it down toward the ground.

JT lies there on his back, eyes open but not seeing anything, the letter opener sticking crudely out of his neck and a pool of blood starting to form under him where it's starting to well and push its way past the object that made the hole in the first place.

JT's dead.

My rapist is dead and I feel like my life has just been ruined.

. . . .

CHAPTER 2

Beck

Fuck, I hate hearing these details. She was almost robotic in her retelling, as if she was reciting merely from a bad memory she tucked deep away so as to protect herself, and it was too painful to bear repeating.

"All these months, I wanted him dead," Sela whispers in a voice laced with pain and regret. "But now that he is . . . I don't want that. What the hell have I done?"

I can't stand it. I'm pissed she put herself in that position, but the depth of her anguish is making my hair stand on end. JT deserved her retaliation, but she's not seeing that right now.

Right now she needs validation that her soul hasn't been tainted. That she was merely ensuring her own life would continue and defending against someone else's attempt to take it.

Pushing away from the desk, I turn to see Sela staring at me with tears pouring down her face and eyes so burned out by grief that they're streaked with redness. I can't fucking stand it, and in two strides, I have her in my arms and lifted from the floor. As I cradle her gently, I tell Caroline, "I'm going to get her cleaned up."

"Beck," Caroline says cautiously. "Wait . . . it was self-defense. We need to call the police. It's bad enough she left the scene, but you cannot go cleaning up evidence off her."

I turn from my sister, noting Sela's head lying heavy on my shoulder as tiny hiccups echo periodically. Caroline rushes to the office door, puts a hand on the knob, and holds up the other. "Just wait a second . . ."

"Open the fucking door, Caroline," I growl at her. "Yes, it was self-defense, but how does Sela prove it? Once they find out that JT raped Sela, there's a damn good chance they'll see that as nothing but a motive for murder. In fact, it will seem more likely since she went there with a gun in her purse."

"But she did nothing wrong," Caroline implores me, even as she twists the knob and opens the door for me. She knows I'll just do it myself. I slide past her, being careful with Sela's body in my arms.

"I know she didn't do anything wrong, but do you think the justice system will see that? The police and DA want convictions, not a messy death with no evidence to support self-defense. I'm not willing to take that chance."

"She has bruises."

"That they'll say were caused by JT merely defending himself," I say bitterly. "Again, not willing to take the chance they won't see it our way."

"There will be physical evidence at his house connecting her," Caroline says as she follows me down the hall to our bedroom. "Prints or some shit like that. That's always how they get the suspect. With forensics."

"Maybe, maybe not," I say as I head straight into the master bath. I hear Caroline close the door behind us, and I have to assume Ally is still happily occupied in front of the TV. Fuck if I want her to see Sela covered in blood. "But I plan to rectify that situation as soon as I get Sela taken care of."

"Beck," Caroline snaps at me in irritation. "Don't put her in that shower until we talk about this. This is Sela's decision, not yours."

"You're right," I say softly, and lower Sela to the tiled floor. Her feet touch solidly, but I keep my arm around her waist, because she looks like a delicate breeze would blow her away. One hand goes to her cheek and I get her attention by tilting her face up so she looks at me.

"Sela," I tell her with a mixture of authority and empathy. "I don't think it's a good idea to go to the police. You'd never be on their radar. They have no clue about your history with JT. I'm going to do everything in my power to ensure they don't find that he's dead."

"But she looks less guilty if she goes to them now," Caroline points outs.

Sela's eyes never leave mine. She never considers Caroline's words, but I feel the need to clarify. "Baby . . . if they come after you, you still have the truth of what occurred. That will always be there."

Caroline makes a frustrated noise but turns away from us, almost as if she's giving us privacy. She knows she's said her piece and she also knows that even though Sela has the truth of what happened on her side, the mere fact she didn't report it right away will be held against her.

But I can't risk it.

Sela has more motive for murder than anyone on this planet. She'll be a district attorney's wet dream as a murder suspect. Hell, until just weeks ago, Sela *was* planning to murder JT. Too many things could go wrong.

"The letter opener's in my car," Sela murmurs. "I wanted to get rid of it but didn't know what to do."

"I'll handle that," I tell her, my thumb stroking her cheek. I'm going to handle so much more than that, but she doesn't need the details.

"Then I'll do what you think's best," she says softly, her shoulders sagging as if she can't handle one more burden.

I lean in, give her a soft kiss on her lips. Chaste. Reassuring.

She can count on me.

"Take your clothes off," I instruct Sela as I stride over to the huge walk-in shower and turn the water on. She complies immediately and without any regard for Caroline, who now stands in the doorway, watching us both with a nervous bite to her lip.

I gather up the clothing . . . the gray hoodie that I have no clue where it came from, blood-soaked T-shirt that leaves her skin rusty brown when she peels it off from the sheer volume that leaked through and dried. Sela disrobes like a robot, eyes almost dead. I take each piece of clothing from her, balling them up tightly, and when she's completely naked, I put my free hand on her lower back and gently urge her into the shower. She complies with no hesitation, stepping under the hot spray, and I try not to notice the immediate swirl of blood around the tile flooring as the water hits the remnants of JT that are left on her body.

Turning to Caroline, I lean in and whisper, "When she's done, you get her dressed and into bed. Then you pour every bit of bleach I have in this condo down that drain, you hear me?"

Caroline's eyes widen in fright, and because she was so adamantly against this, I think she'll complain. Instead, she just nods her head, and I know that our course has been set, she's on board with me and Sela. She may not agree with the way I'm handling things, but she'll help to protect the secret we're slowly creating, one lie at a time.

I walk out of the bathroom, acutely aware of Caroline following me. When I hit the hallway, she murmurs so Ally can't hear us. "What are you going to do?"

"I'm going to JT's house and I'm wiping that place down so there's no trace of Sela. Then I'm going to make sure these clothes and the letter opener never are found."

"I'm scared, Beck," Caroline says in a quavering voice, and I immediately feel crushing guilt that she's been dragged into this.

"It'll be okay," I reassure her, pulling her into me for a tight hug. She clings to me desperately and I press my lips to the top of her head. "I promise it will be okay."

But right now, I feel an impending doom over us all.

The letter opener and bloody clothes can wait. Potential prints and DNA cannot.

I went down to Sela's car, using the extra key fob I kept secured with my Audi's key to gain entrance. She wasn't stupid . . . having apparently grabbed paper towels from JT's house to wrap the murder weapon in. This told me she had presence of mind after it was all said and done. It also told me she ventured into other parts of the house that would have to be cleaned up.

But it was late Monday afternoon, heading into early evening, and to my knowledge, JT wouldn't have any visitors. I should be able to slip in, wipe everything down as best I could, and leave without anyone being the wiser.

I briefly thought of disposing of the body, and while I haven't completely ruled it out, I'm not sure that's a good use of my time. More important, getting rid of bloody clothes and a small letter opener won't be hard. Disposing of a full-grown male body is another matter, and it only increases my chances of getting caught. I need a quick in and out, and hope to God I'm able to leave nothing but a cold body with no evidence that will point Sela's way.

I drive to Sausalito, my brain on overdrive trying to mentally walk through everything I'll need to do to clean his place up. Before I left, I had Sela go over everything in a bit more detail with me as she was drying off from the shower. Caroline was in the laundry room, in search of Clorox that I was pretty sure I had.

According to Sela, who seemed more in control of her emotions but spoke in a detached sort of way, everything happened in the den. I was sure I had her exact path and every potential item she could have touched. She confirmed she also went into the kitchen and grabbed paper towels to wrap the letter opener in so she wouldn't get any blood in her car, as well as snagged a gray hoodie sweatshirt of JT's from the coatrack in the foyer. It wouldn't take me long to wipe shit down, but I was not looking forward to the bloody scene.

Sela said there was a lot of blood.

I can't imagine how much is left behind, because it seemed she had all of it on her body.

The thought makes me shudder, but I'm resolved.

I can do this to protect Sela, and that's all that matters.

In fact, maybe wiping down the place isn't going to be good enough. Maybe I do need to suck it up and package JT's body in one of his expensive silk woven rugs, lug it to my trunk, drive him deep into Mount Tamalpais State Park, and leave him for the animals to pick apart.

I could do that.

For Sela.

The miles melt away under my heavy thoughts and before I know it, I'm crawling down JT's street. It's fairly dark and only illuminated by high-end landscape lighting of the houses that sit secluded by privacy plantings. The lots aren't big, but the neighborhood is well established and the bushes and other plants give each home a protected, enclosed feeling.

This bodes well for me.

It should help me get in and out without being seen.

The road takes a meandering turn east, where it starts running parallel to Richardson Bay, and as I come out of the curve, I immediately see the pulsing flare of blue lights. Before I can even see JT's house in the distance, I know those are the lights of police cars.

I know they're at his house because they've been alerted to a murder that's occurred.

It means I'm too late.

I slow down as I observe three police cruisers sitting in front of JT's house about three hundred yards in the distance. A few neighbors stand out in the street, their bodies nothing more than black shadows against the lights of the Sausalito Police Department.

"Fuck," I mutter as I turn right into the nearest driveway, my heart thundering madly in my chest with newfound anxiety.

JT's been found and now the shit's going to hit the fan. I've officially lost all control over the situation.

I glance down to the console clock and I figure I'll be getting a phone call before too long. Perhaps even a visit from the police.

Of course, they'll contact his parents first, but I'll be next as a close family friend and business partner. It will probably be a visit. They're going to come see me because I'm one of the people who knows him the best, and I'm also going to be an automatic person of interest because I stand to get an entire multimillion-dollar company free and clear with his death.

I slam the Audi in reverse, and with my pulse pounding so hard I'm afraid I'll stroke out, I force myself to calmly ease off the brakes and coast slowly out of the driveway. I turn back and head the same way I came in, my eyes flicking constantly to my rear-view mirror to see if anyone notices me turning away.

Will they recognize my car?

I'm too far away for anyone to see my license plate, but probably not too far to identify the car's color, make, and model. If just one cop happens to see me, notes my maneuver, and thinks it's suspicious in any way, they'll match the car up to me.

Then I'm fucked . . . because there's no sane reason I should be out for a drive on my partner's street, see police cars, and turn around. An innocent partner would speed up to the scene of the crime and demand to know what's going on.

But I don't do that. I continue to drive away, terrified a cruiser will start after me, but ultimately making it away safe and hopefully without notice.

I head back to The Millennium, my mind now racing with all the things I need to do to get ready to face the shitstorm that's coming.

CHAPTER 3

. . . .

Sela

"I made you some tea," Caroline says from the doorway of my bedroom. I sit up in the bed, brace my back against the pillows and headboard. I'd been lying here staring at the ceiling as the sky darkened, waiting for Beck to get back. Caroline hasn't said much to me since he left, and I watched her with a weird detachment as she cleaned out the shower and poured almost a full bottle of bleach down the drain. I think neither of us said anything because it seemed just terribly poor form to discuss disposing of murder evidence.

Caroline was washing a part of my sins away.

Beck was currently off wiping up the rest of them.

It was self-defense, I remind myself.

Murder, my guilty conscience says back.

My fingers involuntarily rub against the splotches of purple that rest at the base of my throat, compliments of JT's cast pressing down on me. I swallow and make myself take note of the slight pain that occurs as I do so.

I do this to remind myself that JT was choking me to death. I had no choice but to swing that letter opener. I hadn't planned it, but perhaps by the grace of God I found the strength to protect myself.

A repulsive half snicker, half sob explodes from my mouth and I immediately slap my hand over it. My eyes well up with tears even as a laugh bubbles up and tries to push its way out. So ironic that I killed him with a letter opener, since I had imagined using that exact implement when I visited his office to meet Karla for lunch all those months ago.

Caroline walks into the room, rounds the bed, and comes to my side, which sits closest to the window-wall. She looks at me without judgment for JT's murder and doesn't seem affronted that I'm trying hard not to laugh. She smells faintly of Clorox so she has no room to judge.

"What's so funny?" she asks carefully as she sets down the cup of tea on the night table beside me before sitting down on the edge of the bed near my hip.

I reach over for the tea, using the simple action to distract my rampant thoughts and get my bearings. I pick up the cup, bring it to my mouth, and blow on it before I take a tentative sip. It's hot and I don't even mind the slight scalding to my tongue and roof of my mouth, which also helps to distract me.

Peeking over the edge of the cup at Caroline, I say, "I once visited JT's office. He wasn't there but I looked inside and envisioned killing him in there with his own letter opener. It was a pipe dream then. It's just funny to me that little fantasy of mine came true."

Caroline smiles at me with understanding. "Nothing wrong with a little inappropriate laughter. Or those types of fantasies."

I smile back at her as best I can, but it's thin and without any genuine force behind it. She sees that. She knows it.

"It was more than fantasy," I tell her with brutal honesty. Caroline just helped clean up evidence of my crime so she needs to know the full truth of what I did. That my original intention was not a silly dream but an actual plan to kill the man who destroyed my innocence.

Tears well up in my eyes again and I blink hard against them, taking another sip of my tea to ward them off.

It was self-defense, I tell myself.

Murder, my subconscious sneers at me.

Caroline turns slightly from me while I get myself under control and stares out the window, which overlooks the Financial District. She looks just like Beck. Same eyes, nose, and perfectly shaped smile.

Same moral character.

Although she wanted me to go to the police, she never hesitated to jump on board with Beck to help protect me by trying to erase my crime. The image of Caroline bent over with yellow rubber gloves on, scrubbing down the shower and then pouring bleach down the drain, ensured she became complicit in my crime.

That will be forever burned in my brain.

She's just helped me try to get away with murder, and she did so because she loves Beck and Beck loves me. It's overwhelming to me that I feel extraordinarily close to this woman that I hardly know at all.

"I'm sorry about what JT did to you," Caroline says softly as she turns to face me.

I'm almost relieved by her statement and avoidance of the subject of blood and bleach, but it's still a sobering moment as I realize that I can't say those words back to her.

I don't think she should know what JT told me in those last moments before I killed him. I can't think of any good reason why I should visit that pain upon her, and I'm sorry . . . closure just isn't a good enough reason. She's better off not knowing who her rapist was than to know it was her half brother.

So while I can't divulge the horror of that knowledge to her, I can reach out and accept her offer of sisterhood that we now share.

"I'm sorry you went through the same thing," I murmur.

"Beck was my rock," she says as she leans a little closer to me, her blue eyes focused intently on mine. "I wouldn't have survived if it wasn't for him. There isn't anything I wouldn't do for him."

Her message is clear.

"Including helping him cover up the fact I murdered someone," I whisper the obvious.

She shakes her head. "Including helping him protect what's his. And JT got what he deserved. It was either kill or be killed, Sela, and you did what you had to do to survive. It's not the first time in your life you've endured something horrible, and it probably won't be the last."

I stare at her, my eyes threatening to fill with tears again, but I command them to stay at bay. It's time to move past what I did.

"We should have gone to the police," I say with a sigh, still struggling with my biggest doubt. It would have been risky, and yes, there was a good chance they wouldn't have believed me. But by staying silent, I ensured that Beck and Caroline just became my partners in crime, and I never wanted them at risk.

Caroline shrugs and stands up from the bed. She turns to me, slipping her hands into the back pockets of her jeans. Looking down at me, she says, "What's done is done. Beck's handling it now and we need to trust in what he's doing."

I nod in agreement but hating every minute we wait for him to return from what could be either a fool's or a hero's mission.

"Why don't you come into the kitchen," Caroline says. "I made some tuna fish salad. I'll fix you a sandwich."

My stomach rumbles, and it hits me I haven't eaten since breakfast. While you would think the fact I murdered someone in a grisly fashion not five hours ago would suppress my appetite, I find myself strangely famished.

I nod and roll off the bed. Grabbing a pair of jeans from the dresser, I slip them on and follow Caroline down the hall.

"Is Ally okay?" I ask hesitantly. When I came into the condo, she was too consumed with TV to do much more than give me a sideways glance and mumble, "Hey, Sela," before turning her eyes back to the flat screen. Luckily, the hoodie I stole from JT covered the blood, so even if she had paid more attention to me, it's unlikely she would have seen anything to traumatize her.

"She's fine," Caroline assures me in an undertone. "She's a smart kid and senses something, but she's also happily watching her favorite show. I fed her while you were in the shower and she'll probably fall asleep on the couch before too long."

I glance at the couch as we walk into the living room, and Ally is lying there with a soft chenille blanket, normally kept in the hall closet, tucked around her. Her eyes are drowsy looking as she stares at *Sofia the First*. I want to go over to her, stroke her soft hair and act as if nothing's wrong. I want to joke with her, see her dimples and bask in the joy of a little girl just hanging out at her Uncle Beck's for the night.

But I don't because I'm afraid I might crumble from just her sweet ordinary child ways, which would be too much goodness for me to comprehend right now. Ally *is* the one good thing that came out of all this family's horror.

So I walk past her and follow Caroline to the kitchen, but just as we cross in front of the foyer, I hear the key slipping into the dead bolt of the door and I pause to see Beck walking in.

My heart slams to almost a complete halt, my chest constricting and the breath going stale in my lungs. He looks scared and stressed, and while there's probably a million different possibilities that could cause that, my first thought is that JT isn't dead.

Caroline stops in midstep, but rather than freeze to inaction, she turns to grab my elbow and pulls me three steps into the foyer so we are almost toe-to-toe with Beck as he closes the door and engages the lock.

"What's wrong?" she whispers so Ally doesn't hear us.

Beck's tired eyes pass over Caroline briefly, but then slide to me where they shimmer with frustration. "The police are at JT's house. They've found him."

"But how—" I start to say, because how in the fuck was he found so fast?

Beck ignores me, turning to Caroline. "Get Ally and get out of here now. I expect the police will come to pay me a visit. Could be tomorrow, could be in five minutes, so get out of here now."

"But—" Caroline says in astonishment.

"Get the fuck out of here now," Beck whispers harshly but still so low that Ally is oblivious to us. "I want you far away from here when they show up. I don't want you becoming a potential witness to anything associated with JT."

"What's that mean?" I ask, stepping into him and putting a hand on his chest.

His gaze comes back to me. "By virtue of my long relationship with him, I'm going to be a potential suspect. They're going to come and talk to me. I don't want Caroline involved."

I spin toward her and give a quick jerk of my head toward the living room. "He's right. Get Ally and get going."

Caroline's no fool. She doesn't spare us even a second more before turning away and hurrying into the living room. I hear her say, "Come on, honey. Let's get your shoes on and head home. It's getting late."

"I don't suppose I could talk you into packing a bag and heading to your dad's?" Beck says softly, and I turn back to look at him with raised eyebrows. He doesn't look apologetic over his suggestion. "We'll say you went there right after school to spend a few days with him. Your dad would cover."

I shake my head almost violently and practically growl at him. "Don't even fucking think about trying to shield me from this, Beck. If they come, then I'll be here by your side, and if they even think you had anything to do with this, I'm telling them every goddamn thing that happened."

I expect him to argue.

I expect him to be angry at me, because I know he's in full-blown protective mode.

I expect—at the very least—for him to look annoyed at me, because after the mess I've created, he deserves to at least look a bit put out.

Instead, he snatches me to him so roughly my head snaps, but then I'm engulfed in his arms, which wrap around me tight. He squeezes me hard and his voice is desperate. "We'll get through this. I swear we will."

I nod against him, not because I believe what he's saying, but because he needs to believe that I trust in him right now.

The sad truth, however, is that I think that both of us are getting ready to fall down the rabbit hole and there's not going to be any way out for us.

CHAPTER 4

. . . .

Beck

The knock on the door comes sooner than I expected, and only a little over an hour since Caroline and Ally left. I've been lying on the couch spooning with Sela, waiting for the other shoe to drop when they show up. The TV's been on, but neither one of us is absorbing. My hand is idly stroking her hip, wanting nothing more than to carry her into bed and for us to pretend none of this happened.

That means I could strip her down, eat her out, fuck her hard. All of the stuff that's been so damn good and that I've taken completely for granted.

But instead, Sela gives a quavering sigh when she hears the confident knock and we both push up and off the couch. Our eyes meet briefly and we both take a deep breath.

"Just do as we discussed earlier and it will be okay," I whisper.

She nods, her face pale but her gaze determined.

I turn away from her, square my shoulders, and head toward the foyer. I hear the creak of leather as Sela lies back down on the couch, presenting the picture of lazy Monday evening happiness of just vegging out in front of the TV and streaming some mindless comedy we found on Netflix.

I present the same, and it was done intentionally. I'd put on a pair of sweatpants, a ratty T-shirt, and my hair was flattened on one side from resting against the pillow on the couch. I hoped to look like a guy who wasn't just a few hours ago getting ready to wipe down a murder scene and potentially sink a body deep into Richardson Bay.

Putting my eye to the peephole, I need to determine who would be sent to my house.

Uniformed cops or plainclothes.

I see a white, middle-aged man and a black woman probably in her late twenties. Both in dress pants and shirts without jackets, the man sporting a loosely knotted tie. Both are clearly detectives; I know this not because I can see their badges, but by the somber yet superior looks on their faces. Still, I school my features and try not to look overly surprised when I open the door.

Had they been uniformed cops, my eyes would be wide with concern.

But I think the best tactic at this point is to feign ignorance because for all I know, they could be Amway salesmen.

I look at them expectantly as I swing the door open, but add a tinge of annoyance to my voice. "Can I help you?"

The male cop, who has dark receding hair and a slight belly, pulls a badge I now see firmly clasped to his belt and holds it up to me. "Mr. North . . . I'm Detective Paul DeLatemer with the Sausalito PD."

My gaze lands hard on the badge he holds up and then I pinch my eyebrows inward. A pained expression takes over my face. I go on the offense and blurt out, "Something's happened to JT, hasn't it?"

This throws the cop off, as I'd hoped, and he turns to look at his partner, who shoots him a look of wary surprise before she turns to me. She also holds up a badge and says, "I'm Detective Amber Denning and yes . . . something's happened. May we come in?"

I appear stunned for a moment, and then remember my manners, my voice sounding high pitched as I step back and wave them hurriedly in the door. "Yes, I'm sorry . . . please come in."

They step into the foyer and I close the door behind them.

"Sela," I call out, letting a touch of fear coat my words as I turn toward the living room. She pops up from the couch, as we'd discussed, and looks confused for a moment to see the detectives standing there. It's an amazing piece of acting if I do say so myself.

Her throat is covered by a lightweight turtleneck she put on, because if we were going through with this whole charade of denial to the police, then they couldn't see the bruises on her throat. Sure, they could have been from a fall or even a sex choking game that got out of hand, but it was best for there not to be any notice or questions about it. Doesn't mean I didn't take pictures with my cellphone though, which I downloaded into an encrypted file on my computer. Just in case we needed the proof later.

Sela's worried gaze flies to mine and I croak, "They're here about JT."

"Oh no," she whispers, hand flying to her mouth to cover it.

She looks so worried for the man who raped her, I almost burst into a spontaneous round of applause. I hold my hand out to her, and she scurries toward me in a move of solidarity and support. My arm goes around her waist and we both turn to face the detective with worried expectation.

Both of them look at us in empathy for the impending bad news they're going to deliver, but I don't have a doubt in the world they're scrutinizing every word out of our mouth and every bit of body language we're conveying.

"Can we sit down?" Detective Denning says. Her voice is crisp and forged with authority. She may be young, but I can tell she's a professional when it comes to awkward situations.

"Of course," I say as I gesture to the dining room table.

Denning takes the end chair, which I find to be a subtle indication that she's the partner in charge, despite being the younger of the two and a minority as a black female. DeLatemer takes the seat to her right, on the far side of the table, while Sela and I sit to her left.

I scrub my hands over my face, back through my hair, and then huff out a sigh filled with regret and fear as I pin a direct look at Detective Denning. "How bad is he?"

"Excuse me?" she responds.

"JT," I say with a touch of frustration. "How bad did they beat him up this time?"

I don't need any heightened sense of awareness to know I've shocked the cops sitting at my dining room table, and I can tell that the direction of their early investigation may have just gotten a little more interesting at this tidbit. Sela and I had a quick but unanimous decision on how we were going to handle the cops when they showed up.

We could either wait for the bad news to be delivered and hope our manufactured reactions of grief for a dearly departed friend and business colleague would be genuine enough to fool them, or we could go on the offensive and lace enough truth into the story that it would throw the scent off of us.

"Mr. North," Detective DeLatemer says from across the table in a gentle voice. My eyes slide over to him and I stare at him with a look of dread because I can hear it in his tone that he's getting ready to drop a bomb on two poor unsuspecting people. "Your partner, Jonathon Townsend . . . I'm sorry to have to tell you this, but he's dead."

Sela lets out a gasp of horror and her hand comes to my shoulder to grip me in comfort. I make a choking sound and slump down in my chair where I mutter, "No . . . they wouldn't have killed him . . ."

My voice trails off . . . my eyes lower to the dark teak wood and I clasp my hands together tightly. I can feel the heavy stares of both detectives as they take in my reaction.

Perfectly on cue, Sela's fingers dig into my shoulder and she says, "It's not your fault, Beck."

"I'm sorry," Detective Denning says, her voice still firm and in control, but there is an edge of confusion that gives me heart she's buying our hasty act. "But what's not your fault?"

My eyes snap up to hers and I try to mix in some shades of self-loathing when I tell her the parts of the story I believe to be pertinent. "JT got into some gambling trouble. Owed four million dollars to someone in Vegas. They want to collect and they paid him a visit on Sunday. Beat him up pretty badly. He called me from the hospital—"

"Which hospital?" DeLatemer interrupts me as he pulls a small pad of paper from the breast pocket of his dress shirt along with a pen. He clicks it once and starts scribbling.

"Marin General in Greenbrae," I supply helpfully.

"And he was beaten up?" Denning asks.

I nod effusively. "Yeah . . . bad. He didn't tell me what happened at first. Just wanted me to take him home, but then he eventually told me about owing the money."

"Who did he owe the money to?" DeLatemer asks as he looks up from his writing.

I shrug. "He didn't say. Just that he owed the money for a

gambling debt and that they threatened to kill him if he didn't pay up."

"They give him a deadline?"

I nod at DeLatemer. "Three days, I think he said."

"And you weren't worried about that?" Detective Denning asks, and I turn my gaze to her. Her expression is cool, perhaps even a bit doubtful.

"Of course I was worried about it," I snap at her, maybe with too much force, because Sela's fingers dig down into my muscles in warning.

I blow out a frustrated breath, mutter a "sorry," and then look to Detective DeLatemer with what I hope are bleak and guilt-filled eyes. "He asked me for the money and I didn't give it to him. If they killed him, then it's my fault for not bailing him out, right?"

The detective hunches over and writes more notes. I wait for another question, but nothing comes. I turn to look at Sela, and although my back is now to Denning, I still make sure to look at Sela with the same angst and guilt I just gave to the cops. "If I'd just given him the money . . ."

"Don't," Sela says urgently. "You can't think like that."

More silence while DeLatemer scribbles. I keep my mouth shut because I don't want to overdo it. Sela's hand falls from my shoulder and she grabs my hand. I smile at her and she squeezes me reflexively. We appear to be broken.

I think.

"I find it interesting you haven't even asked what happened to your partner," Detective Denning asks, and I turn in my chair slightly to look at her.

I go for a hesitant but confused look. "What do you mean?"

Her brown, almond-shaped eyes could be considered soft

looking. But now they hold reserved belief mixed with focused curiosity. "I mean I think most people would be curious as to how he was killed. I mean . . . it was one of the first things his parents asked when we went to see them."

I curse internally for the oversight, but before I can defend my completely manufactured actions, Sela says, "What does it matter to Beck how JT died? Why would he even want those gory details when he's clearly blaming himself for it even happening in the first place?"

I want to turn to Sela and kiss her, but instead I let my shoulders sag with the weight of my guilt, and I don't even bother to answer Detective Denning's question. I let her think that I've got enough troubling my soul without needing to compound it.

She startles me though when she stands from the table, pushing the heavy end chair away with the backs of her legs. DeLatemer jots down one more thing and then stands up, cutting a curt smile down at me. Sela and I also stand up, on edge and waiting to see what happens next.

"Mr. North . . . I'd like you to come down to the station and give a formal statement," Detective Denning tells me.

My mind races, and while I thought this was a small possibility from the start, I'm suddenly torn as to what to do. The stress of our charade is heavy, but we've maintained what I believe to be an easily believable story. But they'll want to dig more and they'll want alibis.

That's not in doubt.

"Actually," I say with an apologetic smile but command in my voice—the voice of a man with an advanced degree who runs a multimillion-dollar company. "I'd be more than happy to come and give you a formal statement. But not tonight, and you'll have to arrange it with my attorney."

"And why do you feel like you need an attorney?" Detective

DeLatemer asks, and I'm surprised by the challenge in his voice. I thought of him as the good cop in this duo.

"I don't," I reply smoothly without losing eye contact with him. "But right now, you've told me my childhood friend and business partner is dead. The only place I'm going to be tonight is at his parents' house, offering them comfort and taking it back from them. It's what family and friends do in times such as these."

"But you want your attorney there?" DeLatemer presses, and while I refuse to take my eyes off him and look at Denning, I can feel her smirking.

I flash a grimace at him and make no secret of my disgust. "Detective DeLatemer . . . I get you want to solve JT's murder, and there's nothing more I want to do than help you achieve that goal. But whether I talk to you tonight or tomorrow, with or without an attorney, it's not going to change the fact that I have more important things to do tonight. I'm sure you understand."

He gives me a knowing smile, but I see a hint of triumph in his eyes because I evaded his question and we both know it. He tucks his pad of paper and pen back into his pocket and doesn't respond to me. Rather, he walks around the dining room table and heads to the front door. Detective Denning turns to follow behind him.

Sela and I watch as they open the door, and I feel like I won't be able to properly breathe until it shuts behind them. DeLatemer steps through and Denning follows, but she pauses just before she reaches for the knob to pull it closed behind them.

"We'll be in touch," she says as she stares at me expectantly.

I nod back at her.

"Very interesting," she says, almost as an afterthought.

"What's that?" I ask her, knowing I have to ask but dreading the answer.

"We never said JT was murdered," she says and I see suspicion sizzling deep in her eyes. "Just that he was dead. You used the word *murder* just now."

Sela steps forward, and before I can stop her, she sputters, "Well . . . that was just a common sense assumption when you show up at the door—"

I grab her by her upper arm and squeeze gently. "Honey . . . Detective Denning's just doing her job. She wants to find the truth and she's trained to pick up on those things and press them to her advantage."

Sela doesn't say anything else.

Denning inclines her head at me, almost as if she's silently saying touché, but as she pulls the door closed behind her, I know without a doubt that she didn't buy the load of crap we were just feeding her.

CHAPTER 5

. . . .

Sela

Beck slips his key into the lock of the condo door and silently opens it. He pushes it open all the way and motions me in ahead of him. It's almost one A.M. and both of us are exhausted from stress, lies, and a lack of sleep.

We've been at JT's parents' house in Sausalito, just two miles from their son. Neither Beck nor I wanted to go there, but we felt it was what innocent people should do. We both knew the police had us in their sights, and while they might also be following the theory that JT was killed by a Vegas bookie, they were not going to leave us alone.

The time we spent at Candace and Colin Townsend's home was dreadful. We arrived to find Beck's parents were already there, because of course they were going to call their closest friends first with the awful news. JT's mom was wailing in the arms of her husband, who eventually gave her a Xanax to calm her down. It wasn't until she polished off a vodka tonic that she finally slipped into sort of a silently numb state of shock where she sat on a velvet couch while Beck's mom patted her hand in an awkward show of comfort.

Beck's dad though?

You could tell he was devastated, more so than Colin Townsend appeared over the news of the death of his son. He faced the windows of the library, where we were all congregated, and stared out into the blackness. He barely acknowledged Beck when we arrived and was clearly distracted. I wondered if he was trying to manage some type of internal pain that he may have been suffering as a father.

We weren't surprised when Beck's mom called us not five minutes after the cops left to deliver the news. Beck, in turn, told his mom about the cops being there and that we were on our way.

Again, we really didn't want to go, but it was what was expected of a grieving friend and partner of Jonathon Townsend. As Beck's girlfriend, I was expected to go as well, although what I really wanted to do was open up a bottle of wine and drown my misery over what has gone down as the single worst day of my life.

Yes . . . even worse than the day I was gang-raped.

Killing another human being—even one who brutally violated me—was more traumatizing and damaging to my soul than I could have ever imagined. I was such a fool to initially even think it was an appropriate course those months ago, and now with the benefit of hindsight, I wish with all my might that I had never concocted the foolish plan to kill JT. I wish I would have gone straight to the police and let them handle it. I wish I'd turned to my dad to let him comfort me when I learned my attacker's identity.

In this moment, I even wish I had never stepped foot in the ballroom of that Sugar Bowl Mixer where my intent was still to confront and kill JT, but instead I met Beck, his business partner, who enslaved my body, and later my heart.

Yes, I'd even give up Beck if I could go back in time and change things so I wouldn't have this guilt pressing down on me.

And it's not just guilt that I took another life. I think given time, I'm going to be able to accept that in that moment I had no choice. I was reacting on survival instinct and I think most people would have done what I'd done.

But I don't know if I'll ever be able to forgive myself for the course of events I started with my stupid plan for vengeance, which led to the police knocking on Beck's door and looking at him as a potential suspect.

I will never forgive myself.

Beck did an admirable job at the Townsends' of portraying the devastated friend but also the one with strong shoulders who bore everyone else's grief. We "learned" some details of what happened to JT from his parents, who were contacted soon after his body was found.

Apparently, his private chef who cooks for him a few times a week walked into the bloodbath a mere twenty minutes or so after I stumbled out of JT's house. When I think about how close I came to being caught, nausea rolls within me and I have to fight it back down. I have to fight with my own need for self-preservation not to offer up a prayer of thanks for letting me escape before his cook arrived.

JT's dad recounted to us that the police told them that JT was stabbed in the neck with a sharp object, but that it hasn't been recovered, and it appeared to have struck his carotid artery, causing him to bleed to death pretty quickly.

Yup. I can attest to that.

They also told his parents that they believed JT knew his attacker because there were no signs of forced entry.

Can also attest to that.

Finally, they confirmed that there was some type of struggle before JT died, but until forensics could finish their investigation, they couldn't guess as to what occurred in the minutes before his death.

I could tell them the details but I won't. I promised Beck I wouldn't and I'd let him handle this.

We stayed for a long time, finally leaving the Townsends' home around midnight. The long drive back into the city was silent, both Beck and I lost in our heavy thoughts.

I wanted to talk to him. I wanted to say something comforting to him.

I wanted to pour out my guilt and beg his forgiveness again for even getting him into this mess.

But he had put up a wall, and I could sense it as clearly as if he had told me point-blank that he needed some space. His body was stiff with tension, his jaw locked tight when I'd turn to look at him in the glow of the dashboard lights. He never said a word to me on the way back, seemingly fine to suffer in silence rather than with my support.

This confused me and hurt me, and yet . . . I really didn't know how to even strike up the right type of conversation that would assure me that he still loved me and give him the emotional support he needed.

At this point, I'm so confused about where we stand that I feel like I'm on the verge of a complete breakdown.

Beck moves quietly down the hall toward our bedroom and I follow behind, flipping off lights as I go. He immediately goes into the bathroom, shutting the door softly behind him. I can hear him in there using the toilet and then flushing. The water turns on, and I can envision him washing his hands. A few more moments of silence, and then he opens the bathroom door, pulling his shirt over his head before he steps out. When the material clears his face, he finally looks at me standing by the bed and I have to hope he sees the look of need on my face.

I need him to say something.

Just one tiny word or even a smile that lets me know that while he's burdened greatly by everything that's happened, it hasn't changed his feelings for me.

Instead, his eyes sort of pass over me and he turns to the closet to deposit his shirt in the clothes hamper.

"Beck," I call out desperately, my voice heavy with need and fear.

He immediately whips around to face me, his gaze filled with worry. "What's wrong?"

My eyes roam all over that face, and I try to take in every single feature that gives me a hint as to what he might be feeling in this moment. From the mussed-up hair indicating a long day without a comb to it, to the fatigue lines around his eyes, to the deep furrow in his brow as he looks at me. His eyes don't shine but have turned a dull matte and his shoulders hang low.

He takes a tentative step toward me but doesn't say anything.

The silence is almost damning, and my gaze sort of drifts to the window where most of the Financial District buildings are darkened except for strategically placed architectural lighting.

Perhaps we're finished.

"Sela . . . what's wrong?" Beck asks softly, and I look back at him. He's standing in the same spot, staring at me expectantly.

"Do you still love me?" I blurt out, and those fucking weak-assed tears start to build up again. "After all this trouble I've caused?"

For a split second, he doesn't react, but just stares at me impassively. Then it's like a curtain is lifted over his face and understanding makes his eyes soften with empathy as he gets everything about me in one clear moment.

Two long steps and he's in front of me.

His hands go to the sides of my head, hold me in place, and he leans his face down until our noses are almost touching. "Of course I love you."

"I'm so sorry," I whisper, the tears making a fool out of me as they spill out.

"Don't," Beck orders me, his eyes flicking back and forth between my own. His command is almost harsh, but his voice gently cradles my battered self-esteem. "Don't you apologize for a thing to me. You did nothing wrong."

I blink and more tears fall. "If only I'd—"

"Don't," he orders me again. "I'm not going to listen to it. If you've got some insecurities about what there is between us right now, then you ask them and let me reassure you, but don't go about doing it by way of pointing a guilty finger at yourself. You hear me?"

I blink, clear the wetness from my eyes, and nod at him in understanding. It's not that I wholeheartedly agree with what he's saying to me, it's just that I know a different way that he can reassure me that I still have his heart and he has mine.

Pushing to my tiptoes, I press my lips against his and speak against them urgently. "I need you."

"You've got me," he says, causing his lips to open, and when he tilts his head slightly to the right, I tilt mine in the opposite direction and slip my tongue into his mouth for a deep but brief kiss.

When I pull back, I look up at him and say, "I need you to fuck me."

Beck's eyes have been flatlined for the past several hours, burdened with death and consequences, but with those simple words fire sizzles and his jaw tightens. "You want me to fuck you? Right now?"

"And hard," I murmur with a nod, pressing my body into his. I feel his dick starting to swell and give a little grind against him. "Really hard."

He doesn't answer me but responds by spinning me around, pushing me into the wall and then stepping up against my backside. I feel every single inch of him, even with the barrier of clothing still between us. For the first time in hours, I feel connected to him, despite the way in which he's tried to protect me and the ways in which we banded together against the detectives' questioning.

Only with the physicality of his touch and the fire I just saw in his eyes can I truly be assured that things might be okay between us.

Beck nuzzles his cheek up against the side of my head as his right hand slips down the front of my sweatpants and straight into my panties. He pushes his fingers straight into me, going deep. He makes me squirm and plead, "More, Beck. I want more than that."

He gives a dark rumble of a laugh. "I'll give it to you, love. Always trust that I'll give it to you."

Beck moves his fingers in and out of me, his lips on my neck and whispering filthy promises peppered with reassurances.

You think my fingers are driving you crazy, Sela? Just wait until I fuck you with my cock. Then you'll see how much I burn for you . . . always.

Beck drives me wild until I'm begging for it, and then my pants are gone and apparently so are his, because he's driving his cock into me from behind while I'm pressed up against the wall.

He holds still for a moment, gets his bearings, and then pulls my hips back slightly all while pressing a hand in between my shoulder blades to keep my torso against the wall. Placing his teeth at my shoulder, he gives me a tiny nip and whispers, "What you and I have, Sela . . . no one will ever comprehend it. No one will ever come in between it. But it's real and it's ours, and I'm never letting it go."

I sigh out a long breath of relief over his words as well as pent-up sexual frustration. I circle my hips and get Beck focused back on the task at hand.

As requested, he fucks me hard, his pelvis slapping against mine. In between grunts of pleasure, he whispers in my ear, "Is this what you wanted, Sela? Is this how you wanted me to prove that you're still mine?"

I nod, gasping and writhing with no control over my actions.

"Don't ever doubt it," he tells me after slamming deep and rotating his hips. "Don't ever doubt that you are mine and this pussy is mine and that I'm never giving it up. I'm going to do whatever it takes to protect what's mine."

My orgasm explodes in response to his proclamations . . . his thrusts . . . fuck, I don't know what it is, but when Beck declares that I'm his, my body acknowledges it by surrendering every piece of control and ownership of feeling to him.

That orgasm didn't belong to me.

That belonged solely to Beck, and we both know it.

. . . .

CHAPTER 6

Beck

I can't explain the heightened sense of awareness, but I come wide awake and realize that something is wrong. I immediately know Sela's not in bed with me and the bedside clock says it's just past five A.M.

We didn't go to sleep until nearly two, and that's because I was busy fucking reassurances into my girl.

I fucked her hard up against the bedroom wall as she requested, and when she came, I pulled out and threw her down on the bed. Put my face between her legs and made her come again.

Flipped her onto her stomach and rode her hard and fast from behind, and because she wasn't coming again fast enough for me, I pressed a finger in her ass and that did the trick. She screamed in relief . . . release . . . pleasure . . . all of it. Only then did I finally let loose, pouring every bit of myself into her.

Only then did we let the trauma of the day overcome us, and we fell to the mattress together, immediately succumbing to sleep.

By all accounts, I shouldn't be awake. I'm beyond exhausted from the mental stress of the situation, and yet I'm hyperalert as

I realize that Sela's not here and the leaden feeling in my stomach tells me there's something wrong.

I hastily roll out of bed, grabbing my underwear from the floor and putting it on.

"Sela?" I call out, unable to bear the wait of a search through the condo.

I almost collapse with relief when she answers back softly, "I'm in the living room."

I find her there on the couch, legs curled under her and an empty cup of tea on the coffee table. She's sitting in the warm glow of the end table light, wearing nothing but one of my T-shirts. Her new blond hair is no longer a shock to me, and because it suits her so well, I can't really even remember how gorgeous she was as a brunette.

"What's wrong?" I ask her as I sit on the middle cushion right beside her. I angle my body to face her, throwing an arm over the back of the couch.

I expect her to hit me up with another plea to let her confess to the cops, because I know she's questioning our course of action. But I'm not about to let that happen, because I don't doubt it. Sela's story would be too improbable and I know the Townsends would put their weight and money behind the investigation so as to not have their son's reputation tarnished. I also know that motive is paramount and she had the ultimate reason to kill him. I just can't risk that the police would be open-minded enough to entertain a self-defense claim, when Sela went to JT's home with a weapon.

Bracing myself against her plea, I'm stunned into momentary inaction when she says, "I didn't tell you everything that happened before I killed JT."

My mind races as I flit through the details she'd given me, but most of that involved her physical actions so that I could be sure

I cleaned up everything. But past that, the story that led up to her killing JT is actually sparse. I don't put that on Sela's doorstep though, as I was rushing her into the shower so I could in turn rush to JT's house and take care of business.

Then the cops showed up.

Then we went to the Townsends'.

Then we fucked hard and went to sleep.

"What happened?" I ask encouragingly, although I know deep in my gut that what she's getting ready to tell me could be a game changer. I have to force myself to look at her with open acceptance of whatever may come out of her mouth.

She doesn't pull any punches. "JT knew you were his brother."

A zing of adrenaline courses through me, but immediately recedes. It's an interesting fact, and one that surprises me, but I'm not sure that it's harmful or helpful to us at this point.

"The reason he called me over there . . . his plan was to get you to let him stay in the Sugar Bowl . . . was that he was going to renounce his right to a part of your father's inheritance."

"How the fuck could he do that if he's not even in the will?" I ask astonished. At least I don't think he's in the will. My father said JT doesn't know about his paternity, so I just assumed . . .

Sela shrugs. "He said his mother told him years ago. Said she wanted him to know so that he could claim what was rightfully his."

I consider the truthfulness of what JT told Sela in those moments before he died. I can accept his mom would tell him the truth, because she's a born gold digger. It's why she married Colin and I could see her wanting to make sure JT wasn't denied anything. But for him to use *those* words with Sela . . .

Renounce his rights?

It doesn't make sense. Just because he's a biological child of my father doesn't mean he'd inherit anything. Not if there's a will in place. That I know for a fact, and I also know without a doubt my father has a will. Not that I've seen it, but he's a financial advisor and guru. He knows the importance of estate planning. Fuck, he oversees estate planning for his clients.

He has a will, I'm sure of it.

"You think your father was lying to you, don't you?" Sela asks astutely.

"If JT used those exact words, then yeah . . . sounds like he knows there's a will and that he's in it."

"Which means your dad lied when he said he hadn't told JT," Sela concludes.

"Probably," I mutter as I press my fingers to the bridge of my nose. I mean, it's possible my dad put JT in the will but didn't tell him. Figured it would be a surprise after he died and he wouldn't be here to deal with the negative fallout that such a bomb would cause.

Christ . . . I was going to have to pay my dad a visit and ask him. I think about how devastated he looked last night at the Townsends' and I wonder if he was feeling guilt removing himself from the situation with JT. The Townsends and my parents had no clue last night of the potential Vegas connection to JT, because at the time the cops had informed them of his death, they weren't aware of that connection. But still . . . my dad knew JT was in trouble because I told him to stay out of it without giving him any details.

"That's not the worst of what I have to tell you," Sela whispers, and my eyes fly up to her.

She looks positively green in the face and tears swim in her eyes. She's cried so fucking much the last twenty-four hours and I can't stand it.

My hand automatically reaches out to her, but she holds her own up, palm out. "Just listen to me. What I'm getting ready to tell you is really bad, and I'm sorry for the hurt I'm getting ready to cause, but you need to know everything."

Fuck me.

Paranoia unreasonably takes hold of me.

She's getting ready to tell me it wasn't self-defense. That she carried out her murderous plot as originally intended. Drove to JT's house with the intent to remove him from both of our lives permanently, and somehow . . . not sure how . . . but she didn't use her gun. For some reason, the letter opener was the better deal. Maybe she was going to shoot him and there was a struggle. That totally explains the bruises then.

So it *was* self-defense. I can see the fucking bruises right now from where I'm sitting. She was protecting herself and that's that.

So maybe something else happened.

Is it possible that JT did something else to her?

Raped her?

"It's about Caroline," Sela says, and I step backward from her in surprise, my momentary paranoia completely forgotten.

"What?"

"JT told me something about Caroline, and I couldn't say anything when Caroline was here. In fact, I had no intention of telling her or you this ever, especially not her. But I think you need to know. It's eating at me and I think it's because you need to know. I can't keep the truth from you."

Acid roils within my stomach and a feeling of dread starts at the base of my spine and crawls its way up until my hair is standing on end.

"Tell me," I whisper, my throat raspy from the effort to keep down the backwash of bile.

Sela's fingers twist in her lap, a sure sign she's nervous, but to give her credit, she never loses eye contact with me. "When JT had me on the desk and was choking me, he told me there was one last thing I needed to know before I died."

Oh fuck . . . no, no, no. No fucking way.

I push up off the couch, crack my knee on the coffee table but ignore the pain. I turn away from Sela, afraid to look at her. Afraid to hear what she's going to say.

"He's the one that raped Caroline," she murmurs, the anguish clear in her voice.

For one brief, glorious moment, everything sort of goes white on me. I don't feel, hear, or see a thing. One tiny blessed moment of peace, where I know deep down it's my sanity refusing to acknowledge what she's just told me.

Then everything turns red and lavalike rage sizzles within my veins.

"Motherfucker!" I scream so loud I feel my vocal chords shredding. I bend down, put my hands under the heavy coffee table, and heave it up and over where it crashes loudly against the hardwood floor. "Jesus fucking Christ . . . just no!"

I wheel on Sela, my hands curled into fists and demand, "Tell me that's a fucking lie."

She doesn't respond but just looks at me with sympathy. She doesn't need to defend her statement. I can see the truth in her eyes.

"I'm sorry, Beck," is all she says.

I spin back away from her, sidestep the overturned table, and stalk across the living room to the windows. Crossing my arms over my chest, I stare bleakly out over the darkened waters of the bay and let the weight of this revelation start to drown me.

JT raped my sister.

Drugged her—most likely at the Christmas party—then ambushed her.

And then that fucker smiled at me the next time I saw him, probably laughing inside over that little tidbit of information.

And Jesus . . . JT is Ally's *father*.

Sela's arms wrap around me from behind, her body warm as she presses into my back and squeezes me in comfort. "I'm so sorry, baby. So damn sorry."

I drop my arms and place them over hers, locking my hands on to her to hold her in place. I hold her tightly as she holds me in sympathy and regret for all the things that are killing me right this moment.

I thought I hated JT before . . . when I knew what he did to Sela.

But now . . . I didn't know such an ugly emotion could exist inside of a human. I don't know how I'll survive this feeling, which seems to be clawing its way deeper into me. My hot rage turns into a dark form of acceptance of this truth, but it feels like oily sludge coating and dampening my soul.

I struggle against it.

"Tell me again about how you killed JT," I murmur as I look out the windows. "Tell me exactly what it was like when you plunged that thing into his neck."

"Beck," Sela whispers in admonishment that I'd even let my thoughts go there.

Black, bubbling, putrid, roiling hatred for JT.

"Tell me," I urge her. "Do you think he was in pain? Do you think he was afraid when he realized he was dying?"

She's silent for a moment but then she tells me what I need to hear, even if it's not true. "Yes. He was terrified at the end."

My lips curl upward and the oily darkness rumbles inside of me, pleased to be reliving the vengeance Sela delivered.

"Good," I whisper in relief. "That's real good. Now tell me more."

CHAPTER 7

. . . .

Sela

My gut was telling me that Beck needed to know the truth about Caroline and JT. I was sure it was the right thing to do. But his reaction . . . the bleak despair mixed with helpless rage made me instantly regret my decision. It's the worst feeling to cause pain to someone you care about, but there's nothing I can do to take it back.

When Caroline was raped, Beck stepped up to the plate and took control. He was able to use his love and strength to help her get through it. While it could never remove the pain that event caused, Beck's ability to support his sister also provided an amount of inherent healing for himself.

But now that he knows it was JT who did it?

He has no way to purge the feelings or make things better in his mind. The most I could offer him was the security of my arms around him and a retelling of the grisly way in which I murdered his sister's rapist. It was a momentary balm to him, but it just wasn't good enough.

Beck left the apartment soon after, forgoing a shower and

throwing on a pair of jeans, a T-shirt, and a sweatshirt, saying he had things to do.

I didn't like the sound of that so I asked, "What kinds of things?"

He was distracted as he shoved his wallet into a back pocket and headed toward the foyer for his keys. He didn't answer me.

"Beck," I said firmly as I followed him. "Are you okay?"

He stopped in his tracks and wheeled on me, and the misery in his eyes was almost too much for me to bear. "No, I'm not okay. But I've got to get rid of that letter opener and the bloody clothes."

There was no opportunity to do it last night once he saw the police at JT's house and realized they could be showing up at his place at any moment to tell him about JT. The items were in the trunk of his Audi, and the thought of the police showing up with a search warrant makes me tremble with fear. There was no chance of that happening last night, of course, because his body had just been found, and even I know that a warrant would never come that quickly. They'd have to have a solid suspect, and last night, they did not.

But today?

Well, we don't know what to expect, so we have to get rid of the incriminating stuff.

"I'll come with you," I told him with a smile, because I did not like the way he was behaving. I threw him for a terrible loop with my revelation of JT and Caroline, and his frame of mind was fragile at best. Besides, that was my murder evidence and I should be taking responsibility for it.

"No," he told me, and turned away, grabbing his keys from the foyer table. "I don't want you anywhere near this shit. If I were to get stopped before I can ditch it—"

"You'd go down for a murder you didn't commit," I pointed out reasonably.

"Better me than you," he retorted as he looked over his shoulder at me briefly before reaching for the front door.

"The difference is," I said softly, and it stopped him cold. "I committed the murder and you didn't."

Beck's shoulders sagged a bit and he huffed out a pained breath. "Stop calling it murder. It was self-defense."

He turned to me, shoving his key into his front pocket and taking me by the shoulders. It was a tender move when he bent toward me and touched his nose alongside mine. "You've been through enough, Sela. Since you were sixteen years old, you've been through too much shit. Now let me handle this, okay?"

He pulled back, and for a blessed moment, the pain of what I revealed to him fifteen minutes ago is gone and he's looking at me the way a man looks at the woman he loves, in a way that shows her he will die protecting her.

It humbled me as nothing has ever done, and equally as much made me very sad that Beck even has to protect me in this manner. I didn't deserve his consideration or his security, but he was making it very clear I was going to accept it.

I nodded at him and he gave me a soft kiss goodbye, saying, "Be back later."

I didn't ask him what his plan was. No clue if he was going to chuck the letter opener off the Golden Gate Bridge or bury it deep in the woods. I trusted he'd do it right though, and those items were never going to be found. It brought him one step deeper into the pile of shit I'd created for us, and made him more complicit in my crime.

Which means my guilt compounded even more.

Beck took off and I was left with the prospect of sitting in an empty condo and worrying myself about all the ways in which this whole house of cards could come tumbling down at any minute. I didn't even have the benefit of school to keep me occupied, as I was on break. However, the spring semester was due to start in two days and I had no clue if I'd be attending or in jail. The thought was abysmally depressing.

But it was only one thing upon me that was depressing, and even if I didn't have that, I'd have a million other things. Which meant I needed to square up my shoulders, assume that Beck would be fine today, and do something that would make a difference to myself.

Maybe another.

I called Caroline and asked if she could have lunch with me today.

We met at Willie's Seafood and Raw Bar, which was only a few blocks from where Caroline worked in Healdsburg, where she and Ally live. She looked lovely and chic in a camel wool skirt that came down to her knees, a cream turtleneck, and plaid scarf. I didn't look chic at all in a pair of well-worn jeans, a turtleneck from Old Navy—again to hide the bruises—and cheap black vinyl riding boots. She didn't seem to care, so neither did I.

I watch as Caroline peruses the menu and takes a delicate sip of water. We made some pleasant small talk until now, and as I look at her, it's hard to believe less than twenty-four hours ago, she was scrubbing the shower down with bleach to erase away any evidence of JT that I brought into her brother's condo.

She closes the menu, sets it down in front of her, and gives me a sympathetic smile. "How're you holding up?"

I shrug, needing to talk things through but dreading it at the same time. "It is what it is."

Caroline nods in understanding.

So much understanding.

"I'm sorry what happened to you," I tell her. "We didn't get a chance to talk . . . with everything that happened last night."

She reaches her hand across the table and takes hold of mine. "We've both been through something horrific. No one can ever know what that feels like. But I'm glad we now have each other."

"If you ever need to talk about it," I say to her candidly. While I can't ever let her know the identity of her rapist, I can offer her everything else under the sun if it will help her.

She nods. "Same here."

We both smile at each other, understanding the tentative friendship we first formed at Thanksgiving a little over a month ago is now infinitely stronger by the bond we now share.

"But getting back to my original question," Caroline says wisely—and by that I mean she was wise to the fact I was evading—and gives me a very pointed look. "How are *you* holding up?"

I reach for my water, trying desperately to still the shaking of my hand, but it won't cooperate and Caroline notices. I take a small sip, set it down, and clear my throat. "I don't know whether to feel guilt or vindication," I tell her truthfully.

"I'm going to suggest vindication," she says pertly. And if there's one thing I can be happy about, it's that I've avenged Caroline although she'll never know it.

"For the longest time, I felt it was my fault, you know?" I say pointedly, knowing Caroline will understand I'm talking about my rape. Although Caroline and I have not compared details, I think I have a pretty good idea of the emotions a rape victim goes through, and I bet she feels the same.

"Yes," she says with a sad smile. "Always wondering what I could have done to avoid it."

"It haunted me for a long time."

"Me, not so long," she says matter-of-factly. "Beck wouldn't let me, and I made peace with it, especially after Ally was born. She was something so good that came out of something so bad, I had to believe that it was supposed to happen because I was supposed to have her."

I duck my head, make pretense of rearranging my napkin on my lap so I can furiously blink my eyes, which are welling up with tears brought on by such a well-balanced and loving perspective. When I have myself under control, I look back up at her to find her staring at me with understanding and empathy.

Empathy that perhaps I didn't find peace as easily as she did.

"You know my original intention was to kill JT," I say as I lean forward across the table and lower my voice. "I was going to torture him for the other attackers' identities, and then I was going to shoot him between the eyes."

She blinks at me in surprise.

I nod. "Months ago, when I learned his identity . . . I had plotted to murder him."

"Oh wow," she mutters in dismay, but leans toward me to hear more.

"I had a gun in my purse and walked into a Sugar Bowl Mixer. I was going to entrance him and get him alone, then I was going to kill him. Simple as that."

"But nothing is ever that simple," she hypothesizes.

I give a short laugh. "Exactly. Beck North intercepted me and then sidetracked me, and then eventually made me realize it wasn't the way."

"Well, I'm his sister, so you don't need to convince me how great he is," she chuckles.

"No, I think I do," I say urgently as I bend in closer and whisper. "He's out right now, disposing of murder evidence to protect me. I can't let this go on, Caroline. I need to go to the cops and confess what I did. Beck has been protecting me from the moment we met, but this is too much. Too dangerous. Risky. I can't let him put himself out there for me like that."

Caroline leans back, crosses her arms over her stomach, and examines me in a shrewd manner. "You love my brother?"

"More than anything," I breathe out in affirmation.

"Then you should trust in him," she says simply, and then winks at me.

Before I can respond, Caroline's attention is caught by the waiter walking up to us. "Are you ladies ready to order?"

"I'm going to have the lobster roll with a side of fruit," she says, and hands her menu over.

"I'll have the same," I say, also giving up my menu, not having bothered to even open it. Food isn't high on my priority list.

Once the waiter turns to leave us, Caroline continues. "He's a smart guy, Sela. He's doing what's best, and yeah . . . while my initial gut instinct was to go to the cops, in hindsight I think this is right. You went to your rapist's house with a gun."

"Because he invited me there," I point out.

"And JT's going to confirm that to the police how?" she asks sarcastically, and then ignores my narrowed gaze because she's not playing along with me. While I wanted to come here and solidify the bond Caroline and I have as rape victims, my number-one priority is getting her on board with me to convince Beck I need to go to the police and put an end to all of this.

But she's not playing nicely.

"This is your brother we are talking about, Caroline," I tell her harshly. "He could get in serious trouble. He as much as told me that they'll be looking closely at him because they always look to those closest to the victim."

"But he didn't do it," she points out. "There's no evidence tying him to the murder."

"But—"

"Just let it go, Sela," Caroline says softly. "I get why you feel the way you do. Trust me . . . Beck does too. But this is stressful enough without you constantly worrying about the correct course of action to take or second-guessing Beck. I'm telling you . . . let it ride. Give Beck this one and stand by his side now that the decision has been made."

I want to argue. I want to argue until I'm blue in the face, until she agrees with me. Hell, just last night she thought we should go to the police. But now she's firmly in support of what's going down, and that was clearly evidenced by the way she jumped into action to help conceal the crime because her brother—her savior—asked her to. She's not going to change now.

Taking a deep breath, I let it out and try to pour out all of my anxiety about the situation with it. It totally doesn't work, as I still feel the telltale cramp of worry deep in my chest. But I smile for Caroline's benefit and nod my head. "Okay. I'll let it ride."

"Good," she says with a curt smile, then turns serious. "Now . . . how is Beck doing?"

How is Beck doing?

You mean after I told him that JT raped you? After he realized that JT was Ally's father? After it became painfully clear he could do nothing about it and has turned his rage and bitterness inward and now I'm really concerned about his mental state of mind?

"He's fine," I assure her, because I don't want her to worry about her brother. There's nothing she could do anyway because she'd never understand his pain right now. So I take that burden solely on my shoulders, and I go on to tell her lies that Beck seems completely in control right now.

. . . .

CHAPTER 8

Beck

I break out of the forest densely populated with Monterey cypress and coast redwoods and into a small meadow where my car sits about three hundred yards on the other side. I'm holding my sweatshirt, marked with grime and sweat, loosely in my hand. I'd long ago taken it off because the weather was unseasonably mild, in the high fifties, and I've been using it repeatedly over the last few hours to wipe my face.

I had no solid game plan for where to dispose of the letter opener and bloody clothes when I left the condo, as I was absolutely driven to get out of there as fast as I could so I didn't have to look at the pity on Sela's face for me. True . . . these incriminating items had to be ditched somewhere far away, but I ran from Sela and her brutal truths because I couldn't fucking handle thinking about it.

I looked at Sela, eyes filled with regret for needing to deliver such hurtful words, and all I could imagine was JT leering over her . . . relishing in telling her that he raped my little sister.

Too much.

Overload.

Had to get out.

And I drove to Uvas Canyon in the Santa Cruz Mountains, stopping once to fill up my car and grab a can of lighter fluid and a pack of matches from the convenience store, all of which I paid cash for. I'd been out to Uvas Canyon Park a few times during my Stanford days. I chose it because it's lushly and densely wooded and there's only six miles of marked hiking trails on almost twelve hundred acres of forest. That means there's a lot of isolated areas where people won't venture and where I could safely hide the murder evidence. My only other implement, other than the backpack that carried the weapon and clothes wrapped in a garbage bag, was my Garmin running watch, which was equipped with GPS. I made sure to put that on versus my Breitling, and I was set to protect Sela as best I could.

I hiked deep into the woods, off the main trail and pushing my way past thick underbrush and fallen, rotted trees. I had intended to bury the letter opener, but immediately realized that wasn't going to work without a shovel or axe to chop my way through roots, so I kept my eyes lifted upward to the trees until I spotted exactly what I wanted: a tree that was half dead, easily climbable, and with a rotted crevice about fifteen feet up in the trunk. It was almost too easy to scale my way up, using a cracked branch hanging at a downward angle, and I was stuffing the letter opener deep into the rotted section that was blackened with shadow because the indentation was so deep. When I got back to the ground, I couldn't see the letter opener from any angle.

I then turned east, went deeper into the woods, and consulting the map periodically, knew I was in an area that would almost guarantee total privacy. Couldn't guarantee there wasn't some other whack job out here trying to hide a body or something, but I knew I had to take a calculated risk to get rid of the last remnants of evidence I possessed. I put Sela's T-shirt and bra soaked with JT's blood and his gray hoodie that had some transferred spots of blood on it in a small clearing I made free of leaves and sticks. I then used my hands to scrape as much damp earth and wet leaves into a small pile to help me extinguish the fire after it had done its job.

I poured a small amount of lighter fluid on the clothes and said a small prayer that I not be caught and that I could get the fire out before anyone smelled the smoke and became curious. I lit a match and tossed it on the pile, and to my dismay, it took a fuck of a long time for the clothes to burn. I had to use more lighter fluid, adding it carefully when the fire would die, until I was confident nothing could be identified. I didn't burn the clothing to pure ash, but I burned most of it away, and what was left was disfigured enough that I knew there'd be no amount of DNA they could ever pull off of it.

At least that's what I hoped.

I easily put out any remaining embers with the dirt and wet leaves and a general stomping of my tennis shoes around, then I gathered the mess that was left and hiked south for several hundred yards where I was able to stuff them beneath a rotted tree that had fallen to the ground. I pulled dead brush to help camouflage the blackened remnants of burned clothing, not much of which was left, but I wasn't too worried about it. Chances of a hiker coming by this area and seeing the clothing was virtually nonexistent to my way of thinking. Even if they did, chances of them even alerting police was even smaller. And if that did happen, I didn't believe there was any way they'd connect that to JT's murder.

I felt I had done all I could.

So with hands completely filthy with dirt and my shirt soaked with sweat, I trudged back through the small meadow, my eyes pinned on my car the entire time. Just waiting perhaps for someone to drive by and see me; placing me in a very strange place at a very strange time in my life. I knew if I could just make it back to the condo unaccosted and get into the shower to wash away the evidence of my crime of concealment, Sela and I could rest easier.

When I get to my car, I take a moment to vigorously scrub my hands on my jean-clad thighs, removing most of the leftover dirt I accumulated to extinguish the fire. I wipe my sweaty face one more time with my sweatshirt before tossing it onto the passenger seat along with the empty backpack. After expelling a deep breath of completion, I get into my car and turn it on, cranking the A/C up so I can cool down.

I take a moment to check my messages and see I have two voice mails.

The first is from my mother and it's short, to the point, and completely offensive to me.

Beck . . . this is your mother.

No shit.

Just wanted to let you know the Townsends have arranged for JT's funeral to be held on Friday at two P.M. They'd like you to give the eulogy and I accepted on your behalf. Oh, and will you talk Caroline into coming? If there's one function she should attend, this is it.

Yeah, Mom . . . that sure as fuck isn't going to happen. No way is Caroline going to give you even a moment's consideration, and I'm sure as shit not going to let her attend the funeral of her rapist.

But joy . . . looks like I'll be giving a eulogy for the man who defiled her and Sela. Oh, the things I'd really love to say . . .

I delete my mom's voice mail and listen to the second, which is from Sela, very brief and just letting me know she decided to drive to Healdsburg to have lunch with Caroline. I'm not surprised. I imagine she's trying to talk through every angle of how we made a poor decision by not coming forward, but I also know Caroline will stay firmly on my side. It's just the way things are between us.

But I also expect it's because she and Caroline now understand they have a deeper bond with each other, forged by circumstances that I cannot truly comprehend. For this, I'm glad that they each now have a true confidante if they need to discuss what happened to them.

Except they now have one difference. Sela has identified her attacker. Caroline never will.

Laying my head back against the cushioned rest, I take a moment to analyze what JT said to Sela. He was clearly telling the truth that he knew about our relation to each other. So he wasn't lying in an effort to get ahead.

I have to assume that fucker wasn't lying when he told Sela about raping Caroline. I suppose there's a small chance he did that just to torture her, but mostly I think he did it because he was a sadistic fuck.

Regardless, I'm pretty sure he was telling the truth.

But the thing I can't get past is the DNA evidence. DNA was collected from Caroline and we were told that there was no match. If JT really raped both women, it should have matched up to the evidence collected from Sela's rape. I suppose the most logical explanation for it not matching up is that perhaps Sela was confused about whose semen was in her hair. She thought it was JT's, but she had two other attackers. Perhaps it was their semen.

But another explanation bothers me and I hadn't thought much about it before, but I do now. When Dennis had gotten a copy of Sela's criminal investigation file, he said the paperwork for the Combined DNA Index System—CODIS—wasn't in the file. He was sure it was an oversight, but it could have slipped through the cracks.

I consider calling Dennis. He flew out to Vegas last night to deliver the money to VanZant for taking the dive, then he's heading to Ireland. After that Panama. The man is on a much-needed vacation and he more than earned some peace from my crazy shit for a few days, even though I'm quite sure he wouldn't be put out to check on that for me.

Still, I hesitate to make the call partly because it truly shouldn't make a difference to me. While the matching DNA would be unequivocal proof that JT raped both the loves of my life, I also have Sela's word, and that's as good as DNA in my opinion.

But mostly I don't call him because if I did, he'd naturally want to know why I'm asking, and I sure as fuck am not going to let one other single soul in on what went down with JT. If I call Dennis, I'll have to tell him JT's dead. If I ask about the DNA matching, he'll connect the dots, and then he'll probably push at me for details. It's too risky, and hence my decision is made not to involve Dennis.

At least not yet.

But if things get dicey later, and I need a man with his particular skill set to help Sela and me out, I'll make the call with no hesitation.

Lifting my head from the cushion, I put the car in drive and pull onto the gravel roadway that will lead back out to the main park road. I need to get home and get cleaned up. I've got some calls to make on behalf of the business. I'd sent an email out late last night to the entire company about JT's death, as I knew it would hit the news and I didn't want anyone to be caught unaware. I also called Linda and asked her to personally call Karla to let her know. I told the staff I'd be in on Wednesday, but that I would need the day off to help make arrangements for JT's funeral.

It was a lie.

I needed today off to do whatever I could to erase Sela's part in JT's death so she wouldn't get caught and she could live her life in peace as she deserved.

Mentally going through a to-do list, I know the next few days are going to be brutal. I'll have to play the grieving partner and friend, prepare a eulogy for a man I despise, deliver it with more acting skill than I needed with the cops, and figure out how to soothe the company employees who will no doubt be traumatized by all of this.

But that could all wait until tomorrow.

For now, I needed to get home.

To Sela.

CHAPTER 9

. . . .

Sela

Despite the nearly hour and a half drive each way to Healdsburg, and the hour we spent having lunch, I still beat Beck back to the condo by almost thirty minutes. I was waiting on pins and needles, not because I was nervous about what he'd just done for me today, but because I wasn't sure how he was processing his pain about what he learned about Caroline's rape.

When the front door opens, I immediately rise from my perch at the dining room table. His eyes slide to mine and he gives me a tired but confident smile.

"Hey," he says as he shuts the door, locks it, and tosses his keys and wallet on the foyer table. His face is streaked with dried sweat and dirt, and the front of his jeans are filthy. In his other hand, he has his sweatshirt balled up and I can also see it spotted with dirt.

"Who won?" I ask as I walk toward him. "You or the pig?"

"Excuse me?" he asks, brows furrowing inward with confusion, and I know he must be completely exhausted in both mind and body to not get my joke.

"It looks like you just wrestled a pig in mud," I point out as I circle my fingers around his wrist, pulling the sweatshirt out of his other hand. I drop it to the floor and turn toward our bedroom, pulling Beck behind me. "Let's get you cleaned up."

He follows me, content to let me lead. He doesn't say a word, but I don't need him to. I don't care or worry about what he did with the letter opener and bloody clothes. I knew from that brief smile he gave me just a moment ago that it was handled in the best way possible.

I lead Beck straight into our master bath, releasing my hold on him to start the shower. It's not lost on me that he was doing the very same thing for me just about twenty-four hours ago. Then he was wanting me to clean away the blood of my crime. Now I want him to clean away the grunge of his.

When I turn around, I find Beck stripping down. This disappoints me slightly, because I had wanted to do that for him. I want to take absolute care of him right now.

Without hesitation, I start taking my clothes off, starting with the awful cheap boots I'm wearing. Beck doesn't act surprised, and even though I know he's depleted, his eyes still wander over my body with a quiet flickering of heat in them. When his pants come off, I can see he's starting to get hard just from watching me disrobe, but that's just going to have to wait.

I reach out and take him by the wrist again, leading him into the shower. While Beck prefers us taking a bath together in his huge garden tub, I'm a fan of his shower. It's huge . . . at least six by ten feet with three walls of pristine white tile and the fourth side mostly open with just a half wall made of clear glass blocks. There's a wide bench that runs the length of the shower, but my favorite part is the various valves and sprays that offers a huge overhead waterfall, nine individual body sprays set into three of the walls as well as a multifunction hand shower that Beck has used numerous times to get me off. It has three different pulse speeds that are divine.

But that's for another time, because the minute I pull Beck into the body sprays, he lets out an almost pained sigh of relief.

"Feel good?" I murmur as I watch him tilt his head back under the waterfall to wet his hair.

"Mmmmm-hmmmm," he responds with his eyes closed.

I reach over and grab the bar of soap from a corner tiled ledge, and I rub it into a froth with a washcloth. Then I methodically take my time and go over every inch of Beck's body, starting first with his hands because they are the filthiest. I take great care with them, using a nailbrush to help get the dirt that's caked under his nails. When they're practically sparkling, I reload the washcloth with the bar of soap and start at his neck and work my way down. Over his shoulders and across his upper back, where I gently wash over the tattoo that's half red phoenix and half dragon.

By the time the washcloth hits Beck's abs, he's trying to wash me as well, his hands coming to my body in a natural way that can't be helped. He's never been one to sit back and let me just do things to him. He always wants to be touching me, focusing on my sensations first, his second.

I bat his hands away, telling him to be still and let me finish. He responds with a slight growl, makes an attempt to drop his hands by his sides, but when my washcloth hits his ass, they come back up again. Granted, they merely rest on my shoulders, his thumbs stroking my wet skin, but they don't make any further move so I let them stay.

Because as long as his hands are being good, I can concentrate on my task.

I bring the soapy cloth back around front, across his hip and over his lower abs, pushing upward to get his chest a second time. Only because I love his chest so much. It's a fabulous chest, well defined with a smattering of hair in the center. It's also clean and doesn't need my attention anymore, but I can't help it. I love touching Beck.

Ultimately, my mistake is when I lift my face to take a peek at his. I find him staring down at me with the most intense look I've ever seen. Blue eyes flashing at me like a blinking neon sign that's advertising his emotions.

Love.

Lust.

Protectiveness.

Vulnerability.

Yes . . . that last one. Him looking vulnerable.

That gets me.

My eyes drop back down to the washcloth and I try to speak, but my voice is raspy with emotion. I cough and try to go for a light, casual tone so he doesn't see just how much a single look from him can move me so deeply. "Thank you for what you did for me today."

With lightning speed, Beck's hand is under my chin, tilting my face up again. Same flashing signs of emotion in those ocean-blue eyes, but a new urgency there. "There isn't anything I won't do for you, Sela."

"I know," I whisper back to him, slowly moving the cloth from his chest down his stomach.

"I'll do anything to ensure you never go down for that—"

"I'll do the same. I'll never let you go down either."

He smiles at me . . . a bit amused at my proclamation because it impedes on his white-knight territory. "Neither one of us is going down. How 'bout that?"

"I can live with that," I breathe out.

"Good," he says, his eyes now lighting up with a different kind of look. One that makes my knees go weak. "Now how about dropping that washcloth and using your hands on me."

I arch an eyebrow at him but drop the cloth to the tiled floor, where it lands with a wet splat. I take his semi-hard cock in my hand and give him a squeeze. "Like this?"

His eyes close and he licks his lower lip. "Just like that."

My other hand cups his balls, rolling them around and then running my finger along the delicate skin behind them. "How about this?"

He groans. "Yeah . . . that's good too."

"Bet my mouth would be better," I observe as I stroke his slick skin until he's fully hard in my hand.

"So much better," he agrees in a guttural voice.

I release him, bring my hands to his waist, and turn him toward the shower bench. He blinks in surprise but lets me push him down until he's sitting and I step in between his legs.

"But first," I say with a playful smile as I reach for the shampoo, "let's get your hair washed."

"You know it's dangerous to tease me like that, Sela," he warns, and the dark promise in his voice causes a tremor to run up my spine.

I shrug like I don't care, but I do.

I so care that he's beyond turned on by me.

I care so much about this man that I want us to consume each other completely.

Holding the shampoo bottle in one hand and the other going to his shoulder for leverage, I haul myself onto him to straddle his lap. His straining cock bumps between my legs and I let out a quavering breath that simple, inadvertent touch causes.

Beck's hands come to my hips but he doesn't try to push me down onto him. He merely holds me steady while I flip the top open from the shampoo and pour a small amount into my hand. The bottle drops to the bench and then my hands are in Beck's wet hair, my fingers massaging his scalp and working up a lather.

I know it feels good to him because he gives a rumbling sound of appreciation in his chest and his head falls forward until his face is pressed into my neck. I feel his mouth open and suck against me lightly, his fingers digging into the flesh at my hips.

"That feels so good, Sela," he murmurs as I go a little rougher in my ministrations, hoping to work out some stress and tension for him. But then he pushes down on me slightly and raises his hips; that amazingly large and hard shaft rubs right against my pussy and reminds me of my earlier intention to suck Beck off.

Reaching up, I grab the hand shower, flipping the tiny valve at the base that will let water through.

"Let's get your hair rinsed," I tell him as I gently wave the shower wand over his head while he tilts it back. As the soap runs free, and then clear, I tell him with brazen promise in my voice, "I'm going to give you a blow job that will make your eyes cross."

"Uh-uh," he says with a shake of his head and a wicked gleam in his gaze as he takes the wand from me, lowering it until the hose is stretched fully before releasing it. "That's just not going to work for me."

I start to ask why not, because hello, I've gotten really good at my blow jobs, but then he's reaching between us and bringing the head of his cock right to my center. My hips involuntarily rotate, dragging him into me slowly.

"That's it," he encourages me in a low voice, his hands now back to my hips. "I want you to fuck me, Sela. And do it slow, okay?"

"Okay," I practically wheeze out, because not only is the feeling of him just inside of me—just waiting for me to fully impale myself—incredibly intense, but the way in which he's giving me some control is almost too much to bear.

Beck is always the one driving when we're fucking. Always the one in control. Always the one who determines the pace and the position.

It's something I've never minded because I adore him being

in control. It makes me feel immensely cherished and it's a huge turn-on to know that he's so confident in his skills that I would never want to ever give that up.

I slide my hands from his shoulders, up the sides of his neck, and then cup his face. I press my mouth to his and kiss him briefly before pulling back. Placing my forehead against his, I take a breath in, hold it, and then drop my body so I can take him all the way into me.

Inch by delicious inch, I slowly sink onto his cock, feeling the stretch and tiny sting that always comes because of his size but quickly melts away into the most exquisite of pleasures my body has ever felt.

When he's buried as deep as I can take him—that point where the head of his cock presses almost uncomfortably against that magical place inside of me—I give him another quick kiss before I start to move.

While Beck has commanded that I fuck him and do so slowly, he ends up using his hands on my hips to help guide me along. He does indeed let me raise and lower with sweet leisure, but after a few moments, he forces me to go a little faster. I try to push against the deep thrusts he's demanding because that very magical place inside of me is super sensitive to Beck's dick and will have me screaming like a banshee in no time.

And I want us to come together.

It's my favorite thing in the world to do with Beck.

My legs tremble as I try to slow it down a bit and Beck uses his superior strength to push past my stubbornness. He thrusts upward with his hips, slamming me back down so our skin slaps loudly past the hiss of the shower, and my body starts tightening with an impending orgasm.

"Slow down, Beck," I huff out as he has me practically bouncing up and down on him.

"Pick it up," he counters wickedly, and then surges up off the bench after slamming upward deeply. He turns, and with sure footing presses me into the wall with three of the imbedded shower sprays, causing water to spray every which way once my back hits them.

Then Beck is back in complete control and he starts to really pound me hard. He thrusts into me with carnal grunts and animalistic growls. He hits my G-spot over and over again, and all I can do is hang on for the ride, my legs trying to lock around him but flopping uselessly while he holds me up under the backs of my thighs.

"Fuck that feels good," Beck groans on a deeper-than-deep thrust, and that's all she wrote for me.

My orgasm tears free, and in that moment of superior bliss, I can't care that I left Beck behind because it's the most intense, wonderful feeling in the world.

So intense that I barely notice that Beck goes still within me and then grinds his pelvis hard against mine as he mutters, "I'm coming, baby. Deep in that pussy of mine. Coming so hard."

Those words . . . the fact I can feel him jerking inside of me . . . knocks a mini orgasm loose and I cry out with a relief I didn't know I needed following that super orgasm he just handed to me.

My head falls forward until it's resting on Beck's shoulder and he nuzzles the side of his face against my wet hair.

"Good, Sela?" he asks me, and I can hear the smug confidence in his voice.

We haven't had much to smile about lately, but that causes one to break free. "So good, Beck. So very good."

"And that's the way it's always going to be," he says softly, and all I can do is hope and pray that he's right and that our days together aren't numbered.

CHAPTER 10

. . . .

Beck

I wanted to do something normal after having the most bizarre and nerve-racking morning of my life. It's not every day a man hides evidence of a crime to protect his woman.

Feeling mellow after that amazing shower sex, and a bit calmer than I was this morning after discovering the truth about Caroline and JT, I suggested we walk down to the market and pick up something to cook for dinner. It's not something Sela and I do often, preferring to dine out because we're both so busy, and neither one of us is that great in the kitchen on a regular basis. She agreed and we returned with some chicken breasts marinated in pesto sauce, along with some tomatoes, mozzarella, and basil for a simple salad. On impulse, I bought a can of whipped cream and figured we could have dessert in bed later that night.

Working companionably side by side, I prepared the salad while she got the chicken ready to bake. We both sipped on a nondescript Cab we also picked up, both of us okay with the silence. We'd been talking about so much heavy stuff lately that the quiet was actually a bit soothing.

But she broke it all too soon.

"So . . . where did you—"

"Don't ask, Sela," I warn her, and then lean over and swat her on the ass. "You don't ever need to know."

Because no way in hell she needs to know about my trek into the deep forest to conceal what she did. I don't want her ever being put in a position of having to make a choice to reveal that information or not in the future if she was pressed to give it.

I expect her to push at me, but she merely gives an acquiescing sigh and says, "Fine."

"But I am going to be all nosy and ask about what you and Caroline talked about at lunch today," I tell her without an ounce of shame.

She turns that lovely face to me, her lips quirking in amusement. "Don't ask."

"Tell me," I demand. "Or I shall be forced to put you over my knee."

She snorts, picks up the pan of chicken, and places it on the top rack of the oven. After closing the door, she turns to me and says, "If that's the consequences for holding my tongue, I'm not telling you a damn thing."

I jerk my chin upward in acknowledgment of her right to stay silent before placing the knife on the counter. I pick up a dish towel, casually wipe my hands, and then lay it back down. I do this all while Sela watches me with anticipation of my next move.

Which comes lightning fast.

I lunge at her and she squeals, so shocked at my move that she practically runs in place. I bend down, put my shoulder to her stomach, and lift her up over my shoulder. She squirms and I slap her lightly on the ass. "That's just a taste of what you'll get."

I'm not sure, but I think I hear her sigh an, "Oh yes" as I carry her into the living room.

Falling onto the couch, I manage to twist her on the descent so she comes to rest lying across my lap, and before she can even think to struggle, I bring my hand down hard on her ass. She yelps from the sting and then says in the sexiest voice ever, "God . . . you better do that to me tonight in bed. And repetitively."

I laugh and pull her up into a sitting position, turn her so she straddles me, then hold her by the hips. "Tell me what you two talked about."

Sela gets a redolent smile on her face, which is indicative of the fondness she holds in her heart for Caroline. I'm not sure if it's solely because they share in a horrific experience or because they both love me, but I know without a doubt that these two will become extremely close one day.

If we can get past all this shit.

Bringing her hands to my shoulders, Sela leans in and kisses me quickly on my lips. When she pulls back she says, "I tried to get Caroline on my side to gang up on you so you'd agree to let me go to the police and tell them what happened."

I stiffen and my amused smile turns into a glare.

Before I can chastise her though, she says, "Relax, stud. She talked me off the ledge."

My body instantly deflates, and while I've been in protective mode of Sela since she showed up bloody in my office yesterday, I don't think I realized how strong she still felt about this issue. I thought it was a dead horse, but apparently it needs more beating.

"There's no reason to go to them," I tell her with what I hope is my most reasonable voice. "Do I need to go over how I came to this conclusion again?"

"One more time," she says, her eyes somber and searching for me to say something that will make it okay in her heart to not step up to the plate and take responsibility.

I sigh with slight agitation but I give it to her one more time again. "Sela . . . you and I both know that you had no choice. It was clearly self-defense. But there are no unbiased witnesses to the event, and the police are going to focus on your motive. You have a good one and you know it since you were in fact planning on killing him at some point. And let's not forget that you went into his home with a gun."

"When you say it like that," she says softly, eyes lowering, "you make it sound like I'm totally guilty."

"No," I say urgently, bending my head and getting into her space so she'll look at me. "I make it sound like we have a fucked-up legal system and you got caught in a really shitty situation that doesn't have a good resolution. So we're making the best of it, and right now, if we're lucky, there's going to be nothing that ties you to JT's death."

"But they could come after you—"

"There's nothing that ties me either," I remind her, although I'm painfully aware that I have just as much motive as she does. If the police ever get wind of that, they are going to sniff very hard at me.

A knocking on my door jolts my senses and Sela and I both go utterly still, our eyes locked on each other. Twenty-four hours ago, the police were knocking on that same door to tell us about JT.

Sela slowly climbs off my lap, smoothing down nonexistent wrinkles in her jeans. I push up off the couch and touch my knuckles under her chin. I smile at her encouragingly and whisper, "It's all going to be fine. I promise."

She nods at me uncertainly but puts on a brave face. I walk to the door and hesitantly look through the peephole, expecting beyond doubt to see Detectives DeLatemer and Denning standing there.

Instead I see the pinched face of my mother, and for a brief moment, I almost wish it was the police coming to question me further.

I open the door, swing it wide because it would be rude not to invite her in, and say, "Mother . . . this is a surprise."

Helen North is unequivocally a stunning woman, and she's dressed impeccably in something that's probably labeled Chanel or Halston. She cuts me a sharp look and walks in amid a swirl of designer perfume before whirling on me as I shut the door.

"I'm very worried about your father, Beck," she says without any preamble. "I think you need to talk to him."

With a sigh, I pinch the bridge of my nose while briefly squeezing my eyes shut. "What's wrong?"

"I don't know," she says in a clipped formal tone. No warmth in her concern. "He's been holed up in his office since we got the news about JT and won't come out. He won't talk to me. I'm extremely worried."

She says all of this in a rush, and as she does so, I notice her leaning in toward me imperceptibly, her eyes flicking back and forth between my own.

As if she's trying to gauge my reaction to her words?

And then it hits me . . . she knows about JT being my father's son. I'm not sure how she knows, because fuck, I thought only my dad, JT's mom, and I were in on the dirty secret. But seems like everyone knows, and I have to wonder if Colin Townsend does too.

It's what I hate most about my family. The deceit and the lies and the cover-ups. Ironic that I'm perpetrating a cover-up myself, but that's different.

Then again, it's always different when it involves the one you love, right?

Because I don't have the time, inclination or mental fortitude to even begin to get into this with my mother, I play dumb. "I'm sure he's just upset over the shock of this. It's been hard on all of us."

She shakes her head almost violently to deny my denial of the truth she wants, and that's when her attention is caught by Sela standing in the living room. My mother goes stock-still and I turn to see Sela looking back at her like a deer caught in the headlights. She swallows hard and says, "Hello, Mrs. North. It's good to see you again, although I'm sorry it's under these circumstances."

My mother definitely has rude down to a science, particularly when she believes someone is beneath her. I tense up knowing she's not going to be nice to Sela.

And she's not, leveling her venom in a masterful way. She turns her back on Sela without even acknowledging her greeting. It speaks volumes that Sela's wearing a V-neck T-shirt that doesn't cover the vivid bruises at the bottom of her neck and my mother didn't even notice. Piercing me with a commanding look, my mother says to me with a shooing motion with her hand, "You need to have her leave, Beck, so we can talk privately."

I can't help it. It's inappropriate as hell, but I let out a bark of a laugh at the ludicrousness of this woman who birthed me. And then I can't stop laughing.

I laugh so hard tears form in my eyes and I almost double over, my stomach hurts so much from the hilarity.

My mother doesn't find it so funny and hisses at me, "Honestly, Beckett. You are being disrespectful."

Straightening up, I swipe at the wetness from my eyes, wind down the full-belly laughs to a chuckle before turning it into a smirk. "Disrespectful, Mother? You're seriously saying that when you just disrespected Sela in her own home?"

"We need to talk privately—"

"Or how about when you disrespected your own daughter by trying to keep her rape silent?" I growl at my mom, all humor over the situation having fled and replaced with scorching anger. Years of anger I'd let simmer.

My mother blinks in surprise, as I've never gone head-to-head with her before, not because I didn't want to, but because I was being respectful of her role as my mother. It appears my own respect has seemed to have flown away as well.

"Beck," Sela says quietly from the living room, but I hold a hand out, indicating for her to stay out of it. She closes her mouth, but out of my peripheral vision, I see her turn and walk down the hallway to our bedroom, giving my mother the privacy she requested.

But I don't take my eyes off Mother. They are locked and I'm loaded, the past twenty-four hours having created such a stressful burden on my shoulders it didn't take much for me to snap.

Just a quick little visit from Mommy Dearest.

"Or how about the disrespect you've shown to your granddaughter . . . your own flesh and blood?" I ask my mom quietly but with no less menace in my attitude. "Wanting her to be aborted."

My mother pales slightly but sticks her chin out aggressively. "I stand by that advice; Caroline didn't need—"

"You don't get to talk about Caroline to me," I say, cutting her off, and walk into her space. Leaning my head down, I come almost nose to nose with my mother, anger vibrating within me for all of the terrible ways my mother failed as a mother. "You don't get to talk about Ally. You don't get to talk about your worries about Dad, or the fact your house was once featured in *Architectural Digest*. You don't get to talk about anything with me, Mother. I'm done with you."

She gasps, bringing her hand to flutter at the gold necklace that sits at the base of her throat. "Beck . . . you don't say things like that to your mother."

I know I shouldn't say it, but she opened the door too wide for me not to. Besides, she clearly doesn't get what I'm saying or that she's been a miserable failure.

So I say it. "You're not my mother. Now, if you'll please leave."

She stares at me a moment, and I might have considered her potentially part human if she'd have at least the moral grace to look as if I hurt her feelings. Instead, her eyes go cold and she squares her shoulders. "I'll have a talk with your father about this."

I turn from her and open the door. "You go right ahead and do that, Helen."

I have to literally bite down on my tongue not to throw JT in her face. I want to say, *"You go right ahead, Mother, and talk to Dad about all of this. Ask him about JT too. You want to know why he's so upset, ask him about JT and what he really means to him."*

But I don't.

The minute I said I was done with her, I meant it.

I'm done.

CHAPTER 11

. . . .

Sela

My heart aches for Beck.

For many things and in many ways.

But hearing him tell his mother he was done brings about a sadness that feels like a heavy, suffocating blanket upon me. I can't imagine, because my mother was wonderful and there's not a day that goes by I don't think of her and wish I had her back. To think that Beck's maternal experiences were so horrific over his lifetime, that it would be a relief to cut that poison from his life, is almost too unbearable to even consider.

I leave the sanctity of the bedroom behind once I hear the door shut behind his mother and find Beck in the kitchen. The oven door is open and he's checking the chicken.

"I think it's done," he says, sensing my presence behind him.

"Let me see," I say as I walk up, put a gentle hand on his back, and peer in the door beside him.

It looks about done, but I won't know for sure until we cut those puppies open and see if they're cooked through. Beck grabs two pot holders and nudges me aside with his hip, pulling out the pan of baked chicken. It smells delicious and I'm starved, even though the events of the last few minutes have left a sour taste in the back of my mouth.

I pull a fork and knife from the cutlery drawer and cut into one of the breasts. As I pull it apart to look at it, Beck says, "So . . . back to our original discussion . . . what else did you and Caroline talk about at lunch today other than going to the police, which I'm assuming is a subject that's been thoroughly discussed and won't be discussed again?"

My jaw drops slightly and I turn to look at him. "Don't you want to talk about what just happened with your mother?"

Beck tilts his head to the side and gives me a sympathetic smile. "Poor Sela," he says with gentle mockery that's not meant to hurt but to let me know he finds me silly in my concern. "Wanting to romanticize a nonexistent mother-son relationship."

I huff out a curse and swat him on the chest. "I'm being serious."

"So am I, babe," he says before leaning in for a quick kiss. His eyes are somber but his tone is oddly light. "You saw me do something I should have done a long time ago. I cut the poison out, and frankly, I feel better for it."

My skeptical look rings through loud and clear, but I give him some concession. "If you're sure, then fine. But if you want to talk about it, lay it on me. I've got loads of advice and sweet sentiments to get you through."

"You are a silly girl," he says, and turns to the cupboard to grab two plates. "But seriously . . . what did you and Caroline talk about?"

"God, you're like a dog with a bone," I grumble as I take a plate from him and put a chicken breast on it. I set that down on the counter and take the other. "But if you must know, we skirted around the edges of our respective rapes. I think we'll probably discuss details in the future with each other."

"Go on," he says as I hand him another plate with the second chicken breast. He turns and puts a few pieces of tomato and mozzarella, which still need to be finished off with basil and balsamic, onto both plates.

"What do you mean, go on?" I ask evasively, as I go to the fridge and grab the fresh basil. Like a coordinated team, Beck grabs the balsamic sitting beside the stove top.

"I mean, tell me what was said about me," he says in exasperation. "And don't try to pretend I wasn't discussed."

I shrug and begin shredding basil by hand over the tomato and mozzarella while Beck drizzles balsamic. "She wanted to know how you were holding up. I told her you were fine."

"You lied to her."

"Because I know you're not," I affirm. "But she doesn't need to know that."

Beck nods but remains silent. We grab the plates, forks and knives, and head into the dining room, Beck pausing to grab two bottles of water from the fridge. We sit and start on our meals. I'm beyond famished and know the way I'll shovel the food in will not be pretty.

As he cuts into his chicken, Beck says, "There's an awful lot of lying going on."

I look up at him, a bite of mozzarella halfway to my mouth. I lower my fork. "What do you mean?"

"You told Caroline I'm fine when I'm not—"

"To protect her," I point out.

He nods understandingly. "Yes, I get it. But it's made me think about all of the deception that's been going on . . . for fuck's sake, for most of my life. My parents lying to the outside world that we were a happy family. Covering up Caroline's rape. Not acknowledging Ally. My dad and JT. All of that . . ."

"Not telling the police what really happened with JT," I add softly.

He ignores that. "Covering up JT's death aside, because that ship's already sailed, I'm just tired of all of it, so when you saw me cut my mother out, that was the first step in correcting some of that shit."

"I can understand that," I say neutrally, because I don't really think he's telling me this to justify his actions with his mother.

"I think I was disloyal to Caroline," he says quietly.

And there it is. I knew there was something else driving this.

"How?" I ask simply.

"By still having a relationship with my parents after what they did to her," he murmurs, laying his knife and fork down. His eyes are so sad when they look at me. "I should have cut them out then. I should have chosen Caroline and Ally completely. I should have made my stand for what was right, and by not doing it, I was just as complicit in their rotten ways."

I don't even know what to say to this, because sadly, I think he may be right. I never understood really why Beck maintained a relationship with them, although it was nothing more than a few get-togethers each year. But it wasn't for me to judge and it still isn't.

The one thing I do know without a doubt is that Caroline never looked upon Beck differently for choosing to give them a small sliver of his life.

"When we were at lunch today," I say as I reach across the table and cover his hand with my own, "I was telling Caroline about how for the longest time I thought getting raped was my fault. That I brought it on myself."

Beck nods and doesn't attempt to disillusion me on that feeling. We've discussed this before . . . many times . . . and he knows those feelings, while complicated and misplaced, had credence in the past.

"Caroline had felt the same way," I continue. "Not surprising. I think a lot of rape victims probably feel a level of culpability."

He watches me carefully, understanding damn well that I have a point to all this.

So I make it clear. "I told Caroline it took me a very long time to come to grips with that, and do you know what she said?"

Beck shakes his head.

"She said it didn't take her all that long to get past that," I tell him, my eyes boring into his. "She said you wouldn't let her. That you were her rock and savior. That you helped her find peace. So I guarantee you she doesn't give a shit if you have a Christmas drink or a slice of birthday cake a few times a year at your parents' house."

He sighs long and loud, flips his hand over, and squeezes mine. "I know. You're right."

"Damn tootin' I am," I say with a smile, and then pull my hand away so I can eat.

Only getting hungrier here.

"I think we need to tell Caroline that JT is the one who raped her," Beck says quietly, but his tone doesn't diminish the force of the bomb he just threw at me.

"What?" I ask, stunned beyond any further words.

"She needs to know the truth. It's going to hurt like hell, but it will give her closure. She'll be able to stop the wondering who did it, and I know you understand that, Sela. You're going to be left wondering about your other two attackers."

And fuck if he isn't right. It's gnaws at me every day not know-ing who committed those atrocities on me along with JT.

"Are you going to tell her that JT was her half brother?" I ask hesitantly, because that's the twist to the twisted story that Caroline will be forced to hear from us.

He nods. "Yeah . . . and I know it's a loathsome thought, but fuck if I can be wigged out by it. I see Ally and how good and smart and funny and kind she is, and there's nothing of JT in her. She's pure Caroline, and that is how I'm choosing to look at it."

And damn . . . my heart. Right there that got me. It flutters with little happy wings of joy that I have someone as amazing as this man.

"I wish I had known you back when . . . well, you know," I tell him with a sheepish smile. "Caroline's such a lucky woman to have had you by her side."

"You got through it just fine without me," Beck says, and then picks up his utensils. "But you got me now and that's what really matters, right?"

"Right!" I agree, and pick up my fork with mozzarella still speared on the end.

I bring it to my mouth but then stop again when Beck says, "There's something else that's been eating at me."

I lower my fork and sigh wistfully at it. Beck snickers and says, "Eat your food and listen while I talk."

"Okay," I say, happily picking it back up again and placing the cheese in my mouth before I can be stopped again.

"The DNA's bugging me," he tells me while he works on cutting up his chicken.

I nod and speak around the food in my mouth. I know what he's talking about because it's caused me a little worry too. "You mean that if JT raped both Caroline and me, how come the DNA wasn't matched up?"

"Yeah," he says, deciding to dice the entire chicken breast before eating as he continues to throw his thoughts out to me. "It could be that JT lied to you. Told you he raped Caroline just to torture you a bit before he killed you, and I wouldn't put it past that sadistic fuck to do that."

"But you don't think he lied," I observe as I spear a piece of tomato.

He shrugs. "I honestly don't know. The other plausible explanation is that something happened on the police side of things and the DNA didn't get entered in correctly. I mean . . . no clue how that shit works, but people are fallible. Computers are fallible. Who knows?"

"And Dennis did mention that he didn't see the documentation in the file about sending the DNA in to the database . . . whatever that was called," I add.

"That's right," he agrees, and finally puts some food into his mouth. He chews, swallows, and then repeats as he contemplates what this all means.

Finally, he lowers his fork again and says, "I need to know, but I'm not sure how to go about doing it."

"Just call the investigating officer in my case. Simple as that."

"Maybe," he says hesitantly. "But I'm a little worried about drawing attention to us right now. And we certainly can't tell them why we're questioning it. It's just extra motive to pin on us. So, I don't know. It doesn't feel right, but then again, it's the easiest thing to do."

"Have Dennis get involved?" I suggest.

And I can tell by the look on his face that he's already considered this. "He's on vacation, and I hate to bother him."

"What the fuck ever, Beckett North," I scoff at him. "Dennis is a friend and he'd jump all over this in a heartbeat."

"And he'd ask us questions," he points out, and now I understand his hesitancy. "I don't want to drag him in any deeper."

"Well, we don't have to decide right this minute," I tell him as I pick up my utensils again. "I say we finish dinner and relax the rest of the night. God knows we need a little downtime away from all of this worry and stress."

"And we have whipped cream," he says with a husky laugh.

"Exactly." I pop the tomato into my mouth and chew through my grin at him.

Beck's phone starts ringing from the kitchen and he stands up to retrieve it. As he's walking away from me, he looks over his shoulder and adds, "But I don't think we tell Caroline until we know for sure about the DNA. Agreed?"

"Sure," I say with a nod of acceptance. It wasn't going to matter if we told her tomorrow or a few weeks from now.

Beck disappears into the kitchen, and before it can ring a third time, he answers, "Beck North."

He's silent for several moments, then I hear him say with resignation, "Sure. I'll be there at two."

He disconnects without even saying goodbye and I know this because he suddenly appears in the dining room before me.

"That was my attorney," Beck says in a low voice filled with tension. "The police want me to come in and give a formal statement tomorrow. He's arranged us to meet there at two P.M."

The food in my stomach seems to turn to lead as a heavy feeling of unease settles in. All thoughts of whipped cream and relaxation are now gone.

Tomorrow the police will talk to Beck, and while they certainly may want to just pick his brain about the potential of a bookie killing JT, my gut instinct says they're putting a narrowed eye on Beck because of his close relationship with his partner.

A kernel of fear forms in the center of my chest and I imagine the worst.

Beck going down for my sins.

. . . .

CHAPTER 12

Beck

I don't know this attorney, but he seems more than capable. My buddy Robert Colling, who is a domestic attorney, recommended this guy, Doug Shriver, to represent me in dealing with the police. I'd called Robert not long after the cops showed up at my condo on the night JT died and essentially told him the basics that he needed to know.

That being JT was dead under suspicious circumstances and the cops wanted to talk to me further.

Robert called Doug, and Doug called me.

We spoke for fifteen minutes and he advised me it would be best if we not only cooperated in the investigation but were proactive in setting up the meeting with the detectives as they requested. And so this is where I am now, waiting in a large conference room at the Sausalito PD that isn't what I expected from watching a few episodes of *Law & Order*. The room's brightly lit with large windows letting in sunshine. The opposite interior wall is solid, clear glass with vertical blinds that are open so we can see the hallway that's lined with individual offices with detectives' names on brass plates beside each door. The room almost has a boardroom feel to it, as the conference table is oval shaped and done in cherry wood with eight chairs around it covered in burgundy leather.

Doug and I had met an hour before this meeting at a nearby coffeehouse, along with Sela, who's back there waiting for us. He's an interesting-looking fellow, not one I would immediately associate with a big-time criminal defense attorney. He's probably about sixty with curly hair worn short and completely grayed. He can't be any taller than five five and wears a nondescript navy suit with a smart yellow bow tie. Horn-rims complete the look, which is more retired professor than courtroom shark.

Even though Robert recommended Doug, I'd done research, and the guy had some seriously big cases under his belt and was known for representing high-profile celebrities who got into trouble. He assured me that he wasn't going to let me answer anything that could be construed as incriminating, but that we wanted to be as open as we could so they would be assured we had nothing to hide.

I struggled not to laugh when he said that. I guess poor Doug looks at all potential clients as innocent.

The conference room door opens and Detective Denning walks in, carrying a cardboard tray with three large lidded cups. She kicks the door closed behind her and gives a quick nod to me and Doug as she rounds the opposite side of the table from us and sits down. Pushing the tray toward us, she says, "Coffee if you want some."

Doug grabs a cup but I don't. It might be paranoid, but I'm not about to leave evidence behind. "Thanks but no," I say politely. "I've already had my one allotted cup for the day."

"Would you like some water?" she asks.

"I'm good."

"All right then," she says leaning back in her chair, also ignoring the coffee. "My partner is handling some other things in the investigation so it's just us today. And this is just sort of an informal get-together so we can get more information about this theory that Mr. Townsend was killed for a gambling debt."

I nod with an understanding smile but she's not fooling me. Informal get-together my ass. I didn't miss the mounted camera in the corner with the red light that popped on as soon as Detective Denning sat down at the table. She doesn't have a notepad or computer with her, and I'm sure she wants this to appear as a friendly little meeting so I'll open up.

"I'm sure you've noticed the camera," she says, jerking a thumb over her shoulder at it.

Yup. Noticed that.

"We're recording this, and for the record, can you state your name?"

"Beckett North," I reply.

"And you're represented by attorney Doug Shriver, who is in attendance with us today, correct?"

"Correct."

"Mr. North, I'd like to know more about this gambling debt you say that Mr. Townsend owed to someone," she says almost lazily, and I get the distinct impression she really doesn't care about it.

So I tell her everything I know, leaving out, of course, the way in which I orchestrated VanZant to take the fall. I tell her about JT calling me to pick him up at the hospital, and how he told me he was in deep with a Vegas bookie. That he'd lost two million and doubled down on the VanZant fight, who we know as a matter of public record got his ass handed to him. I told her JT seemed panicked and how he begged me for the money, and yes, I even admitted to her that I didn't agree to give it to him at first. I didn't particularly like admitting this, but I knew I had to.

"Did there come a point when you agreed to bail him out?" she asks.

I nod. "I told him I'd give him the money plus an extra million, and he wouldn't have to repay me, and in return I wanted him to sign over ownership of our business."

She doesn't seem surprised by this at all, and that makes me nervous.

"Why did you want ownership of The Sugar Bowl?" she prods.

"Because he was clearly making terrible financial decisions," I hedge. She doesn't press me further.

"And did he agree to those terms?"

I shrug. "I have no clue. I was expecting him to call me and let me know his answer the day he died. He only had three days to deliver the money to the bookie and I told him I'd need some time to get some funds liquidated."

"If they gave him three days to pay the money, why would they bother killing him before the deadline?" she asks as she leans back in her chair.

"No idea," I tell her. "Why did they beat him up so soon after he lost the bet?"

"That is the million-dollar question, isn't it?" she muses, and then flashes a grin. "Or the five-million-dollar question as it may be."

I don't laugh or smile back.

Detective Denning now leans forward in her chair, placing her forearms on the table and clasping her hands. Gone is the casual cop, and now I'm seeing one who has determination in her eyes.

"Mr. North . . . you'd actually been having quite a bit of trouble with Mr. Townsend of late, hadn't you?" she asks slyly, and I know she absolutely knows the fucking answer to this question and it's not a stab in the dark. She's clearly been busy looking into JT and me regarding The Sugar Bowl.

"It's not a secret," I tell her candidly. "He'd been spiraling out of control. Drugs . . . gambling. I was afraid he'd drag the business down."

"In fact, you've tried to buy him out on more than one occasion, correct?"

Fuck. I'm guessing she's talked to JT's business attorney. My attorney can't reveal that information because it's protected, but JT's attorney could sure help out the investigation.

"That's correct," I say, but don't offer an explanation.

"And the way I understand your partnership agreement"— *yup, she's talked to JT's attorney*—"you couldn't force him out unless he did something criminal that affected the actual business itself, correct?"

"Yes," I grit out, and feel myself starting to get angry at the way she's piecing this all together.

"So the drugs and the illegal gambling debt wasn't something that could get him out, right?"

"Right."

"In fact, you could almost say that the only way to get him out was for him to willingly agree to a buyout—let's say for five million dollars—or if he was dead?"

I don't answer her question but instead ask her, "Detective . . . are you insinuating I killed JT to get him out of the business?"

She shrugs, sits back in her chair. "I'm not insinuating anything, Mr. North. I'm investigating all angles."

"Well you don't seem to be taking it very seriously that his gambling debt probably got him killed," I retort.

"We've thoroughly checked all of Mr. Townsend's phone records and computers. We can't find any communications whatsoever with anyone remotely related to gambling," she says.

"He used a burner phone then," I suggest.

She ignores that and says, "What is interesting though is that there was a call Mr. Townsend made to your girlfriend just a few hours before he died. And she called him back. Any idea what that was?"

I was prepared for this because I knew the police would easily find that information. "Yes. Sela told me he left her a voice mail while she was in class. She called him back and he said that he wanted to talk about the buyout. Wanted her to help convince me not to kick him out."

"And what did she say?" Detective Denning asks.

"She declined to get involved," I tell her. "Told JT it was between me and him."

"And that was it?"

"That was it."

"We'll want to talk to her about that," Detective Denning says with a smug smile.

"By all means," I say politely. "I'm sure she'll be happy to cooperate."

Then my head is spinning slightly as she changes tactics on me. "Mr. North . . . our forensics team has already gathered quite a bit of evidence from Mr. Townsend's home. Blood, prints, hair, fibers. The usual. We're rushing the processing on those."

"Your point?" I ask, but I already know the fucking point.

"Would you be willing to offer a DNA sample so we can exclude you as a potential suspect?" she asks with dead seriousness, leaning forward again and carefully evaluating my reaction.

But before I can say anything, Doug says, "Not without a warrant."

Now fuck, that makes me sound guilty, so I say, "Detective, I'll have to follow my attorney's advice, of course, but I can tell you, I've been in JT's home many times. I'd be surprised if my DNA wasn't there."

She nods, knowing that's most likely true. "What about your girlfriend?"

"What about her?"

"She's been in his home too?"

For all the planning and talking Sela and I have done over the past two days, this was not discussed, and I feel like an idiot for not considering I'd be asked this. My normal human reactionary programming wants to deny it, but I force myself to pause. Chances are they are going to find some evidence of Sela being in that house, so I tell my first bald-faced lie to Detective Denning and pray it doesn't bite me in the ass. "Yes. Sela and I had dinner there with JT one night at his invitation."

"When was that?"

"December twenty-eighth," I tell her as my mind flies mentally through my calendar. "I believe it was a Monday night."

That was the week that I had been playing nice with JT, hoping to gain his confidence and trust knowing that he'd be approaching me for money soon. I hope to fuck he didn't have some other plans that Monday night that would show up on a credit card receipt or something.

Detective Denning stares at me a moment, perhaps considering the truth of my words. But finally she nods in acceptance before she says, "Just a few more questions, Mr. North, and I'll let you get out of here."

"Sure," I say, feeling some stress coming off my shoulders that this is winding down.

"Mr. Townsend was your half brother, correct?"

Fuck. Detective Denning has been very busy, it appears.

"That's correct."

"Wasn't common knowledge, was it?" she asks with an almost lecherous smile.

I shake my head. "Just me, my father, and JT's mother."

"Well, Mr. Townsend knew, didn't he?"

I hope my look of surprise seems genuine. "Now that I did *not* know."

Well, didn't know that until yesterday when my girlfriend told me that JT told her that, but whatever. Denning absolutely doesn't know that.

"Really?" she asks skeptically.

"Really," I say firmly. "I only knew because I overheard a conversation between my dad and JT's mom when I was young. I talked to my dad about it maybe twice since, but it was a very hush-hush secret. My dad even told me specifically that JT didn't know."

Suck it, Dad. You're going to have to fend for yourself on this one when they come knocking on your door to ask you about this.

"That's not what your father told us," she says with an almost feral grin at me.

Goddamn that motherfucker.

"Then he lied to me," I grit out.

"In fact, he told us that his will left half to you and half to JT if your mother predeceased you both," she seems to relish in telling me.

Again, I try to look surprised, because I sort of figured that was true, based on JT's offer to rescind rights to my dad's fortune just before he tried to kill Sela and she, in turn, killed him. "I'm sure your investigation into that has been thorough, Detective Denning, but again . . . I had no knowledge of that, and frankly, I don't give a shit. I have no need of my father's money."

Her eyebrows raise slightly and that might even be a pinch of respect I see, but then she cuts my legs out from under me again. "Did you know that your sister was explicitly cut out of your father's will?"

"I didn't," I say guardedly.

"Why do you suppose that is?" she asks with her head tilted to the side.

"I suppose it's none of your goddamned business," I say as I lean forward in my chair, Detective Denning finally having succeeded in getting under my skin. "Caroline doesn't have a damn thing to do with anything."

"All right," Doug says with a hand to my shoulder. "I think Mr. North has been more than patient and forthcoming with you, Detective. Wrap it up."

"Mr. North . . . where were you on January fourth between the hours of noon and five P.M.?"

Knew this was coming too.

"I had lunch at Michael Mina with a colleague, ran to the market after, and then went back to my condo," I tell her.

"And who did you have lunch with?" she asks.

"Dennis Flaherty. He runs a security and investigations firm."

"And what was the purpose of that meeting?" she pushes.

"I'm afraid that's confidential because of patent issues," I tell her smoothly. "But it had to do with security work for The Sugar Bowl."

She nods in acceptance of that, but I know she'll check it out. She's too thorough not to, and I'm glad Dennis is out of the country for a while, and equally glad I did not call him, because I'm sure my phone records had been checked too.

"Anyone that can vouch for your time while at the condo?" I ask.

And I tell her my second bald-faced lie. "My girlfriend, Sela."

"Anyone not as . . . biased?" she asks with a smirk.

"Oh, I don't know . . . she's my girlfriend. She can be pissed off at me for any reason, especially when she's PMS'ing."

Hello snarky, smartass Beck North.

Denning stares at me a moment and the smirk never slides off. Finally, she turns her eyes to Doug and stands. "That's all I have. For now. I'll be in touch if I need anything further."

Doug and I don't say a word but watch her round the conference room table and head for the door. When she places her hand on the knob, she pauses and turns to look at me. "Did you know that just this past November, an appeals court struck down a prior ruling that the death penalty was unconstitutional in California?"

"I remember seeing that in the news," I manage to say, even though my stomach is threatening to rebel against me the minute she said *death penalty*. "What's the point?"

"It's just that capital murder charges are called for if the murder happened for financial gain," she says lightly.

Fucking bitch.

"Then I expect when you find the bookie that killed JT, you'll be filing those charges, right?" I can't help but ask.

She doesn't respond to me but nods her head slightly. "Have a good day, gentlemen."

CHAPTER 13

. . . .

Sela

I flip through the textbook I had picked up this morning at the university bookstore for my class entitled Perception and Sensation, which is scheduled to start day after tomorrow.

I've got nothing but time to kill while I wait for Beck while he gets interviewed at the police station and I sip on my second cup of tea. Beck and I have been busy today. We left this morning for his office, where he gathered everyone in the largest conference room they had. People were standing shoulder to shoulder, three to four deep in the area around the table, as they all listened to Beck talk with heartfelt grief over the passing of JT. A few cried, most had stoic looks on their faces. Karla wasn't there and I assume she was too consumed with grief to come in today.

In fact, Beck had told everyone that he was closing the offices down except for nominal tech support until next Monday, and then I waited around while many of the employees came up to Beck to express their condolences. Within an hour of arriving, we were out the door and headed to the bookstore so I could get my materials for spring semester. We then had a quick lunch and headed to Sausalito, where we met with Beck's attorney about an hour prior to his scheduled "interview."

But let's be honest . . . it's an interrogation.

And the minute they both walked out of the coffeehouse and left me behind at approximately 1:50 P.M., I became a mess worrying about what was happening.

By two P.M., I didn't wonder anymore. The coffeehouse door opened, which caused a jingling from the bells attached to the door, and I saw Detective DeLatemer walk in. His eyes came directly to me and I knew without a doubt that this was a planned visit on his part. The detectives were splitting Beck and me up, and hitting me by surprise while Beck was sequestered in a planned meeting.

Devious, and my palms immediately started sweating.

He saunters up to me, not even bothering with pretending this is a chance meeting by going first to order some coffee. "Miss Halstead . . . imagine running into you here," he says with an affable smile.

"Yeah, imagine that," I say dryly.

"Just came in for my routine caffeine fix," he says as he turns toward the counter. "Can I get you anything?"

"I'm good," I say with a nod down at my tea.

"Be right back," he says with that same cheerful smile.

I watch as he puts his order in and patiently waits for them to make it, hands tucked casually into his dress pants and rocking back and forth on the balls of his feet. When he has coffee in hand, he turns back my way and sits down at my table without invitation.

"Studying?" he asks as he looks down at my textbook before taking a sip of his coffee.

"Just scanning," I say pleasantly, forcing myself not to look and sound like a guilty-as-fuck murderer. "Have a class starting soon for spring semester."

"What are you studying?"

"I'm getting my master's in counseling psychology."

"Interesting," he says as he sits back comfortably in the small café chair. "My daughter had considered a degree in psychology but eventually went with social sciences."

"She can pursue a lot of noble careers with that," I say so we can hopefully keep this small talk going and avoid the harder questions I know are coming.

"So, I'm not going to bullshit you," he says, getting down to business. "I know Mr. North is at the station now talking to my partner, and I knew you were in here. Thought I'd knock out a quick interview. We were going to request a formal one of you anyway."

"Appreciate the straight shooting," I say, and I truly mean that.

"You know you have the right to an attorney to be here if you want," he offers.

I wait for him to go on, but he remains silent . . . watching me.

"I thought my list of rights were much longer," I mutter.

He laughs and it's genuine. He's totally the good cop. "I only read you your Miranda rights if I arrest you. I've got no intentions of doing that right now unless you want to confess to Mr. Townsend's murder."

My tea almost explodes violently out of my gut but I manage to give what I hope is an amused chuckle. "Yeah . . . I most certainly won't be doing that because it wouldn't be true."

"So you're good talking then with me right now?" he presses.

"Sure," I say, but I want to pick up my textbook, conk him over the head with it, and run.

To Mexico.

Beck can find me later.

"Well, we're obviously taking this information about his gambling debt very seriously. We've received the records from Marin General and there's no doubt he had the snot beaten out of him. We also verified that Mr. North came to pick him up, so we think that's credible evidence that Mr. North wasn't involved in that."

You think?

"But we're running low on finding anything else," he says, and then just waits for me to say something.

I try to wait him out, but the silence is too unbearable so I say, "Well, I don't know anything about it. Only what Beck told me after he came home that night after JT got beat up."

DeLatemer nods. "I'm sure Detective Denning will cover that more with Mr. North. And I'm sorry, but I have to ask, can you account for your whereabouts on January fourth from noon to five P.M.?"

I nod confidently. "I was at school and classes got out around twelve thirty. I went to the condo to study. Beck got there about two P.M."

"Gotcha," he says like we're buddies having a beer together. "So, you had roughly an hour and a half that your whereabouts can't be verified, correct?"

I give an amused laugh. "Well, the doorman at my condo can verify what time I got back from class, I'm sure. But Detective, if you think I had time to get to Sausalito, kill JT, and get back before Beck arrived, good luck in trying to figure out the logistics on that one."

He laughs along with me and gives a carefree shrug. "Hey . . . you know I have to ask these things, right?"

"Of course," I say kindly, and try to look at him with open honesty as he proceeds to ask me all my darkest secrets.

"So . . . tell me about JT and Beck's relationship. I understand they were friends for most of their lives, and then of course, hey . . . what a success with The Sugar Bowl, right?"

"Incredible," I agree with a smile. "But I'm afraid I don't know much. Beck and I haven't been together that long, and frankly, I've only been around him and JT together a few times."

"But has Beck said anything to you about strained relations?"

"I think every business partnership probably has that, right?" I say vaguely. "But nothing comes to mind as being troublesome."

"And you said, you've only been around them both a few times," he says as he picks up his coffee. He takes a sip, sets it back down. "Tell me those instances."

"Let's see . . . I met JT briefly at a Sugar Bowl Mixer, same night I met Beck. Then another time in Beck's office, both of those times only for a few minutes. Then Beck and I had dinner with him one night at a restaurant and he brought a date. And then the last time was at Beck's parents' Christmas party. Again, that was only for a few words."

"Any other times?"

"Nope. That's it."

DeLatemer nods. "And what did you think of Mr. Townsend?"

And here, I cannot lie. I just can't.

"I didn't care much for him," I tell the detective. "I found him arrogant and a misogynist. But I was polite to him because I didn't want to come between him and Beck."

"Did Beck know how you felt about his partner?"

"Probably not," I lie to his face. "I kept that stuff to myself. Didn't want to be that nagging girlfriend, you know?"

"Are you saying Beck had no clue of your feelings? I mean, he seems like a pretty nice guy. And if Mr. Townsend is as much of a jerk as you say he is, surely that's not news to Beck, right?"

"Well yeah . . . Beck knew those things about JT," I admit, but I feel like this is a slippery slope. "But it was business, you know."

"But Beck wanted JT out of the business, didn't he?"

Christ. Definitely a slippery slope.

"Yes," I have to say truthfully, because clearly this cop knows this for sure. "They had discussions."

"More like arguments, right?"

"I guess," I hedge. "Beck doesn't really get into a lot of details about that stuff with me."

And shit, shit, shit. That just made me sound so guilty because it was completely evasive.

I can feel a bead of sweat trickle down my spine. I wait for him to drop the next hammer on me.

But instead, he picks up his cup of coffee and stands. "Well, I don't want to take any more of your time. I think I've got what I need here."

Not sure if that's good or bad, but I smile at him politely. "Glad to help."

He nods his head and gives me a wink. "Have a nice day, Miss Halstead."

"You too," I murmur, and watch as he walks out of the coffee shop, and I have to physically restrain myself not to run out after him.

Call out, *Wait, Detective. I did it. I killed JT.*

I want to do that because it's patently clear to me that they're focused on Beck, and I can't bear the thought of him taking the blame on my behalf. I can't even think about the possibility of arrest.

But then I have to remember Caroline's words that I needed to trust in Beck that we were doing the right thing. I had to remember Beck's confidence and determination that we were doing the right thing that was best for both of us at this moment.

I force myself to try to calm down. I take deep breaths, hoping to get my heart rate back under control. I tell myself over and over again that this will all work out for the best.

CHAPTER 14

Beck

The church is overflowing with people, which doesn't surprise me given the large circle of people that JT knew. What does surprise me is that his parents are having his funeral service in a church. They must have given a hefty donation to the St. Luke's United Methodist Church in Sausalito to have the funeral here, because JT and his parents weren't Methodist. They weren't churchgoers at all. I expect they chose to have his funeral in the house of God because that would be expected by polite society, and after all, news of JT's death was in all the papers. There's no way Candace and Colin Townsend would want to be caught with pictures in the society page of JT's service being held in something as common as a funeral parlor.

Sela and I were surprised when Caroline showed up at the condo this morning, dressed in a long-sleeved black dress with black high-heeled boots. I took one look at her when I opened the door and said, "You didn't have to come."

She gave me a light, backhand slap to my stomach and I gave an equally fake doubled-over *ooph,* and she breezed by me into the condo. "I didn't come for you. I came to see Sela."

I laughed because I know my sister. She came for both of us.

We made a unanimous decision to leave for the funeral a bit late to put us there with no time to spare for socializing once we arrived.

The church is overflowing with cars and we have to park in a public lot a few blocks down. Caroline insisted on following us in her car because she was going to head straight back to Healdsburg after the service. By the time we walk up to the chapel, it's only a few minutes before the service starts and I'm surprised when we're met at the chapel doors by my father looking upset.

Because Sela and I walked in together holding hands, and Caroline followed behind us, my father's eyes come first to me, then Sela, then back to me without even noticing Caroline.

"You're late," my father says by way of greeting. "I was afraid you weren't going to come."

"Why in the hell would you think I wouldn't come?" I ask, affronted that he gives me so little credit.

"We'll talk about it later," he says dismissively. "After the service. But your mother and I saved you a seat up front."

He then has the grace to look at Sela, and I'm surprised he remembers her name. "Hello, Sela. It's good to see you again."

"Hello, Mr. North," she says with polite reserve. Like me, she's written my parents off and isn't going to spare them much more than common decency.

"Well, come on, you two," my father says impatiently, and I'm surprised his invitation includes Sela. My mother would certainly have a cow if she knew her husband was fraternizing with the riffraff.

"Actually, we're going to sit back here with Caroline," I say to my father, and he blinks in surprise, then his eyes immediately cut over my shoulder to see his daughter standing there. He hasn't seen her in almost five years . . . not since the rape.

He appears confused for a moment and I think he might even be compelled to say something to her, but then an organ plays a sad melody indicating that the service is starting and his mouth clamps shut. He merely nods at me and says, "We'll talk after the burial."

I nod back, wishing this day would just hurry up and get the fuck over. Why the hell you have to have a service and then a separate get-together at the gravesite is beyond me. Why can't it all just be done there at once?

To say I'm a little on edge since the meeting with the detectives yesterday is an understatement. I came out of the police station with Doug on my heels feeling relatively okay about matters. Sure, they asked tough questions but nothing that would be beyond circumstantial evidence that I'd killed JT.

Of course, my bubble was deflated a bit as we walked to the coffeehouse and I pointed that out to Doug. He said, "Mr. North, most murders are proven based only on circumstantial evidence. There's hardly ever anything in the way of direct evidence unless there's a witness who observed what happened."

That put me in a pissy mood, but when we walked into the coffeehouse and I saw the look on Sela's face, my mood got darker without even knowing what was causing it.

I went berserk when she informed Doug and me about the surprise interview from Detective DeLatemer, but Doug managed to calm us down and told us not to worry. He seemed confident that neither one of us said anything that was incriminating and that we just needed to remain calm.

Easy for him to say, especially after Sela and I got back to the condo and compared notes on the questions we were asked. And the immediate and most noticeable fuckup was that I lied and said Sela had been at JT's house for dinner and Sela didn't mention that to DeLatemer when he asked all the times they'd been together.

Sela started crying when she realized, not because she was afraid for herself, but because she was beyond wigged out that I was in the crosshairs now. It took me forever to calm her down, and when no amount of talking, sweet words, or stroking of her back would work, I ended up stripping her down and making her come with my mouth. That stopped the tears, but it didn't stop her worries. She tossed and turned all night, and neither one of us slept a wink.

The day after was no better, with both of us having too much time on our hands and nothing to do but wait for something bad to happen. Luckily, nothing did happen yesterday, and I feel marginally better that once we can get through this funeral, we can start leaving some worries behind.

Caroline, Sela, and I sit several rows back from the front and JT's casket, which is closed, and a large portrait of his smiling face beside it. I have no clue why it's closed. Not sure if that was his preference, his parents', or perhaps the gaping holes in the side of his neck couldn't be hidden. Regardless, I'm thankful, because I sure as fuck don't want to see him. Not that I'd mind taking some sort of satisfaction in said gaping holes, but I want to hurry up and forget the son of a bitch. The last time I saw him he was beaten to a pulp, and that's not a bad way to remember him.

Candace Townsend cries during the entire service. Her husband sits stoically to her left. My father sits to the right of Candace and I notice their shoulders touch the entire time. My mother sits to my father's right and quietly dabs at her eyes with a handkerchief.

My eulogy goes as expected. I keep it short and sweet. So fucking sweet. I talk about my childhood friend with genuine emotion. I tell a few funny stories about JT. I commend his amazing business sense and his confidence in me, for which I would not have had the opportunity to help create The Sugar Bowl. I talk about a life snuffed out far too early, and that the world is a little darker without him in it. I get through all of this without a single hitch in my well-rehearsed speech, because I want people to believe I'm devastated over the loss of my friend.

"I know we're all grieving," I tell the crowd as I look out over the sad faces. I didn't prepare any type of formal speech but just had some index cards with jotted notes. "But we should all take some measure of happiness in knowing that JT is in a better place. Rest well, buddy."

And by that, I truly mean "burn in hell," but the mourners don't need to know that.

The graveside service is short, with only a few words spoken by the pastor before JT's casket is lowered into the ground accompanied by Candace's wailing. I expect Colin will medicate her with Xanax and whiskey later.

Sela, Caroline, and I stood at the perimeter of the crowd, quietly watching this last ode to JT's life. I expected it to feel bittersweet to me, that my friend had fallen so low. But there's no bitterness at all. Only sweet relief he's dead and out of our lives. I expect that makes me one cold bastard, but knowing what he did to my sister . . . to my Sela . . . I can't seem to find any shame in my thoughts.

As the mourners start to disperse, I watch as my father touches his hand to my mother's elbow and nods my way. She spares me the briefest of glances, says something back to him with flattened lips, and he leans in to kiss her on the cheek.

To calm her down maybe?

I watch as he clasps Colin on the shoulder, murmurs a few words, and then bends to give Candace a hug. It's so clear to me, their familiarity with each other. It's almost embarrassing the way

Candace's fingers clutch desperately to my father's shoulders, and I nearly smile when I see my mother watching every bit of it like a hawk. Sela told me at Christmas she thought my mother knew about my father and Candace, and I've often wondered.

Didn't really care, but I wondered.

Now I'm pretty sure Sela was right.

My father turns and starts making his way through the crowd to us. I turn to Sela and Caroline. "Okay, ladies . . . that's your cue. Better get gone while the gettin's good."

Caroline smirks and goes on tiptoes to give me a kiss on my cheek. After the funeral, we decided that Caroline would take Sela back to the condo so I could talk to my father alone. I bend down and give Sela a swift kiss, and then watch them walk out to the roadway that curves through the cemetery where our cars are parallel parked.

When I feel my dad's presence behind me, I turn around to face him.

"That was a good eulogy," he says, but there's no genuine praise in his voice. It's filler . . . an icebreaker . . . nothing more.

"I wanted to talk to you about your mother's visit the other night," my dad says uncomfortably. I know he's being made to have this "talk" with me at my mother's behest.

"Save your breath," I tell him as I hold a hand up. "I told her I was done and I meant it. I'm done."

"Just like Caroline then," my dad observes bitterly.

"That's no one's fault but yours and Mother's," I tell him. "And if I'm being honest with myself, I should have cut ties with both of you when you so callously tossed aside your daughter who had been raped."

I can't gauge the look on my father's face. I can't tell if it's anger or sadness. It's this weird mixture maybe of the two, and he mutters, "Now all my children are gone."

Still your fault, Dad.

Well, JT's not your fault. That's strictly on himself, but what-ever.

Now that the unimportant shit is out of the way, turns out this talk was opportune because I've got some shit on my mind too. "You told me at the Christmas party that JT didn't know he was your son."

My dad jerks in surprise and his jaw drops.

"He knew," I say confidently.

"How do you know that?" my dad asks.

I provide the easiest lie. "Because he told me a few days before he died."

My dad's gaze cuts over to where Candace stands with Colin, accepting handshakes and air kisses from friends. "Candace felt he had the right to know, and I couldn't argue with that."

"And you left him half of your estate," I throw out in accusatory fashion, not that I care, because I don't. I do it so my dad thinks I'm emotionally invested in this argument and perhaps he'll be more genuine with me.

"Of course I did," he says heatedly and with self-righteousness, and it doesn't occur to him to find out how I know this. "He's my son."

"And cut Caroline out," I growl at him.

"She was lost to me."

"Then why all the secrecy?" I say with unfiltered disgust. "Why not have just admitted all of this to me when I asked you about it at Christmas?"

"I don't know," he says loudly as he throws his hands out to the side in frustration. Then he lowers his voice. "I don't know. It was just awkward and you caught me off guard."

"And lying comes easy to you," I interject.

He lets that one go. "I knew it was going to make you angry

so I just avoided it. And yes, he's in my will, but I didn't tell you because I didn't want to deal with the messy fallout."

"No, you were just going to leave that for me and Mom to deal with if you died, right?"

He doesn't answer me because there's nothing to justify such a cowardly act.

"Well thanks a lot, Dad," I say with derision. "Your failing to clue me in on these little tidbits is making me look every bit a murderer right now."

"What?" my dad gasps.

"I was called in for questioning by the police. They seemed to take a lot of pleasure in beating me up about your illegitimate son and the fact he's entitled to half your estate. Seemed to think that gave me plenty of motive for murder."

"But you wouldn't," my father says in outrage on my behalf.

"Yeah, why don't you call the detectives and tell them that," I say snidely. "I'm sure that will ease their minds. Make them forget all about me and trying to pin this shit on me."

"I'll call the district attorney right now," my father says. "He's a member of our club and I know him well."

"For fuck's sake, Dad," I curse at him. "I don't want or need your help. And besides . . . it's only about twenty-eight years too late for you to start acting like a dad."

"Beck, please," he begs me for understanding.

"Why didn't you at least call me and tell me the cops came to talk to you about JT and your will? You could have given me a heads-up."

He shakes his head vigorously. "They didn't talk to me. I swear it. If they knew about the will, it was from Candace. She knows I left half to JT."

"So your mistress was in on your grand estate plans, but I'm betting Mother knows nothing of it, right?" The condescension is thick on my tongue.

My dad deflates. "I'm going to tell her . . . at some point. I'm just not sure how."

"Here's a clue, Dad," I mock him. "She already knows. Trust me on that."

My dad's jaw drops open and I can't help but wonder how he could be that ignorant after all these years.

"One more question," I say, ignoring his eyes swimming with pain and a need for mercy from me. "How long has JT known?"

I need to know this. It's so fucking important I know this.

"Candace told him when he was eighteen," my dad says, his voice sounding lost. Utterly defeated.

Rage spikes within me.

I thought I was past JT and his evil ways. I thought I was starting to find some peace with it now that he was dead.

But knowing that fucking evil son of a bitch knew Caroline was his half sister and still raped her anyway . . . I want to jump on the casket as it's lowering into the ground, rip that son of a bitch out of there, and repeatedly stab him again and again. I want to dismember him.

Mutilate him.

Obliterate him.

I'm so overwhelmed with hatred for that man that I can't even spare my father another thought. I turn away and start stalking toward my car, trying to find some measure of peace that I've cut the remaining poison from my life with that conversation with my dad.

. . . .

CHAPTER 15

Sela

"I'm so glad that's over," Caroline says as she navigates her way through the city. I'm grateful she didn't mind bringing me back to the condo, as I really had no desire to listen to Beck have it out with his dad. By him not having revealed the full truth to his son, he made him look at the least a fool—at the worst a murderer— by letting him be blindsided by the cops. The fucker should have told Beck the cops were asking about it. That would have given Beck a better opportunity to be able to address those motive concerns by the police.

"So what do you think your brother and dad are talking about?" I ask curiously from the passenger seat. Caroline drives a late-model four-door sedan. It's clean and in good condition, but certainly not the car of a daughter of millionaires. And yet she doesn't seem to give two fucks about losing out on all that money. One of the reasons I like her so much.

"Well, I suppose the conversation will be short and to the point. Beck won't entertain discussion about our mother. Once he draws the line in the sand, he stays on his side."

I nod, because I also suspect this is true, and it makes this line of conversation dead. Caroline has no clue about JT's relation to her dad or that she's been cut out of the will to make room for the bastard son. She has no clue that Beck intends to squeeze the truth out of his dad once and for all about who knows what.

But again, Caroline doesn't know that. She will one day when Beck is ready to give her the full truth, but I don't see that happening anytime soon. At least not until we can figure out the issue with the DNA.

Last night Beck and I talked more about it, and given the fact Detective Denning showed interest in Beck's relationship with Dennis after he became a partial alibi for Beck, we decided resoundingly that we wouldn't call Dennis about the DNA issue. He will happily stay ignorant drinking beer in Ireland and fishing off the coast of Panama none the wiser. Hopefully this will all have died down by the time he comes back.

However, we're not going to wait to start on the DNA. It's eating at both of us with the need to know, and it's also delaying us in telling Caroline the truth. So I'm going to call the detective who investigated my rape and ask about the DNA, as I shouldn't trigger any suspicions for asking.

At least we hope that doesn't occur.

"Did you read the paper today?" Caroline asks me.

I nod glumly. News of JT's death has been all over, even hitting national news, given the controversial nature of The Sugar Bowl. So not only were the entertainment media all over this, but mainstream news was watching it carefully. With the murder of a high-profile businessman, reporters everywhere were waiting to pounce once a break in the investigation occurred.

"I can't stand to see the speculation about Beck," I tell her. While it hasn't been prolific, attention has been called to the fact that Beck was asked to give a formal statement to the police. In the news world, they practically translate that into a conviction, and I'm seeing more and more stuff about Beck popping up. While we tried really hard to ignore it yesterday, I couldn't help but surf the Net, devouring any news I could find to see what the public opinion was, but equally hating myself for doing it.

Beck kept a lackadaisical attitude about it, but still . . . I know it has to be weighing on him a bit.

"Listen," Caroline says in a tone that indicates she's getting ready to lay some serious wisdom on me. "Beck's been in the public eye his entire professional life. He's got the backbone for it. A little mention or speculation isn't going to hurt him, and if anything, it's probably good for The Sugar Bowl. Sort of like free marketing."

I snort. "Way to make lemonade out of lemons."

"I'm just saying, you've got to stop worrying about him so much."

"I can't help it," I say softly, my fingers idly playing with the hem of my black skirt. I paired it with a gray sweater and finished off my funeral attire with a black scarf around my neck to hide the bruises. "I love him too much not to."

Caroline sighs and her hand reaches over to take mine. "I'm so glad Beck found you."

"Even after the shit I brought into his life?"

"Shit and all," she affirms.

Caroline circles the block the Millennium sits on, intent to drop me off at the front door. But as we arrive, we see several reporters camped outside, as well as two marked police cars and an unmarked one.

"Fuck," she hisses.

"You don't think they're here for—"

"Let's go park in the garage," she says. "I'm going up with you."

Moments later, Caroline pulls into one of Beck's reserved spaces and we're riding the elevator up to the condo. The minute we step out, my heart drops with a resounding thud. The door to the condo is wide open and I can hear sounds from inside. Voices . . . a camera snapping . . . the sound of drawers being opened.

Not once do I believe we've been broken into.

I hurry to the door, Caroline hot on my heels, and as soon as I enter, I rear backward at the amount of people inside my home. Uniformed cops, plainclothes cops, and technicians wearing blue windbreakers with the words Bureau of Forensic Sciences on the back. They're everywhere . . . taking pictures, searching cupboards, flipping couch cushions, placing labeled bags of evidence into large plastic tubs with lids.

"Jesus Christ," Caroline whispers fearfully.

"Ahhhh . . . Miss Halstead I presume," I hear from my left, and see a tall, blond woman in her early forties walking down my hallway toward me. I peg her as an attorney right away, given the charcoal-gray skirt with matching jacket, sedate white silk blouse, and sensibly heeled shoes. She has a badge clipped to her jacket pocket.

She strides up to me, those long legs eating the distance quickly, and I want to walk backward away from her because she has *bearer of bad news* written all over her smug face.

"I'm Assistant District Attorney Suzette Hammond," she says briskly, and doesn't offer a handshake, but nor do I expect one. We are not friends or even business acquaintances. We're hunter and hunted. "We're here executing a search warrant. Detective Denning is in your room and she has a copy for you."

"You can just come in here without invitation?" Caroline asks with irritation.

"That is the purpose of a search warrant," the ADA answers dryly. "You see, criminals don't just go around inviting the police into their homes to search for evidence."

"We're not criminals," I tell her. "You won't find anything."

"Disposed of all the evidence, have you?" she asks, leaning toward me with a smile.

I have no idea if she's joking with me or not, but I'm saved from the expectation of answering that question when she adds, "Doesn't matter if you did or didn't. I've got enough regardless of what we find here."

"Enough what?" I ask.

The bitch holds her index finger up and wags it at me with a stern look. "Uh-uh, Miss Halstead. Not about to give away all my secrets."

The room spins a bit on me at the implication of that statement and Caroline's hand comes to my elbow for support.

"And you are?" Hammond asks Caroline.

"Caroline North," she answers with her chin up. "Beck's sister."

"Pleasure," the attorney responds, and then turns back to me. "Now, since this is your home, you can be in here while we conduct our investigation, but I'll need you to stay out of our way. Park yourself at the dining room table and we should be done in a few hours."

"A few hours?" I whisper with stunned disbelief. It already looks like they've been here for hours with a wrecking ball.

"We want to be thorough," she says with a playful grin, and it pisses me off this woman is enjoying tearing people's lives up this much. I believe I might actually hate her.

"What the fuck is going on?" I hear from behind me and spin around to see Beck standing in the doorway. His gaze sweeps the open interior of the condo, finally landing on me with carefully veiled agitation.

The assistant district attorney says, "Ahhh . . . Beck North. I recognize you from the news coverage."

"And you are?" he asks.

She doesn't respond but instead says, "I'll be right back. Don't go anywhere."

We watch as she spins on her sensible shoe and heads back down the hallway to our bedroom. Beck steps in immediately and whispers, "What's going on?"

I lean into him, hands on his chest, where I can feel his heartbeat racing away. "She said they had a search warrant. Denning has it back in the bedroom with her."

His eyes cut to the hallway quickly and then back to me. His hands come to my shoulders and he squeezes. "It's fine. It's going to be fine. There's nothing here for them to find."

I nod quickly in agreement, not because I actually agree but because I'm terrified to doubt his word and jinx the fuck out of us.

The clicking of heels alerts us to Hammond returning and we look over to see Detective Denning following behind her. She doesn't look smug the way the attorney does, but she does look motivated. Hammond stops in front of Beck and me and folds her arms over her chest to watch as Denning walks up to Beck.

"Mr. North . . . this is a search warrant signed by Judge Reyes this morning authorizing the Sausalito Police Department and District Attorney's office to enter your home to search for evidence. The summary of probable cause presented is there if you wish to read it as well as a list of the items we're looking for."

Beck takes the document and opens it up as it's folded into thirds, but before he can read it, Denning hands him another document. "And this is another search warrant for your Townsend-North office. We already have a team there conducting the search."

Irritation flashes on Beck's face as he takes the warrant. He's not worried though. There's nothing at the office at all that will aid them.

"And finally," ADA Hammond says as she uncrosses her arms and reaches into the inside of her gray jacket. She pulls out another document, folded into thirds as well, and my stomach cramps in fear. She hands it to Beck. "This is a warrant for your arrest, Mr. North, for the murder of Jonathon Townsend. I'll give you a moment to read it, but then I'm going to ask Detective Denning to place you in custody."

"What?" I practically screech at the top of my lungs. "No . . . you can't do that."

Before I even know what's happening, Beck is pushing the warrants at Caroline, who takes them without question, and his hands are on my shoulders, his fingers digging in with painful pressure so he gets my attention. He's very aware we have an audience but he pins me with an intent look.

"Sela," he says calmly. "It's going to be fine. I've done nothing wrong, so you've got nothing to worry about. Now I want you to take these warrants and call Doug Shriver. Have him meet me at the police station. He'll handle everything, and you're going to sit here with Caroline and relax while we get this figured out. I'll handle this, okay?"

Translation: *You are absolutely not going to say a fucking word about your involvement in JT's death. You're going to sit back like I'm telling you to do, and we're going to let this play out.*

"Okay?" he asks again.

I'm forced to nod my acquiescence because he's asking me to do so.

To trust him.

Beck pulls me in, moves his hands from my shoulders to my face, where he cradles it gently. His eyes look at me with such tenderness and fierce love that I immediately start to cry. He leans in and gives me a kiss, and when I mean a kiss, I mean a kiss. It's openmouthed, deep, and possessive. He doesn't give a fuck we're being watched and he's making sure I understand that I am his and he's going to protect me no matter what.

"That's very touching," I hear Hammond's bitchy voice penetrate through the kiss. "But it's time to go."

Denning steps forward, pulling a pair of cuffs clipped to her belt. "Mr. North . . . if you could turn around and put your hands behind your back?"

"Do you have to handcuff him?" I ask pleadingly.

"It's protocol," Denning responds briskly.

I watch in despair as Beck is handcuffed. She then puts one hand on his elbow and leads him to the door. She says, "Mr. North, you have the right to remain silent. Anything you say, can and will be used against you in a court of law . . ."

Her voice drones on as I follow them numbly out the door, Caroline right behind me and Hammond following all of us. When we reach the elevator, I start to follow them in, but Denning says, "Miss Halstead . . . you really should stay here."

Her voice actually sounds sympathetic.

"I'm going down with him," I say firmly, and I dare her to tell me no. This elevator and this building are mine by rights. That man is mine by rights.

She nods and pulls Beck to the side to make room. I enter and stand by his side, Caroline behind me and Hammond in last to stand in front of us as the doors close. Hammond actually taps her shoe and hums a little song I don't recognize, but it's a happy tune and I can tell she's eating this up.

I hate her.

I press in closer to Beck, touch my arm to his. He doesn't respond but he doesn't need to. I know how he feels.

When we get to the lobby, our doorman, John, looks stunned to see the procession walking toward him. His eyes go to Beck's in shocked surprise but he scrambles to open the door.

And the throng of reporters swarm us as we step out.

That fucking bitch tipped the reporters. It's all clear now. Her smug attitude. The triumph in her eyes. Denning pulls Beck to the side toward the unmarked car, but I'm rooted to the spot as I watch Hammond almost trot down the three steps to come to stand before the reporters.

"Miss Hammond, are you taking Mr. North into custody for the murder of Jonathon Townsend?" a reporter calls out, but I can't see who it is. So many of them are holding up recording devices and others are snapping pictures.

"Yes," she says with a confident smile. "Mr. North has been served with an arrest warrant for the murder of Jonathon Townsend. We'll be booking him today and he'll be arraigned tomorrow. Now, I've got some time to answer questions, but let's try to do it in an orderly fashion."

That fucking bitch. I want to claw her eyes out. She's a media whore, plain and simple. She's eating up the attention and she's going to use Beck to put her name in the spotlight.

I turn back to look at Beck as Denning is helping him into the backseat with a protective hand on his head so he doesn't bump it. He looks at me briefly, mouths the words *I love you*.

I mouth the same words back to him, and hope to God I get to tell him that in person again sometime soon.

· ·

CHAPTER 16

Beck

I'm led into the courtroom of the Marin County Courthouse in cuffs, but I'm spared the khaki-colored jumpsuit I was given last night to sleep in while I enjoyed overnight accommodations at the Marin County Sheriff's Department. Sela had brought one of my suits to Doug, who met with me in a private counseling room just off the courtroom where my arraignment would be held. He went through the process again of what would happen, although he'd talked to me about it briefly last night after I'd been booked.

He tried to be reassuring, telling me the evidence was all circumstantial, but I was not reassured, since he told me just a few days prior that most convictions were based purely on circumstantial evidence. The arrest warrant was lean on details, but he said it met the probable cause standards. Motive and DNA were mentioned, but none of that surprised me. The police had made it clear they felt I had plenty of motive in the questions they'd asked me, and like I told them, I'm sure my DNA was all over JT's house, since I'd been there numerous times in the past.

My eyes immediately go to the front row behind the defendant's table, where I'll be sitting with Doug, and I can feel my body swell with confidence when I see Sela and Caroline sitting side by side. I give them an encouraging smile but they're hard-pressed to give it back. I can see terror in both their eyes.

Just behind them, I see Linda sitting there, her gaze holding me solidly with support and sympathy. She presses her fingertips to her lips, kisses them, and sends it to me with a subtle blowing of her breath. I smile differently for her; it's one of gratitude for her being here. I have to assume my arrest was all over the news and I'm worried sick about the stability of The Sugar Bowl, but I'm going to have to assume our VP of operations will be working closely with all departments to keep things running. That's her job on any given day.

The deputy leads me over to the table I'm to sit at, and I note Doug is bent over at the table set about ten feet from ours, talking quietly with ADA Hammond. She has a stubborn set to her chin as he motions toward a file she has sitting before her and shakes her head to deny whatever he's asking. He straightens up and turns to me, and after the deputy removes the handcuffs, he walks over and gives a hard squeeze to my shoulder.

"Can I say hi to Sela and Caroline?" I ask him, as it's driving me crazy to have them both sitting not five feet away.

He shakes his head and pulls his chair out from the table. "Sorry. Those cuffs only come off for you to sit at counsel table, so go ahead and take a seat."

With a sigh, I look over my shoulder at my lover and my sister and give them a small smile before I sit down beside Doug. The courtroom is abuzz with idle chatter. It's filled to almost capacity and I'm wondering how many of those people are reporters versus perhaps family members of other defendants who are awaiting arraignment. Or maybe even family members of victims.

My head snaps to the right and I look over my shoulder at the rows of benches behind the district attorney's table. And sure enough, Candace and Colin Townsend are sitting there, both of them staring straight at me with cold, hard eyes. My chest squeezes painfully, because while I'm not exceptionally close to them, I'd been fond of them just from years of knowing them, despite Candace's illicit relationship with my father. They've never looked at me with anything but the same fondness coupled with respect for my achievements.

I almost half expect my parents to be close to the Townsends, so my eyes scan the rest of the seats, but I don't see them. Never in a million years would I expect them to be sitting on my side of the courtroom in support of their son, and I can't really expect differently. In the past two days, I'd cut both of them out of my life, and I'm still fine with that decision.

Besides, had they shown up for me, that would have just been all kinds of awkward. My guess is they're both holed up in the house right now probably cowering in shame over what their son has allegedly done.

"All rise," I hear as a door behind the judge's bench swings open and a bailiff steps through calling the room to order. I stand along with every other person in the courtroom. Judge Reyes— the man who apparently signed my arrest warrant—walks up the dais in a swirl of black robes. He's a small man with ink-black hair and caramel-colored skin, and I would have thought he was Latino, but Doug told me last night he was actually from the Philippines but had dual citizenship.

Doug and I discussed Judge Reyes at length last night, because it seems that is the one good thing that has happened to me since I was arrested. Judge Reyes used to be a criminal defense attorney, and while judges are supposed to be impartial, he has a slight bend in favor of the defense side. It's not to say he's going to wave a magic wand and release me, but Doug assured me I couldn't have landed a judge more devoted to ensure the prosecution plays nicely by the rules.

He also told me that nothing much was going to happen today. The arraignment was nothing more than to advise me of my constitutional rights, read the charges against me, and give me the opportunity to plead guilty or not. Then Doug will have a slight battle on his hands to try to get me released on bail.

"All right," Judge Reyes says as he picks up a file from his raised desk. He opens it, peruses a document. "We have the matter of the State versus Beckett North before us."

The judge looks up from the document to me, and Doug stands from his chair and I follow suit. "Mr. North . . . you've been charged with first-degree murder by the state of California. It's my job to advise you of your constitutional rights. First, you have the right to an attorney, and if you cannot afford one, the state will appoint one to you at no cost. I see you're represented by Mr. Doug Shriver though, so that's a moot point. Second, you have the right against self-incrimination. That means at no point can you be compelled to give testimony that could implicate you in this crime. You are also entitled to a speedy trial as well as a trial by a jury of your peers. Now, I'm sure your attorney has gone over these with you, but do you understand these rights as I've just read them?"

"I do, Your Honor," I say confidently, although quite frankly, my knees are shaking.

"And how would you like to plead to these charges, Mr. North?" he asks.

"Not guilty," I reply with even more strength in my voice.

I didn't fucking do it, so it's not like I'm acting.

"Duly noted," Judge Reyes says, making a notation in the file before him. "I'm going to set the preliminary hearing for Monday at ten A.M."

This surprises me. It's Friday and I didn't think things would move that fast.

ADA Hammond stands swiftly from her chair. "Your Honor, the state would ask for a bit more time. The law states the preliminary hearing can be set up to ten days from arraignment."

Judge Reyes sounds completely bored. "Actually, Miss Hammond, what the law truly says is that it *can* be set within ten days of the arraignment. I suppose one could argue that I could set it for tomorrow if I was so inclined to bring you good folks back on a Saturday but as it is, I have a birthday party to attend for my granddaughter so you're off the hook. I'll see all parties here Monday at ten A.M."

Hammond sits back down in a huff.

"Now, let's discuss bail," Judge Reyes says.

Hammond jumps back up from her chair so quickly it slides back and knocks into the half wall that separates the seating gallery. "Your Honor, the state would oppose any bail and requests the defendant be remanded. This was a grisly crime fueled by aggravating factors that will be revealed at the prelim, and the defendant is a danger to society. Furthermore, he is a man of immense wealth and has the ability to flee if he were released."

Judge Reyes, still looking quite bored, turns to my attorney. "Mr. Shriver?"

"Your Honor, Miss Hammond is right . . . this was a grisly crime, but seeing as how they've arrested an innocent man, that shouldn't have anything to do with your decision. Mr. North deserves the presumption of innocence as the law requires. And while we can't do anything about the fact that he is indeed rich, you can set the bail high enough to make it hurt if he runs and merely ask him to surrender his passport, which will ensure he cannot run. Seems quite simple to me."

Man, I love this guy. He's slightly snarky, but so well reasoned you can't argue with what he says. At least I can't.

Judge Reyes nods at Doug and says, "Bail is set at five million dollars and the defendant will surrender his passport until after the trial."

"Your Honor," Hammond says in an almost whiny voice. "If you're not going to remand him, at least order house arrest with an ankle bracelet."

Judge Reyes looks to Doug with his eyebrows raised, conveying it's his turn to counterargue.

"Again, in the eyes of this court, Mr. North is presumed innocent. He has a large corporation to run and over fifty people who depend on him for jobs. He must have the freedom to continue to operate his business. If you must have control over him, simply order him to stay within the state of California unless he has business elsewhere, and at that time, the court can decide whether or not he can travel outside of California but within the boundaries of this country."

Reyes doesn't even pause. "Agreed and so ordered. Is there anything else before I move on to the next case?"

"No, Your Honor," Doug says politely.

"Not from the state," Hammond says in a sulky voice.

"Very well, Bailiff . . . call the next case."

Over the next hour, I'm shuttled back over to the Sheriff's Department, this time without handcuffs, and I'm processed out of their system. I get back my clothes, wallet, phone, and watch. Doug stays with me the entire time while I insisted that Sela and Caroline go back to the condo. He tells me that the preliminary hearing will be nothing more than the state providing their evidence and Judge Reyes will determine if it's sufficient to push this to trial.

Doug tells me that the prelim is going to make or break me.

He never once asks me if I killed JT.

. . . .

CHAPTER 17

Sela

My fingers slide over the track pad on my laptop, the cursor arrow going where I want it to, choosing a new article to read.

Sugar Bowl Founder Accused of Murdering Partner

(AP) San Francisco—The business and tech worlds were stunned Thursday night when multimillionaire founder and program developer Beckett North was arrested for the brutal murder of his partner, Jonathon Townsend. Booked and then arraigned on Friday with a five-million-dollar bond, North was released on his own recognizance but had to surrender his passport.

Just four days prior, Townsend's body was found in his home by his personal chef, who stumbled onto what she describes as a scene "straight out of a nightmare." While the police have yet to release details about the crime, Rosalinda Patane said that Townsend was on the floor of his den with stab wounds in his neck. Sources within the Sausalito Police Department have refused to disclose the murder weapon, which led many to believe it hasn't been recovered.

Townsend and North, who were childhood friends, went on to open up the controversial Sugar Bowl, a dating website that pairs older, wealthy men with younger women. Many claim the site is nothing more than a means to provide paid prostitution, but Townsend had repeatedly denied that claim in interviews, maintaining no money is exchanged . . .

"Jesus," Beck says from behind me in irritation, and I jump in the dining room chair that I'd been sitting in for the past half hour, spending Sunday reading news stories about Beck's arrest. "You've had your nose buried in that laptop for the last three hours. Quit reading that shit."

Okay, so maybe it was three hours, not thirty minutes. But I can't seem to keep track of time this weekend. I'm in a constant state of worry, internal debate, and problem solving.

I get up from the chair and my back screams in protest, confirming that I had indeed been sitting there way too long. I follow Beck into the kitchen and watch as he pulls the refrigerator open and pulls out a beer. He twists the cap, puts it in the garbage, and takes a long pull while looking at me.

"I read a piece by one of the analysts at Court TV and they seemed to think without a murder weapon, it would be difficult to—"

Beck slams the beer down on the counter and foam shoots out the top. His face contorts in anger and he yells at me, "I don't give a flying fuck what reporters or analysts are saying, Sela."

He throws his arms out to the side in frustration and continues his rant against me. "I don't give a shit what anyone thinks about this. What I do give a shit about is that my girlfriend has been moping around this place all weekend and won't even look at me because she's too busy reading shit that's written by a biased media. I'm tired of it, Sela. Tired of you sitting in front of that computer reading stories or constantly flipping channels on the TV, trying to find something that will make you feel better about this shitstorm. Well, I'm here to tell you, babe . . . none of that stuff is going to make it better. It's only going to cause you more anxiety. So give it up and get the fuck on with your life. You're driving me batty."

Outside of that one afternoon when Beck kicked me out of the apartment, I've never seen him angry like this before. Never seen him so close to being out of control. His face is red and his chest is heaving.

"What would you have me do?" I ask quietly, because I'm thinking he's geared up for a fight and I don't want this to escalate.

He takes a deep breath, seems reasonably mollified by my request, and says with a release of air, "Let's go out and do something. Get out of this place for a bit."

"I don't feel like it," I say automatically, and then wince the minute the words are out.

Beck advances on me, coming to a stop when we're toe-to-toe. His lips peel back into an ugly grimace and he snarls, "You don't feel like doing anything. You've shut down and you've shut me out. You wouldn't even let me touch you last night or the night before. Just moping around like you're half dead, waiting for the sky to fall."

A tiny flare of anger pulses within me. "Well, the sky is fucking falling if you haven't noticed, Beck. You're in some serious fucking trouble and I don't know what to do."

He makes a scoffing sound and turns away from me.

"I'm scared," I say pitifully.

"Well join the goddamned club," he growls as he spins back on me. "It's my ass on the line right now, but you don't see me pulling away, do you? You see me trying to keep on living life, right?"

I want to accept his words and give them credence. Hell, I'm sure he's 100 percent right. But right now, I feel similar to the way I did after my rape. Completely lost, unsure of what to do or how to feel, and trying with all my might to resist the urge to just curl inward. I want to ignore all of this mess and live in a world where tomorrow doesn't come, because tomorrow means we are back in court listening to evidence that could take this man away from me forever.

Beck looks at me expectantly, hope in his eyes that I might just step forward and tumble into his arms. Apologize for my bizarre behavior over the weekend and snap myself out of it.

But I can't. I know things are hard on him right now, but they're equally as hard on me. Not only am I terrified of what will happen, I'm loaded with guilt so heavy I feel like my back will break from the sheer weight of it. Because let's face it . . . this is all my fault. One could even take it right back to my sixteenth birthday, where it all started. Had I just listened to Whitney at the mall and never gotten into the car with those boys, wanting to prove how grown up I was, Beck wouldn't be in the position he is now.

"Fuck this," Beck mutters when I don't say anything, and stomps out of the kitchen. He grabs his keys off the foyer table and pulls the door open.

"Where are you going?" I ask, because our building is surrounded by reporters and I'm worried about him facing that.

"Out," he says curtly, and then he's gone, slamming the door behind him.

That wasn't our first argument, but it was the nastiest and it leaves me completely restless. I pace the entire condo several times, resisting the urge to call Beck. I eventually give up the compulsion because at this moment, he probably needs distance from me.

My phone ringing startles me and for a moment I can't tell where the sound is coming from. But then I notice it's muffled and realize it's in my purse, which is on the floor in the bedroom. I run back to it, figuring it's Beck and I intend to say "I'm sorry" when we connect.

When I pull my phone out, a tiny thrill of excitement flushes through me at the prospect of making things better for him with a genuine apology and hearing his beautiful voice on the other line, but instead I see an unrecognizable number with a 408 area code. That's Santa Clara, my home county.

"Hello," I say hesitantly after I tap the answer button.

"Sela?" a man's voice asks me just as hesitantly. "It's Detective Bruce Remmers."

I immediately recognize the deep baritone voice of the incredibly nice detective who investigated my rape ten years ago. I called him on Friday afternoon and left a message for him. Calling Dennis was out of the question so we could keep him off the police's radar, and Beck and I knew we needed to push forward with verifying that JT was indeed Caroline's rapist. Thus we had to match him up to the DNA in my case.

"I got your message," he says jovially. "Had to come into the office and catch up on a few things. It's nice to hear your voice. You doing okay?"

"Yeah," I say with a breathless murmur, both relieved he called me back but also nervous to be opening up this can of worms. "I'm doing fine, actually."

"That's good to hear," he says kindly. "Always knew you were a tough girl and that you were going to make it. So where are you now?"

"I live in San Fran," I tell him, not wanting to waste time with the necessary small talk, but knowing that because he's a nice guy and he's truly interested in me, that he deserves it. "Going to Golden Gate and working on my master's in counseling psychology."

I can hear the pride and respect in his voice. "That is fantastic. Just really amazing, Sela."

"Yeah . . . so, um . . . listen," I say nervously, even though Beck and I thoroughly talked through how to approach my inquiry. "I wanted to ask you about the DNA that was retrieved off me. I mean . . . it's been over ten years now and there's not been a match, and I was just worried . . . you know . . . that maybe something got messed up in the system."

"Sela," he says with that pastoral tone he'd used on me in the past when he was delivering hard news. "You know sometimes rapists just aren't caught. They become more careful. Or maybe they don't rape again because that could have been a one-time-only thing fueled by drugs and alcohol."

I know he's right. He's told me that before. But I press him anyway. "I know. It's just been bugging me lately, and what if it didn't get put into the system properly? I mean, those things can happen, right? Do you think you could maybe check, and just ensure that everything is good on your end? Then I could just put this out of my mind and move on."

Detective Remmers gives a tiny sigh but it's not irritation with me. The man knew how to handle rape victims with the softest of gloves. No, his sigh is because he'll do it for me, and in his heart of hearts he believes he's going to find everything done according to protocol and that he'll be delivering bad news to me yet again that they have nothing on my rapist.

"Sure," he says softly. "I'll head over to cold storage now and pull the file. Call you back soon."

"Thank you so much," I tell him with immense gratitude. After spinning my wheels for two days, feeling utterly helpless about everything, I feel energized now that something is moving. Even if it doesn't directly impact Beck's case, it's one step closer we have to verifying JT raped both me and Caroline, and then we can tell her the truth.

When I disconnect, I immediately dial Beck. He answers after the first ring. "Hey."

"Hey," I say softly. "I just wanted you to know that Detective Remmers just called me. He's going to pull my file and check to make sure the DNA was submitted properly."

"That's great," he says, and his voice sounds lighter. I'm thinking the anger's dissipated.

"When are you coming home?" I ask hesitantly, because I really, really want him to come home.

"In about ten seconds," he says, and I can hear a slight smile in his voice. "I never made it past the elevator."

I disconnect the call, run down the hall, pausing long enough to throw my phone on the dining room table. I scurry to the front door, open it, and see him standing there.

"I'm so sorry," I tell him before flinging my arms around his neck. "I'm sorry I've been such a pain in your ass this weekend."

His arms come around my waist and he hugs me tight to him. "I'm sorry I yelled at you."

"I deserved it."

"No, you didn't."

He pulls back and then kisses me sweetly, a little tentatively.

He's right . . . I told him I wasn't in the mood for sex the last two nights. Not that we have sex every night, mind you, but we do most nights. Or days. Whatever. So I get why he's hesitant and I don't want him to be.

I press my body in tight, my signal to him that I want more than just a kiss.

He doesn't hesitate further. Within moments, our clothes are gone and he's got me on top of the dining room table, pushing my phone down toward the other end so we don't knock it off. He's hot and hard, lodged deep inside of me. He rocks slowly against me, holding my arms pinned above my head while my legs are clamped tight against his ribs. Beck kisses me leisurely while he fucks me, but soon, as with most times we are wrapped up with each other like this, his moves become more forceful.

His thrusts a bit deeper.

When he can't concentrate on the kiss anymore because I know he wants to concentrate on getting us off, he pulls his mouth from mine, releases his hold on my arms, and puts one palm on the table for leverage. He pushes up slightly and then he's able to really let me have it.

The condo is filled with the sound of the table creaking as we fuck and our heavy pants, and I get closer and closer to the finish line.

So close, almost there.

Then my phone rings.

Beck doesn't even stop pounding inside of me, but does look above my head at my phone. "It's a 408 area code," he grunts at me.

"That's Detective Remmers," I manage to gasp out as his cock consumes me. "Should we answer it?"

"No," he groans as he slides in deep. "Let him leave a voice mail. More important things right this minute."

My phone rings three more times but then Beck's hand is in between my legs, rubbing my clit while he fucks me and I don't hear the phone anymore.

"Beck," I cry out as I start to come, my back arching off the table.

"That's my girl," he mutters, and then he starts jerking inside of me with a long groan.

He immediately rolls us to our sides, legs still intertwined and his dick still wedged deep inside me. With his long reach, he grabs my phone and hands it to me.

We're both still breathing heavy and layered in sweat, but I manage to access my voice mail, put it on speakerphone, and we listen.

"*Sela . . . Detective Remmers. I pulled your file, and just wanted you to know, everything was done properly. It was submitted to CODIS and we have a receipt for it. I couldn't find it at first, but it was mislabeled. So yes . . . the DNA we collected is in CODIS, and if the man that raped you gets put into the system in the future, we'll get a match. It was great hearing your voice today. Stay strong and call me if you need me again.*"

My eyes snap to Beck's, who looks just as perplexed as I feel.

"JT didn't rape Caroline," I murmur, as the implication of what I just learned sinks in. JT's DNA from my rape is in the database. It should have triggered a hit with Caroline's case but it didn't.

"He was saying that just to torture you," Beck says. "But thank fuck . . . thank fuck we didn't say anything yet to Caroline."

Yes . . . thank fuck. We would have destroyed her for no reason whatsoever.

. . . .

CHAPTER 18

Beck

The relief I felt over finding out that JT didn't rape Caroline only lasted for a bit. Sela and I dragged ourselves off the dining room table and spent the rest of the day in bed, both of us buoyed by that news.

But now, as I sit back in the same courtroom and listen to the proceedings around me, my stomach gets knotted back up with anxiety again. Periodically, I'll look behind me to see Sela and Caroline there, giving me looks of encouragement. I dared to glance only once at Candace and Colin Townsend, who thankfully weren't glaring at me but were talking quietly with ADA Hammond as she leaned over the gallery wall before court started. Still haven't heard a word from my parents, and that neither surprises me nor makes me feel bad. They're a nonissue in my life.

Doug had said the preliminary hearing could take anywhere from half an hour to several hours, depending on how good their evidence was. If they were building a circumstantial case, it would take longer so they could lay it all out. It was up to the judge to listen to it and determine if there was probable cause to move forward. As Doug explained, it was a low threshold for the district attorney to overcome, the standard being if the facts presented would cause a person to have an *honest and strong suspicion* that a person is guilty of the crime.

This doesn't bode well for me, because all of the financial motives they think are driving me are enough for most people to have a strong suspicion that I did it.

Currently, an evidence tech is on the stand while ADA Hammond leads her through a series of questions about what was found at the crime scene. I watched as they identified color photos of JT's body and bags of hairs and fibers. Doug had told me that it could take weeks for that to all get analyzed forensically, but that doesn't hold up the criminal justice process.

After the tech comes the medical examiner, but his testimony is short and sweet, and nothing surprising. JT died of massive blood loss due to a single stab wound to his carotid artery. The other stab wound was inconsequential. Although a murder weapon had not been identified, they believe it was a letter opener that JT's housekeeper said he keeps on his desk but had never been recovered. The medical examiner opines that the wounds look to be caused from an instrument such as a letter opener.

Then we get to what I believe to be the meat and potatoes of their case. ADA Hammond calls Detective Amber Denning to the stand. She leads her through some questions regarding investigative protocol, eventually leading her up to her interviews with me.

"And how many times did you interview Mr. North?" Hammond asks.

"Twice," Denning replies. "Once at his condo the evening we found Mr. Townsend's body, and then again last Wednesday when he came into the station voluntarily with his attorney."

"What was his demeanor during those interviews?" Hammond asks.

"He did not seem surprised when we arrived at his condo to

advise him of Mr. Townsend's death," Denning says as she flips through her written reports she must have made after. "But he was cooperative and answered our questions. He was also cooperative during the second interview."

I'm glad she doesn't mention the fact I got pissy with her at the end, but I expect that's because she's a professional and wouldn't stoop. Probably irrelevant anyway.

"And in the course of those interviews, did you learn anything that would lead you to focus in on Mr. North as a suspect with a sound motive for murdering the victim?" Hammond asks smoothly.

Denning nods. "Two things stood out. Mr. North had tried to buy Mr. Townsend out of their business on a few occasions and Mr. Townsend would not sell out. He seemed to be battling issues with drugs and gambling, but those weren't factors that could cause Mr. North to terminate their agreement and force Mr. Townsend out. We were able to gather all of the financial records of Townsend-North, and the estimated worth of the company was right at three hundred and seventeen million dollars."

Hammond makes a low whistle sound, like she's astounded to hear that amount, when everyone in this courtroom knows damn well it wasn't news to her. "And what was the other thing that stood out?"

"We discovered that Mr. North and Mr. Townsend were actually half brothers, both sharing Beckett North, Sr., as a father. We learned that Mr. Townsend was going to get half of Mr. North's inheritance."

I can't help it. I look over my shoulder at Colin Townsend, and I can tell by the look on his face that this is not news to him. Either he's always known or the ADA told him so he could be prepared to hear those things in court, but he sits ramrod straight on the wooden pew-type bench and listens with rapt attention.

Then I turn even further in my seat to look at the other person that this *will* be shocking news to. Caroline stares right back at me, her eyes accusatory that I would keep something like this from her. I'm going to have to answer for that secret once we get this shit behind us. Hindsight is twenty-twenty and all that, but clearly, this is something I should have told Caroline a long time ago. Just never thought it would ever have any bearing on either of our lives, but it turns out it's a fact that could end up tearing all of us apart.

ADA Hammond asks a few more questions about her interviews with me, including my alibi. She also brings up the fact I suggested this was done by a disgruntled Vegas bookie who didn't get paid. Denning merely testified that they searched JT's house and office, including phone records and bank transactions, and simply could find no evidence other than the fact he'd been assaulted by unidentified assailants the day before his death.

"Detective Denning," Hammond asks bluntly. "Do you believe Mr. Townsend's death was related to this alleged gambling debt?"

"I do not," she says firmly. "We could find no evidence, and even Mr. North admitted to us that Mr. Townsend was given a few days to come up with the money. It made no sense for this alleged bookie not to honor the deadline, as he stood to get a lot of money."

"Thank you," Hammond says, and then moves on. "Now, in the course of your investigation, did you come up with other evidence that would give Mr. North motive to kill his partner?"

"Yes," Denning says as she flips through her file. "All going to the theory he wanted Mr. Townsend out of the business, but in searching Mr. North's office at home, we found a copy of a signed agreement between Mr. Townsend and a Miss Melissa Fraye outlining the mechanics of a sexual rendezvous that would occur between them that involved a rape fantasy. We interviewed Miss Fraye and she acknowledged she did not sign the agreement. We believe Mr. North was perhaps trying to use that as blackmail to get Mr. Townsend out of the business."

What the fuck?

I start to lean toward Doug to tell him that's absolutely untrue and that I saved that woman from getting raped, but he's busily taking notes.

Denning continues. "We also interviewed Mr. Townsend's secretary, Karla Gould. She said that the two owners' relationship was extremely volatile, involving many arguments that were loud and disruptive in the office. It was always Mr. North coming down to Mr. Townsend's office to instigate these encounters. She had even heard Mr. North on one occasion make a death threat against Mr. Townsend. Overall, it's clear they did not have a good relationship and that Mr. North was trying everything he could to get him out of the business, but was unsuccessful about it."

I can't help myself. I lean in to Doug and hiss, "That's not true. Out of anger I said something like 'I could kill you, JT' or something like that, but it wasn't a death threat."

Doug nods in understanding as he scribbles more notes.

Hammond asks a few more questions, but right now I'm so angry at the way things are being misconstrued I have a subtle ringing in my ears. I say subtle because I don't miss the last question that starts to put the nail in my coffin.

"Detective Denning, anything else from your investigation you believe is relevant?" the district attorney asks.

"After the victim's body was found and we set up a police perimeter so we could start our investigation, we posted an officer to keep an eye on the surroundings. The officer assigned to that duty reported seeing a white Audi A4 turn onto the street where the murder occurred, but then pull into a driveway and leave by the same route it arrived."

"And that seemed suspicious to you?"

Denning shrugs. "Could be, or it could be someone lost, but we did subsequently confirm that Mr. North drives a white Audi A4."

Yeah . . . I hear the gasp in the courtroom from some of the spectators and I want to bang my head on the table in front of me.

"Did Mr. North ever mention to you coming to the victim's neighborhood on that night?" Hammond asks.

"No," Denning says. "In fact he maintains he was at his condo the entire time. We've subpoenaed the GPS records from Mr. North's Audi, but we don't know what that will reveal at this time."

I can't help myself. I turn myself all the way around in my seat to look at Sela and she gives me a halfhearted smile. I try to give it back but my lips won't fucking move. I don't dare look at Caroline again, because I know I won't get a smile from her after the revelation that JT's our brother, so I turn back around. Then Doug begins his cross-examination of Denning, which is very good considering what just occurred. He manages to poke enough holes in her testimony that it's a bit weakened, eventually getting her to admit that all of this is pure conjecture and speculation on a motive that may or may not exist.

Still, by the time Denning leaves the stand, I find myself rubbing my sweaty hands repeatedly on my slacks trying to get them dry.

ADA Hammond stands up and says, "Your Honor, we have one last witness . . . the state will call DNA analyst Michael Carbone to the stand."

"What's that for?" I whisper to Doug.

He shrugs. "Most DNA takes a while to process, but they must have processed something fairly quickly. Relax. Probably just a hair of yours at the scene, but we figured they'd find that."

And yeah . . . they could match that up, because when I was arrested last Thursday, they also had a warrant compelling my DNA. That was done by swabbing the inside of my cheek when I was processed into the jail.

A nerdy-looking guy with dark wavy hair and a huge Adam's apple takes the stand, nervously tugging on his tie. Hammond goes through his background with the Bureau of Forensic Sciences and asks about all of the samples that were retrieved during the investigation. It's boring, tedious stuff that I guess does nothing more than prove the samples are being processed correctly.

"Mr. Carbone, have you managed to process any of the evidence collected at the scene?" Hammond asks.

He nods and in a somewhat squeaky voice says, "A little bit . . . identification of some fibers and such."

"What about DNA?" she asks.

"We've got several samples to go through, but we have processed one fully," he says.

Hammond nods at him to continue.

"We always take a sample from the victim so we can use it to exclude against other samples found at the scene. So we usually run that first. We analyzed Mr. Townsend's DNA, and as we routinely do in all cases, also submitted it to the CODIS national database and we got an interesting hit."

Holy fuck.

My blood freezes in my veins, disbelieving that they are going to out JT as a rapist. There's no way, but then again . . . if they pin my girlfriend's rape on him, *boom*! My coffin is nailed shut with motive.

"And what did the 'hit' reveal?" Hammond asks, and I can hear in her voice that she can barely contain her excitement at the bomb she's getting ready to drop. I twist my head, look at Sela, who is watching the nerd on the stand with wide, disbelieving eyes.

"It actually revealed that Mr. Townsend's DNA matched an unsolved rape," he says with no emotion.

Jesus fuck, this is it.

"Almost five years ago here in San Francisco," Carbone adds, and my entire world spins so hard I have to slap my hands hard on the table to keep my balance. Doug goes stiff beside me and I hear a small pained moan that I know is from Sela.

"And who was the victim in that case?" Hammond prods.

"Caroline North," Carbone says as his eyes shift slightly to mine and then back to Hammond, as if he had to take a peek at my reaction.

"N-o-o-o-o-o," I hear Caroline whimper behind me, and then rustling and something knocking against wood. "Get out of my way."

I spin in my chair to see Caroline trying to push her way past Sela, who's trying to hold on to her.

"Caroline, wait," Sela says pleadingly as Caroline jerks her arm away, manages to get to the end of the row, and runs for the exit doors.

Sela turns to look at me and I want to break down like a baby and cry at the anguished confusion on her face. I know what's in her head right now:

Remmers just confirmed to me that my attacker's DNA was in the system properly.

JT's DNA is now in the system.

It didn't match with mine.

JT didn't rape me.

He didn't rape me and so now I don't even have that to alleviate some of my guilt for killing him.

I don't care at all what the judge says, or if I'm damning my case. I push up out of my seat, bend over the gallery wall, and put my hands on Sela's shoulders. I can hear the deputy coming toward me so I whisper to her urgently. "He *did* rape you, Sela. He admitted it to you. I don't know what the fuck's going on, but don't you even be thinking you got it wrong, you hear me?"

Hands at my arms start to pull me away and the deputy says, "Mr. North, you need to sit back down before I have to cuff you."

The judge taps his gavel slightly on the wooden bench and says firmly, "Okay . . . let's have some order, please. Mr. North, kindly take your seat."

The deputy pulls me back to my chair but I don't break eye contact with Sela. "Go after her," I beg her, and let my eyes cut to the doors where Caroline just went. "Please help her."

Sela nods once and then she's sliding out of the pew and running toward the doors herself. I have no clue what's going to happen to me and I don't give a fuck. I just want Caroline and Sela to be taken care of, and I think my time on this earth where I can do that may now be over.

CHAPTER 19

. . . .

Sela

I can't process what was just laid out in open court for all the spectators and reporters to hear. That Caroline was raped by her half brother, Jonathon Townsend, which is the perfect motive to pin his murder on Beck. Just yesterday, Beck and I had been convinced otherwise.

The minute Remmers told me that my rape case DNA was properly in the database, and knowing that it did not match up with the DNA from Caroline's rape, had both of us assured that JT was lying to me.

But now it appears the opposite is true, and that is what I cannot process. Whatever DNA they pulled off of me was clearly not JT's, and that means I was very much mistaken about his involvement that night.

What if all of my memories, no matter how pitiful or chopped up they may be, are completely false? What if I manufactured much of what happened to me?

No . . . can't process that, nor do I have time.

Beck asked me to help his sister and that is what I'm going to do. My own mind may be all kinds of fucked up now not knowing shit about my attackers, but I've been in that position before. I went years without knowing and it's not going to kill me to go back to not knowing.

The minute I burst out of the courtroom doors, I look left down the hall to the elevator and see Caroline standing inside, tears pouring down her face. A few reporters come out the door behind me and pause, unsure of what to do. Caroline looks at me with anger and misery as the doors slide closed, and that spurs the reporters into action. They run to the elevator and jab at the down button, but I've been in that thing a few times. There's only one that services this part of the courthouse and it chugs at the speed of a snail.

I don't hesitate. I sprint the opposite way and hit the stairwell exit. We're on the fifth floor, and providing I don't bust an ankle in my high heels while hurtling down them, I should be able to catch her.

Down one flight, heels clacking and hand gripped hard on the handrail. Around the landing. Down another flight.

When I get to the bottom floor, I slam open the door and come skidding out into the lobby of the Marin County Courthouse, and immediately spy Caroline heading for the exit door with one hand clasped tightly to hold her purse over her shoulder and her face angled downward so no one can see her tearstained face.

"Caroline," I call out as I start running after her.

She hunches her shoulders and quickens her pace, and beats me to the exit doors by several strides. I rush right out after her and call out again as she starts to cross the one-way street to the parking deck on the other side, being fortuitously lucky there is no traffic to mow her down. With a brief glance over my shoulder, I see the lobby is still reporterless so I kick my run into overdrive, hoping against a twisted ankle, and by the time she's entering the parking deck, I've caught up with her.

If we're lucky, the reporters will chase after nothing down the sidewalk.

"Caroline, please wait," I say as I reach out and grab her by the elbow.

She spins on me in a swirl of spitting anger, jerking her arm away. "You knew, didn't you?" she accuses.

"Yes," I say with a wince, then immediately amend my answer. "Actually, no. It's a long story and we were going to tell you, but—"

"You should have fucking told me," she screeches at the top of her lungs as she takes a step toward me in a menacing fashion. Tears still pour out of her eyes but they are filled with pure malice and not an ounce of pain right now. I expect that will come back later, and I'll take her anger. She deserves to lay it on someone.

"We were going to," I say desperately. "But we wanted to be absolutely certain first, and we learned something yesterday that led us to believe he hadn't done it."

She scoffs and turns her back on me, walking across the concrete deck toward the internal stairwell rather than the elevator. I follow along. "I swear it, Caroline. If you just stop and listen to me, I'll tell you everything."

"As if I could ever believe you," she huffs as she drags a hand across her cheek to wipe away the wetness.

"Well just stop, take a moment, and listen to my story and then make your judgment," I snap at her as I jog to keep up with her long-legged pace.

She stops as I request, so suddenly I almost barrel into her, but I pull myself up quickly. "You see, the thing is—"

"You know," she interrupts me. "I don't know who to be more pissed at . . . Beck for not telling me something I had a right to know, or you for even coming into his life and bringing all this shit with you."

"Me," I say solemnly as I reach out and touch her forearm. "You be mad at me. Beck has always been your champion, so you take every bit of your pain out on me. Okay?"

Tears well up again in Caroline's eyes and her shoulders sag, and I can see the fight completely drain out of her. She looks up to the concrete ceiling above us and says on a disbelieving moan, "Oh God . . . JT is my brother?"

"Yes," I whisper.

"And he raped me?"

"Beck and I honestly didn't think so, but let's go get in your car for some privacy and before the reporters find us. Let me tell you every bit of it, okay?"

Caroline's gaze drops to mine and she nods, spinning back on her heel and climbing up the stairwell to the second level. I follow behind her, trying to calm my racing heart. Too much fucking drama for me to handle. Beck sitting there while evidence mounted against him, a scandalous bomb dropped in open court that will have every news media channel about ready to cream themselves, and Beck's sister destroyed by something she should have been told a long time ago.

When we both get situated in Caroline's car, I angle my body to the left to look at her directly. She sits facing completely forward, almost as if she's afraid to look at me. In fact, her gaze seems superglued to the steering wheel.

"When I was at JT's house and he was on top of me—choking me—he told me he wanted me to know something before I died."

Caroline swallows hard but doesn't look away from the steering wheel.

"He told me that he was the one who raped you," I tell her

softly. "I made a bad judgment call not to tell you and Beck about it that night. But I did tell Beck the next morning, and at first, we thought it best not to tell you."

"You should have told me that night," she whispers, gaze still forward.

"I know," I tell her with full acceptance of that fuckup on my part. "And we pretty quickly realized you should know . . . that we shouldn't keep it from you. Once we thought about it, we knew that you needed that closure and resolution, no matter how painful it may be. As someone who probably will never get that closure, I knew it was just so obvious that you should know."

"But you said you didn't think it was true," Caroline says as she turns to look at me for the first time since we got in the car. "Something must have made you think JT was lying."

I nod. "What we couldn't get our heads around was the fact that if JT raped me and you, the DNA should have matched up. It should have hit when the DNA from your case was put into the system. So that meant either JT was lying or perhaps the DNA from my case wasn't in the system. Last month, the investigator that Beck hired to help us with all this had pulled my criminal file so he could get up to speed. He noticed that a document was missing regarding submittal of the DNA in my case into the national DNA database, so Beck and I wanted to check that out. We had intended to tell you after we verified it."

"And let me guess," she says softly with full awareness of this fucked-up, complicated mess. "The DNA from your case was in the system."

"Yes. Yesterday I talked to the cop who investigated my rape and he verified it was all there. Because I believed JT raped me and that was his DNA, it only stood to reason he lied to me about raping you. There was no reason to tell you at that point."

"You're wrong," she says, a little anger touching her voice.

"You should have at the very least told me JT was my half brother. Well . . . Beck should have. How long has he known?"

"A while," I admit. "But that's something you need to discuss with him."

Caroline gives a tiny, bitter laugh. "For all Beck's bitching and moaning about the secrets this family keeps . . . about him acting all high and mighty about the truth . . . he sure does lie a lot."

"I'm sorry," I tell her simply. Because I am. Sorry she just heard this terrible news and on top of that, has every reason to be pissed at her brother for keeping her in the dark. But it's not my place to fight Beck's battles for him when it comes to Caroline. He's going to have to take one on the chin and resolve this himself.

That is, if he doesn't go to prison for the rest of his life.

Silence hangs heavy in the air as I let Caroline process everything she's just learned. Her eyes slide back to the steering wheel. While I know she's going to be troubled by these events for a long time to come, I also know this woman is strong and resilient and that she will get past this eventually.

"Do you think—" she starts to say, and then abruptly stops, as if she really doesn't want to know the answer to the question she was getting ready to ask.

I hold still, wait for her to determine the level of bravery she needs.

She clears her throat and starts again. "Do you think JT knew I was his half sister when he raped me?"

I internally wince, because this is what makes this story ten times more horrible. But I tell her the truth. "Yes, he knew."

Caroline jerks in the seat and her face pales, her lower lip trembling.

"Beck asked your father that after the graveside service and your dad said JT's mom told him when he turned eighteen," I tell her with brutal honesty. No way I'm holding anything back from her.

"Ally's perfect, isn't she?" Caroline asks in a small voice, and I know what she's wanting me to affirm. That she wasn't touched by the nastiness of rape and incest.

"She's absolutely perfect and she is everything that you are," I tell her truthfully as I put a hand on her shoulder and squeeze. "Out of all of the bad that has happened to you, and even knowing this horrific truth, I know you'll accept every bit of it with the knowledge that you have Ally, and nothing better will ever happen to you in your lifetime."

A tiny sob pops out of Caroline's mouth and she squeezes her eyes shut while she nods effusively in agreement. "I'll take every bit of this nastiness," she says in a quavering voice, then opening her eyes to look at me. "Every bit of it in exchange for the wonderful gift I got out of it."

"No other way to look at it," I agree, dropping my hand to grab hers, which sits limply on her lap. I lace my fingers with hers and squeeze.

Caroline tilts her head and her eyes widen as she realizes something. "The DNA . . . if the DNA in your case doesn't match JT . . . then . . . ?"

I shrug nonchalantly even as a stab of pain lances straight through my heart. Caroline doesn't need to know how bad this feels to me, so I say, "I must have been mistaken."

She shakes her head, and squeezes my hand so hard the tips of my fingers go numb. "I'm sure there's a reasonable explanation."

"Perhaps," I say as I pull my hand away from hers. "But it's a worry for another time. If you're okay with it, I want to get back to the courtroom for Beck. Want to come?"

She nods her head. "Yeah . . . let's swing by the bathroom so I can repair this wreck of a face. I don't want to upset Beck, but maybe it will scare the reporters off if we run into them."

I laugh. "You two . . . your bond is amazing. I know you have a lot of reasons to be pissed at him, but you also have this love that's untouchable. I'm a little envious of it actually."

Caroline smiles at me. "You have the same thing with him. Don't ever doubt that."

And I don't . . . doubt it. But I do worry that might not be a good thing as we try to hold this puzzle of lies together because we're fueled by this love we have for each other.

. . . .

CHAPTER 20

Beck

"After considering the evidence before me, I believe the state has met its burden of probable cause in this matter. As such, I am binding this case over for trial and will set it on the trial docket to commence on April 21 . . ."

The judge's words are still echoing in my head two hours later as Sela and I make our way wearily from the elevator into the condo.

I'd like to say this came as a surprise but it didn't. Not after the motivating factor for JT's murder is the fact he raped our sister, Caroline. There wasn't a judge in the state who was going to let that one pass by, no matter how liberal minded they might be.

After the hearing, Doug, Caroline, Sela, and I all met in the small conference room behind the courtroom. It was a brief meeting and was only for Doug to reassure us not to lose hope. That there would surely be a plea deal offered.

Nope, not even going to consider that.

"And besides," he had said, "with your resources, I'm sure we could hire a competent investigation team that can find the bookie who's behind JT's murder."

Yeah . . . that's not going to happen either, because the bookie or his goons didn't murder JT.

Of course, I wasn't about to tell my attorney that. He may be my attorney and sworn to confidentiality, but I wanted him doing whatever the fuck he could to prove me innocent, and while he might not be able to find evidence of the gambling to connect to JT's death, he could probably find something about the beating being related, and that right there could provide enough reasonable doubt.

Reasonable doubt.

My two new favorite words.

In fact, maybe when Dennis gets back in town, I can have a conversation with him and see if he can give me something to feed to my attorney that will push him in the right direction.

Sela wordlessly heads back to our bedroom while I detour into the kitchen to open a bottle of wine and perhaps put a frozen pizza in the oven. Not the poshest of meals, but I know she doesn't feel like going out tonight, and neither do I for that matter. My phone's already been blowing up with texts from people about me standing trial for murder as well as the secret that JT was my brother and he raped my sister.

Now that I think about it, I'm not sure I'm going back out in public again. Of course, following the trial, that could be a very true statement if I end up in prison, but that's not an outcome I'm willing to even consider. As Doug reminded me, the case is still entirely circumstantial. While money and anger might be motivating factors, Doug believes we'll be able to show that I'm really a guy who isn't moved to violence. I've got hundreds of people who can attest to that. We can build up just as much circumstantial evidence in the opposite direction, and the jury may very well see my side of things.

I hope.

In the kitchen, I open up the freezer and see there's nothing in it but half a pint of ice cream left. Looks like we'll be ordering takeout.

Chinese, maybe.

But I do know we have wine, and I decide on a crisp pinot grigio I have in the fridge. Pulling it out, I efficiently remove the cork and pour two glasses before carrying them back to the bedroom to see what Sela wants to order. I'm ready to get out of this monkey suit, relax, and perhaps cuddle with her after dinner. Maybe watch a mindless movie.

Probably fuck.

That's always guaranteed to get my mind out of my dark place.

When I hit the bedroom, I see Sela in the large walk-in closet taking her skirt off and letting it slip to the carpeted floor. She'd already removed the cranberry turtleneck she had on, and now she looks beyond angelic in snow-white lace panties and bra. Her blond hair blankets her shoulders and falls forward to momentarily hide her face as she leans first to one side, then another to remove her heels while balancing herself against the doorjamb with her hand.

When she straightens up, I'm surprised to see her reach for a hanger and take one of her lightweight sweaters off and put it over her head. After threading her arms through the sleeves, she reaches for a pair of gray wool slacks, pulling them right off the hanger.

"What are you doing?" I asked, perplexed as to why she's getting dressed. Perhaps I misread her exhaustion and desire to go out for dinner.

She jumps lightly and turns to look at me, the slacks held before her. Her eyes are wide for a moment as if she got busted doing something illicit, and then they change right before me into a hardened flatness.

"This farce is over," she says briskly, and shakes the slacks out before her with the intent to put them on.

And I know exactly what she means by that statement, and fuck if I'm going to let that happen. I put the glasses of wine on the long dresser that sits by the door and then I'm on her, ripping the pants out of her hands and tossing them to the back of the closet, where they land on top of a built-in dresser with thin drawers that holds all of Sela's lingerie.

"Beck," she says with anger and frustration, but I don't let her get any further.

"You are not fucking turning yourself in," I growl at her.

I expect her to argue, but instead she throws herself into my arms, and with desperation such as I've never heard, she begs me, "Then let's leave the country. Dennis can get us fake passports. You have enough money to buy us a nonextradition island. Let's run."

"We can't," I tell her softly, one hand stroking her hair, the other her back. "I can't leave Caroline and Ally . . . my business. It's not a good option."

She tears out of my arms, spitting at me like a cat and rage flashing in her eyes. "Then I'm done with this. I'm turning myself in."

"Sela, baby—"

"This has gone too far," she yells as she stomps her foot, her cheeks tinged red with anger. "You are not going down for what I did and you are as good as convicted if you go through with that trial."

"We don't know that," I try to reason with her, even though I can feel myself getting angry at this same old argument we've had time and again. "The judge has only heard their side of the story. We'll put on evidence. They have to prove I was there and I did it and they can't do that."

"They can," she insists. "You've got motive and your DNA will be in that house. You know it."

"The motive is conjecture," I point out. "For every witness they call that says I wanted JT out for the money, we'll have ten that say it's just not true."

"What about the fact JT raped Caroline?" she hisses at me. "How're you going to convince a jury that wouldn't make you mad enough to kill that sick fuck?"

"They can't prove I knew it," I argue.

"Do you even understand the level of crazy you've stooped to by letting this go this far, Beck?"

"It's what you do when you're in love," I tell her honestly.

"You're absolutely ridiculous," she snarls at me, eyes flashing in fury. "You think you're protecting me, but you're not. You think you're protecting the idea of 'us,' but you're not. If you go down, I'm destroyed . . . we're destroyed . . . and that's not protecting me. Stop trying to act like the fucking white knight."

"I can say the same to you, Sela," I growl at her. "You turning yourself in isn't fucking protecting me either. What do you think will happen to me if you get convicted of this? I'm not ready to live with that level of pain, baby."

"It doesn't matter," she screams, beyond reason at this point, as she turns toward the back of the closet, intent on grabbing her pants, putting them on, and then going to the police to ruin both of us. "You can't stop me."

"It does too fucking matter," I yell at her as I grab her from behind. But rather than pull her out of the closet, I push her two more steps until we're flush against the dresser and I have her pinned so she can't move.

She lets out a tiny gasp of outrage and starts to squirm to get away from me, but my hand circles around her stomach, dips into her panties, and I'm pushing a finger inside of her. "And I *can* stop you."

"Stop it, Beck," she grits out, and when her hand locks around my wrist, trying to pull me away, I have a slight moment of doubt.

But I push it far away from me.

"No," I growl into her ear, and because she's no match for my strength, I pull my finger out and sink it back in deep. Her insides flood with wetness even though she pulls at my arm to try to get me away.

"Beck," she says pleadingly. "Let me go."

"I am never letting you go," I tell her, my voice harsh and husky with anger that she'd even think about doing this. "If I have to tie you to that bed and fuck sense into you, I'll do it."

I plunge my finger in and out of her a few more times, add another, and feel a measure of triumph when her grip loosens on my wrist and her hips rotate seeking more contact.

"This doesn't change anything," she seethes, and even though she's practically fucking my fingers right now, I'm surprised by the venom in her voice.

"We'll see about that," I retort, pulling my hand free and rejoicing at her mewling sound of loss. But then she's gasping as I spin her around, lift her up, and deposit her on top of the sturdy built-in dresser. My fingers go into her panties at her hips and I rip them down her legs, which are dangling over the edge. With my palm to her sweater-covered chest, I push on her hard until she falls back against the wall, and then I'm spreading her legs open.

Bending over, I put my mouth between her legs and I eat *my* fucking pussy like a man on a mission. Sela's hands fly to my head, grip it tight, and she pushes my face against her harder. She knows it's my pussy, but she's also reminding me that my lips and tongue are hers.

I hit it hard, letting one hand drop to my belt, where I manage to work it free of the buckle through the magic of multitasking. Sela moans and begs me, and when I sense her getting close, I let my tongue fly against her clit.

"Beck," she gasps, and I have to stop myself from smiling at how easy it was to get her turned around from this ludicrous idea of leaving.

I tongue her harder.

"Beck," she moans again. "Make me come and then fuck me."

I pull back briefly and mutter against her wet lips, "I will."

"Good," she says, pressing me down harder against her. "Because after . . . I'm going to the cops and you can't stop me."

Son of a fucking bitch.

I rear back from her, leaving her hanging high and dry on that massive orgasm that I know was moments away. I swipe the back of my hand across my mouth, and even though her face is flushed with pleasure and I know she'd drop to her knees and beg me to finish her off right now, I also see the fire of resolve in her eyes.

"Yeah, that won't fucking do," I snap at her, enraged she's still even thinking that, but also hard and horny as hell, and more determined than she ever will be.

I use both hands to quickly unbutton my slacks and push them down my hips along with my underwear. I take my aching cock in one hand and snake my other arm around her back, pulling her to the edge of the dresser. Her hands come to my shoulders and she spreads her legs wide for me, all indications that she wants to be fucked. And yet she looks me square in the eye and I know this argument isn't over by a long shot.

The dresser is the perfect height, and with another pull on her body, I have her ass hanging halfway off but her pussy now pressed against my dick. I groan because just that tiny, wet, hot touch has me about crazy with lust for her. I bring both hands to the back of her hips and hold her steady as I slam deep into her, both of our eyes locked on each other in challenge-fueled passion. Her gaze burns bright with rebellion, and I'll be damned if I want to listen to her further arguments while I'm fucking her.

I put a hand to her jaw, press lightly at the joints, and tell her, "Open that pretty mouth so I can kiss it."

She gives me a gamine smile and does as I ask. I lean in slightly, tilting my head, but then my other hand snags the panties I had pulled off her moments ago and I shove them in.

Her eyes flare with surprise and heat before they narrow into a glare. I grin at her and kiss the corner of her mouth. "There . . . now I can fuck you without hearing your ridiculous words."

This pisses her off and she shoves at my chest, trying to push me away from her. I merely get hold of her hips again and pump in and out of her a few times. I'm fascinated as I watch the struggle on her face not to show me how good that feels and to keep that malcontent look leveled at me. Her fingers come to my shoulders and she digs her nails down into me, not sure if that's a sign of lust that she's so turned on or a form of punishment, but fuck . . . it hurts.

So I pull her off the dresser, expecting her to wrap those legs around my hips for leverage, but she starts to scramble off my cock and that just won't do. No way I'm not fucking this pussy now that I'm sunk in deep.

I spin forty-five degrees and push her right into the line of suits I have hung up on a bar that sits high enough that her head clears it easily. I push her into them hard, some of them falling from hangers, and some hangers falling from the bar to rain down around us. I push her all the way back with my suit coats at her back until she's pinned against that side of the closet, and I ram into her hard, holding her in place and grinding against her. She moans, her eyes fluttering in the back of her head, and finally . . . those beautiful legs come around my waist to hang on.

And she needs to hang on.

I let my anger and frustration and anxiety out on her body. I let my fear and love and uncertainty drive the force of my thrusts into her, letting that delicious wet heat cradle me and soothe me. I fuck my misery out on her, burying my face into her shoulder and closing my eyes. I hear her panting against the lace in her mouth and her moans every time I drive deep.

This right here . . . never giving this up, and I'm not going to let Sela destroy this.

Pulling my head up, I find her staring at me, her eyes now completely soft, her spirit completely in the moment with me. I reach a hand up, pull the panties out, and place my lips against hers, all while I push in and out with the force of a battering ram. Little bursts of air pump from her mouth into mine every time I slam in, and her arms wrap around me tight as we kiss.

Never fucking giving this up.

CHAPTER 21

. . . .

Sela

It's a quarter till five in the morning when I walk into the Sausalito Police Department. I left Beck sleeping soundly, utterly exhausted. I left him sleeping with the delusion that I'd be by his side when he woke up.

The only way I was going to be assured of slipping out of the condo was if I could get him into a deep and restful sleep. So after he fucked me in the closet, I urged him to take me to our bed where we kissed, and cuddled, and whispered sweet nothings. I let him make love to me, our eyes locked as we just rocked against each other. I let him extract promises that were nothing but lies while he tenderly fucked me.

"Promise me, Sela . . . you'll give up this idea of turning yourself in."

"I promise."

"Swear it for me."

"I swear it."

"Swear it on your love for me."

"I swear it on my love for you."

We came together and it was so beautiful I almost started crying. Then Beck pulled me into his arms, satisfied that I was put back in my place for the time being, and we fell asleep.

Well, he fell asleep.

I feigned it.

I didn't move a muscle and let him hold me for a few hours, memorizing the feel of his skin, his hair, the pace of his breathing . . . his scent. I inhaled against him deeply, committing it to my deep memory so I'd never lose it.

He never stirred once when I slipped out of bed and quietly put my clothes on.

By the fact he hasn't called me on my phone means he's still in our bed sleeping . . . probably with a contented smile on his face.

Chest pain . . . squeeze of regret.

I turn my phone off, so I won't be tempted to answer it when he calls.

A uniformed cop sits at the curved reception desk and looks at me curiously when I walk in. "Can I help you?"

"Yes, I need to talk to Detective Denning or DeLatemer . . . either one."

"Well, neither one of them are in yet," he says with a smile. "They usually roll in around seven. You could come back . . . there's a twenty-four hour McDonald's about a mile away; you could go get some coffee or something."

"I need you to call them," I say firmly. "Tell them that Sela Halstead is here."

He has no clue who I am and there's no doubt it's crazy that I've walked in here during the dark morning hours demanding he call in a detective.

A flash of irritation across his face. "Miss Halstead . . . I can't—"

"Call one of them and tell them I'm here to confess to the murder of Jonathon Townsend," I say softly and with such honesty he immediately turns to the computer in front of him.

He types a few things on the keyboard as he says, "Just a minute . . . let me look up their cell numbers."

The cop finds them fast as he picks up the desk phone, and with his eyes pinned to me in disbelief the entire time, he calls Detective Denning. "Um . . . I've got a Sela Halstead at reception asking for you to come to the station. She said she wants to confess to the Jonathon Townsend murder."

He listens for several moments and then hangs up the phone. Standing from the desk, he says, "Miss Halstead . . . follow me. I'm going to seat you in an interview room and Detective Denning is on her way in."

I nod and follow the cop through a door that's opened with a code he punches in, and then down to a large room with a conference table. He flicks on the light and points to a seat. "Can I get you some coffee?"

I shake my head. "No, thank you."

"All right," he says as he pulls a tiny card from his breast pocket and gives me a sheepish look as he nods toward it. "I don't normally do this, but Detective Denning asked me to read your Miranda rights."

I just nod, my tongue too thick with fear to say anything.

"You have the right to remain silent . . ."

"You understand, Miss Halstead," Detective Denning says as she sits across from me with her arms folded over her chest and a pissy I-can't-believe-you-woke-me-up-for-this-shit look, "this sounds like nothing more than an attempt by a desperate girlfriend to save her boyfriend."

"I can understand that," I say, wishing that she didn't look so doubtful. "But when you hear my story, you'll believe me."

"Then let's hear it," she says with boredom before flicking a hand toward the top corner of the room. I see a camera there with a red light. "And this is being recorded."

I nod, swallow, and then say, "Ten years ago, Jonathon Townsend raped me."

That gets her attention, as I knew it would, and she sits up straight in her chair. "Go on."

"At least I thought he did. I was sixteen, drugged at a party with Rohypnol, and raped by three men. I remember bits and pieces. A semen sample was taken from me but my attackers were never identified."

She doesn't offer me sympathy, but I expect it's because she either doesn't believe me or she doesn't want to interrupt me.

"Almost a year ago, I was watching TV and I saw Jonathon Townsend on there, and I saw a tattoo he had of a red phoenix on his rib cage. I remember that tattoo . . . it was the exact one I remembered from my attack."

"So you identified Mr. Townsend as your alleged rapist?" she asks.

"Yes," I tell her. "I was convinced he was one of them. One of the others had the same tattoo on his wrist."

"What did you do?"

"I planned to murder Mr. Townsend," I tell her honestly. "It took me six months to get ready for it. I changed my hair color, had to let some facial piercings close up, worked out and lost some weight. Then I joined The Sugar Bowl and my intention was to meet Mr. Townsend, get him alone, and then I was going to shoot him after I induced him to tell me who my other attackers were."

"So you went to his house and stabbed him instead?" she asks incredulously.

I shake my head. "No, I met Beck North instead, and I eventually told him the truth about JT. He convinced me to give up my murderous plot and to go to the police. We had just decided to do that right before Mr. Townsend was beaten up."

"You know if it's true, that Mr. Townsend raped you, that adds additional motive for Mr. North," she points out.

"It does, but Beck never once considered it. In fact, I actually asked him if he'd help me do it and he unequivocally rejected the idea. He's the one who talked me out of giving up that quest. He knew it wasn't the right thing to do."

"All right," she says skeptically. "So then why did you kill him?"

"He called me the day it happened. I had just gotten out of school and he left me a voice mail. I called him back and he said he had an idea he wanted to run by me. He asked me to come to his house to go over it."

"And you want me to believe you were stupid enough to go to the house of a man who raped you?" she asks skeptically.

"You've been right about one thing in this investigation . . . Beck wanted JT out of the company. We were very much relying on him taking Beck's offer of five million in exchange for ownership of The Sugar Bowl, and JT could get out of his gambling debt. We wanted him out of the business before I went to the police so it made the transition smoother. I went to JT's house because I was hoping I could help him to see reason that this was a good deal. I wanted him to take that deal, give The Sugar Bowl to Beck, who is a good and decent man, and then I wanted to go to the police and put JT in jail."

"Tell me what happened when you got to his house," she prods me, and by the fact she's not questioning my story up to this point, I have to take that to mean she believes me to some extent.

I take a deep breath, but before I can answer, there's a knock on the conference room door. The same cop who was at reception pokes his head in. "Detective . . . Beck North is in the lobby, demanding to see Miss Halstead."

Detective Denning looks at me and raises her eyebrows. "Do you want to take a break to talk to him?"

I shake my head. "No. He's here to try to talk me out of it."

Denning nods and turns back to the cop. "Tell Mr. North that Miss Halstead doesn't want to see him."

The officer nods, backs out, and closes the door. Denning refocuses on me. "We were talking about what happened at JT's house."

Another deep breath. "He invited me in and we went into the den. He started—"

"Wait a minute," Denning interrupts. "He hadn't recognized you the few times you'd been around each other."

I give a dry laugh. "I hadn't thought so, but apparently he had. He told me that he knew Beck was his brother and he wanted Beck to let him stay in The Sugar Bowl and he'd in turn renounce his rights to the North estate."

"What did you say?"

"That it wouldn't change Beck's mind," I tell her.

"Then what?"

"He got angry . . . called me a cunt . . . He came at me, so I reached into my purse and pulled out my gun," I tell her candidly.

She blinks in surprise. "You have a gun?"

"It was my mother's," I tell her. "It's not registered to me. It's in my car and you can have it."

She blinks again in surprise, shakes her head as if she can't believe she's hearing this. "Then what happened?"

"JT was crazed with anger. Didn't care that I was pointing a gun at him. Walked right up to me until the gun was pushing against the center of his chest. He actually dared me to shoot him, and I swear to God, Detective Denning, no matter how much I hated him, I couldn't pull the trigger."

She nods in acceptance of that because she knows JT was in fact not killed with a gun.

"He knocked the gun out of my hand and then forced me back onto his desk. He was choking me with his cast on his broken arm. That's when he admitted that he knew who I was." I pause a moment and take a small breath, swallowing hard against the rotten memories. "Said I was one of the best fucks he'd ever had and would never forget someone like me."

Denning doesn't say anything, but she's now leaning over the table, enthralled with my story.

"Anyway . . . he was choking me," I tell her, and pull down the edge of my turtleneck so she can see the bruises that remain on my neck over a week after he choked me, although they're mostly faded. "I couldn't breathe . . . I was dying. I somehow got ahold of the letter opener and I swung at him. It went into his neck and I pulled it out. Then I swung again, I think out of reflex . . . I'm not sure. I was able to push him off me and he fell to the floor. I watched him die. It didn't take long."

"Why didn't you call the police?" Denning asks. "If what you say is true, it would have been self-defense."

"Would you have believed me, given the fact I went to my rapist's house with a gun and then stabbed him in the neck?"

"There's no telling now, is there?" she counters. "There's no evidence left. Blood spray on your clothes, the weapon . . . the positioning of where the gun landed. None of that for us to see now."

"I know," I whisper, looking down at my hands.

"What did you do with the letter opener and your clothes?" she asks.

And this is where I determine the interview is over. I am never telling her what happened to those items. "I'm invoking my right to remain silent."

"What?" she asks in surprise.

"I've told you what you need to know. I've got my voice mail proving he contacted me and the bruises on my neck. If that won't amount to self-defense along with my story, I'll let the chips fall where they may."

"Did Beck North dispose of that evidence for you?"

I say nothing but stare at her with stony resolve.

"Did Mr. Townsend ever admit to you that he raped Caroline North?"

Not answering that one either.

"Did Mr. North help you cover up your crime?"

Silence.

"Did you tell Mr. North what you did?"

Crickets.

"Miss Halstead, if you want me to believe this story, which started out with you telling me Mr. Townsend raped you, why didn't the DNA in your case match up to Mr. Townsend when we put it in the system?"

I look at her sadly and decide to answer in a self-loathing whisper. "I don't know. I think I may have been wrong about all of that."

. . . .

CHAPTER 22

Beck

Shit, fuck, shit, fuck.

Pace to one side of the police reception lobby, turn and pace to the other side.

The young cop sitting duty watches me warily, and I'm sure I'm making quite the spectacle. Mumbling obscenities to myself, constantly pulling my phone out to check the time, even though there's a plain wall clock just behind the reception desk.

I'd woken up and saw Sela wasn't in bed. Didn't even need to call out her name or search the apartment. I could tell by the stillness in the air and the dread pushing down on my chest she'd made a run for the police station to confess. I immediately called her cell but she didn't answer. I then called Doug and told him to meet me at the Sausalito Police Department. I was sure that's where she was.

I'm so angry at her right now I should just leave her here to rot. I should after she refused to speak to me. But I suppose the damage is done and now I have to figure out how to not only get myself out of this mess but get Sela out as well.

Shit, fuck, motherfucker, fuck.

The door to the station opens and I see Doug walking in, looking very different in a pair of dark jeans, a UCLA sweatshirt, and hiking boots. His hair is flattened on one side, and that tells me he rushed out of his home as soon as I called him without even bothering to use a comb.

I jerk my chin to the outside and give him a pointed look. He gets the message, that we need to talk in privacy, and heads back out. Before I follow him, I look back to the cop. "I'm going to be standing just outside. I need to talk to Detective Denning when she's done."

He nods at me, looking completely mystified by the events that occurred this morning. I'm sure he's never encountered someone walking in before to confess to murder.

Doug is waiting for me a few paces from the door, leaning back against the pale red brick exterior of the building. It's not quite seven A.M. and the early morning rush-hour traffic is starting to pick up, but for now we're alone on the sidewalk.

"You said on the phone that Sela came here to confess to killing JT," Doug says to start the conversation.

I nod, and I'm sure Doug knows the look of irritation on my face is not for him. "Yeah . . . She's in there right now spilling her guts. I tried to talk to her but she wouldn't see me."

"Did she do it?" he asks, and I can tell by the tone of his voice he doesn't expect me to admit anything, but I can't hold anything back now.

"Yes," I tell him bluntly, and he physically jerks in surprise, pushing off the building.

"She killed JT?" he asks. "And you didn't think to tell me this as a defense to the charges against you?"

I give him an exasperated look, wondering if this man has ever felt the power of love or the need to protect the way I have.

"I was sort of banking on the fact that *I didn't actually do it* would save me," I tell him dryly. "Handing Sela over was not an option."

"Tell me what happened, and I need the full truth so I can figure out options at this point," he says, and there's no missing the chastisement in his voice.

Taking a deep breath, I give him the short version of the story. "He called Sela to come over to his house. Wanted to get her help in convincing me to let him remain in The Sugar Bowl. He got angry when she wouldn't and came after her. Was choking her. She got the letter opener and stabbed him in self-defense."

Doug's lips flatten out in a look that says, *That's the most ludicrous, unbelievable story that I've ever heard.*

"Just do something to help her," I snap at him.

"Beck, I can't represent Sela," he says, and this surprises me. "My duty is to you, and that's a conflict to represent her. But tell me everything from the beginning so I can figure out if this helps you in any way."

"Doug," I snarl at him in frustration. "I don't need help. Sela does. I need you to do something."

And yeah . . . that last little bit was begging on my part.

He nods at me, holds a finger up, and digs into his pocket. Pulling his phone out, he flips through the contacts and dials someone. When the call is connected he says, "Kerry, Doug Shriver. I've got someone down at Sausalito PD confessing to murder with a self-defense element and is going to need a sharp attorney."

He listens for a moment and then turns to me to ask, "Assume money is not an object?"

I shake my head. "I'll pay whatever the fees are, as well as bail."

Putting his mouth to the phone, he says, "You hear that? Good. See you soon."

When he disconnects, he shoves the phone back into his pocket and says, "You know that story didn't sound plausible. That's going to be hard for her attorney to work with . . . JT getting that angry with her in his own home and trying to kill her just because she refused to help him out."

I blow out a heavy breath, scratch at the back of my neck, and look at him intently. "Yeah, well, there's more to it."

"Such as?"

"JT raped her ten years ago," I tell him. "She had been drugged and only recently realized who he was when she saw him on TV. She was going to go to the police because DNA was taken in her case, but we wanted him out of The Sugar Bowl first. We had a plan we were trying to follow."

"Wait a minute," Doug says holding up a hand. "JT raped both Sela and Caroline?"

"He was a sick fuck, what can I say?"

"But his DNA didn't hit with her rape," he points out.

"Yeah, well that sort of threw us for a loop in court yesterday," I grumble. "I haven't really had a chance to talk to Sela about that, but the most logical explanation is that the DNA taken off her was from one of her other attackers. Her memory is spotty from being drugged."

"Attackers?" Doug asks with disgust.

"Three of them. She thought JT was the one who left the sample behind, but clearly she's wrong. It had to be one of the others."

"Any chance she's wrong in her ID of him?" he asks hesitantly, but it's something I've asked myself already and I know damn well Sela's wondering the same thing.

I shake my head and tell him adamantly, "No. She clearly remembers his tattoo from that night and it's distinctive. But more than that, he recognized her. As he was choking her, admitted he remembered her from that night. Up until then, we thought JT just didn't recognize her. She had darker hair when they first met a few months ago, but apparently we were wrong."

"So he came after her because of that," he posits. "He couldn't take the chance of what she'd do."

"I'm sure he even figured out we were trying to get him out of the business to clear the way to go to the police," I tell him. "He knew it was all crumbling down. The gambling debt, me offering a buyout he could barely refuse, and Sela coming into his life again were no coincidence. Honestly, I could even make the argument JT lured her there with the intent to kill her."

"Now that is something I can finally wrap my head around," he agrees.

"So it's a good defense, right?" I ask, coming around full circle to the reason I called him here. I get he can't represent her and he has what I'm guessing is a very good attorney on the way. But I need to know.

"It's her word against his," Doug says. "What evidence does she have to prove what she's saying?"

"She doesn't," I admit heavily. "The letter opener and clothes she was wearing are gone."

He holds a hand up. "I don't want to know any more about that. That makes me a potential witness against Sela."

Shit, fuck, shit.

This has gotten so goddamned complicated, I'm terrified that there's no way out for either of us.

"Beck," Doug says softly to get my attention. "Sela confessing is not going to make the charges against you go away. You know that, right?"

I nod my acceptance. "I didn't figure it would. It's why I told her not to do it."

"Well, Kerry Suttenson is a fantastic lawyer. One of the best.

She'll do all she can to help Sela. Now I'll certainly make a motion to have the charges against you dismissed, but it's a one-in-a-million shot."

Before I can respond, the station door opens and Detective Denning sticks her head out and looks at us. "Mr. North, Mr. Shriver, let's talk and I'll fill you in on what's going on."

We follow her in, where she leads us to a small office that has her name in brass on the outside of the door. We walk in and I'm surprised to see ADA Hammond there, looking polished and like the cat who just ate the canary.

We shuffle into the small space when Denning motions us inside. She doesn't follow us in but rather pulls the door shut so we are left alone with the district attorney.

"I just wanted to let you both know that Miss Halstead is being booked right now on first-degree murder and conspiracy to commit murder," she says brusquely. "I'll be amending the charges against Mr. North to also include conspiracy."

"What does that mean?" I ask, turning to Doug, who doesn't look surprised by this news.

But before he can answer me, Hammond says, "Your girlfriend's cute, Mr. North . . . thinking that by confessing we'd drop the charges against you. All that tells me is that you were both in on it together, but even if you weren't, we'll let a jury figure it all out."

I open my mouth to tell that bitch to bite me, but Doug lays a restraining hand on my forearm, which silently tells me to shut the fuck up.

"Miss Hammond, I'm going to enter a temporary appearance as Miss Halstead's attorney, just until her attorney can get here. I'd like to see her immediately and I'll stay with her until Kerry Suttenson can arrive."

She looks at Doug with amusement but nods. "Sure, Detective Denning will take you to her and I suppose I'll be seeing all of your bright, shining faces tomorrow morning at the arraignment. This should be fun, gentlemen."

Hammond turns her back on us and I have to restrain myself from leaping onto it, knocking her to the ground, and strangling the breath out of her. I want to pin her down, wrap my hands around that scrawny neck, and choke her until she turns first red, then blue. I want her to fear imminent death and see the look in my eyes that I won't save her, and then I want to bend down and whisper to her, *"You see, bitch. This is what it feels like to be dying. Now tell me that if you had a letter opener in your hand you wouldn't swing it at me right now, just to get one drop of precious oxygen?"*

Instead, I merely fantasize about that and watch as she pulls the door shut behind her, giving Doug and me a few moments of privacy.

"So we'll be tried together?" I take a guess.

"Looks that way," he says. "It's a win-win for them. They get two bites at the apple so to speak, and while they'd be ecstatic to have the jury believe you two were in on it together, they'll be completely satisfied if just one of you is resoundingly convicted."

"Well isn't that a fucking junk punch," I say, and then immediately regret the words. Too crass for a refined gentleman like Doug who is working hard to help me.

"I know what you'll probably say, but I do have to throw this out there, Beck. If you took the stand and testified against Sela, the chances would be much better for you."

"Not going to happen," I grit out.

"Didn't think so, but I have to give you the advice regardless," he says kindly. "And I'm sure that won't be the last time I bring it up to you."

"Duly noted," I say.

"All right," he says, laying a hand on my shoulder. "You might as well go home. Sela's not getting out today, but I don't see any reason why Judge Reyes won't grant her the same bail conditions he gave you. So go home, get some money transferred and ready to put down on her, and oh . . . she'll need something nice to wear tomorrow in court."

I nod, feeling utterly exhausted and helpless at this moment. Doug opens the door and I follow him out. Denning is waiting and she jerks her head down an opposite hallway for Doug to follow her. I head back to the reception area, out of the police station, and cross the street where I'm parked half a block down.

As soon as I'm in my car and pulling into traffic, I call Dennis. It's more than time.

By my rough calculations, he should be in Panama and is probably on a boat right now pulling in some marlin or other sport fish, so I'm not surprised when I get his voice mail. I'm sure it will be sitting behind some calls from the police wanting to verify my alibi the day of JT's death.

"Dennis, it's Beck. I need you to call me ASAP. Sela and I are in a world of trouble. We need help."

I disconnect, knowing that my message is going to knock the breath out of him. I'm sure he's enjoying a nice vacation, drinking beer with his buddies and figuring JT was in the midst of transitioning out of the business and Sela would be having a long-overdue chat with the police about her rapist.

He's in for one hell of a surprise.

I don't head home the way Doug suggested. I make my way to Belle Haven instead because I need to have a very immediate and important talk with William Halstead, Sela's dad. This shit with Sela will be hitting the news quickly and he does not need to be finding out this crap on TV.

He's been kept fully in the loop on what's been going on, and I've talked to him a few times over the last few days when he calls

Sela to check in. I know he doesn't owe me the benefit of the doubt, but he's given it, throwing his full support behind me and trusting in Sela and me when we tell him that I had nothing to do with JT's death.

That's going to make what I'm getting ready to tell him extremely difficult.

As I navigate my way through the rush-hour traffic, I take a deep breath and dial William on his cell phone. Sela gave me his number not long ago but I've never called him yet, so he won't recognize my number.

I'm grateful when he answers on the third ring.

"It's Beck," I tell him. "First, know that Sela is fine, but something bad has happened and I need to talk to you about it."

"Where are you?" he asks briskly, not bothering to pump me for information.

"I can be at your house in about an hour," I tell him. "I'm coming from Sausalito."

"Assuming you won't tell me over the phone, because I can hear it in your voice that it's really bad, meet me instead at the Starbucks in Millbrae; it's on Broadway. We can both be there in about half an hour."

"Got it," I say.

"And, Beck . . . you swear she's okay?" he asks fearfully.

"Physically, yes," I tell him truthfully. "But she's in some trouble and it's going to be on the news soon. I need to fill you in."

"Fuck," he curses low, and it's the first time I've heard him say that. "Okay . . . drive fast. I'll see you soon."

· ·

CHAPTER 23

Sela

Jail sucked. While I was given a cell to myself, the temperature was too cold, the mattress too lumpy, and my blanket too scratchy. The food was barely palatable and the strange noises around me kept me awake all night.

Guess what, Sela? Prison will be even worse.

I try not to think of that just yet, because I've got a million other things to worry about. While it's probably a foregone conclusion I'm going down hard for JT's murder, there are so many other things I need to put right in my life. Mainly I'm worried about Beck, my father, and Caroline, all three who sat stoically behind me through the entire arraignment proceeding. I haven't been able to talk to them, although my attorney, Kerry Suttenson, brought me a navy-blue dress from Beck this morning. It had an open neckline but there was no need to hide the bruises at this point, although they were almost gone.

I had met Kerry briefly yesterday morning after I was processed. Beck's attorney kindly stayed with me until she arrived, informing me that it was a conflict for him to represent me but that Beck had hired me an exceptional lawyer.

And Kerry certainly seemed exceptional. She was tall with dark blond hair that was thick and wavy and serious, deep-set eyes. She commanded attention and her manner was brisk and efficient. I didn't get a single ounce of sympathy from her when we were able to meet for about ten minutes before I was to be taken to the sheriff's department for holding, and I suspect it was because our time was limited. I told her about my history with JT and she nodded while taking notes, pausing every once in a while to clarify an issue.

When we were done, she said, "Sela, I'm not going to lie, self-defense is going to be a hard sell."

I looked at her glumly. "I know . . . no evidence and all that."

She gathered up her notepad and briefcase and stood from the table we were sitting at in a private room. "I very rarely advise a defendant to take the stand in their own defense, but it's the only chance we have to prove it was self-defense. You're going to have to get up there and tell the entire story from the start."

"I can do that," I said in quiet acknowledgment.

I can most definitely do that because I have absolutely nothing to lose. As it stands now, I have not a single thing but my name and the truth, and perhaps life in prison if the jury doesn't buy my truth.

So she left and I went to jail for the first time in my life. I made it through last night, but felt like an utter zombie when Kerry met me at the courthouse. I silently changed into my dress while she went over the arraignment procedure. I only half listened because I'd been through it with Beck and knew what to expect. My attention was piqued a little though when she said, "Mr. North has already made arrangements for your bail so you should be able to go home today."

And now I'm left wondering what home even means anymore as I'm being processed out of the sheriff's department. I'm given a plastic bag that contains my jeans, T-shirt, and tennis shoes I came in with yesterday, as well as my purse. My gun had long been confiscated since I'd offered it to the police, and Kerry told me that my car had been impounded as well to check for evidence.

Kerry walks beside me out of the sheriff's department where I find Beck and my father waiting for me, and I assume Caroline must have gone back to Healdsburg.

Yeah . . . no clue what home means to me right now, but my gut instinct tells me I'll be moving back home to Belle Haven. I know that Beck has to be beyond pissed at me and my breach of his trust is not going to be forgiven easily. I know how Beck feels about honesty and transparency, and the only thing I've shown him in the last twenty-four hours is a woman clouded with shadow and deceit.

Kerry puts a hand on my shoulder and I turn to face her. "I'll see you next Monday in my office so we can get ready for your preliminary hearing. You're going to need to take the stand like we discussed. I think it's worth a shot for Judge Reyes to go ahead and hear what your testimony will be. I think there's virtually no chance he's going to drop the charges against you based on your testimony alone, but we have to take the opportunity to try."

I nod, my head still a little foggy and reeling from everything that's happened. "Whatever. I just want Beck out of all this trouble."

Her eyes stare at me intently for a moment before she sighs. "Yeah . . . well, I'll let you talk to Beck about that."

Not very reassuring on her part, but I still feel good about her representing me. My preliminary hearing is set for Tuesday because Monday is Martin Luther King Day and the courts are closed. But it appears Kerry and I will be working that day to prepare for what I've come to think of as my snowball's-chance-in-hell defense.

"Take care, Sela," Kerry says as she turns away and starts across the parking lot to where she must be parked.

I slowly turn around, bracing myself against the reactions of the two most important people in my world. I simply can't bear to see condemnation and disgust in Beck's eyes; the easier burden is to see the disappointment in my daddy's.

So I look at him first, and find his head tilted with a soft smile of gentle love on his face. In that one look, I know that Beck has told him the entire truth of what happened that night and he still loves me no matter what. My dad opens his arms, and in five steps, I'm wrapped in a hug. I turn my face away from where Beck is standing and put my cheek against his bulky chest while he squeezes me hard.

"It's okay, baby," he practically coos at me. "I've got your back. You're going to get out of this just fine."

My dad . . . my rock. Just like when I was raped.

"It's okay, baby. Your mom and I love you and will protect you forever. You'll never get hurt like this again."

Those were sweet words back then, but I didn't believe them. I was so paranoid about getting attacked again for the longest time, I distrusted every person who tried to reassure me of my safety.

Just like I don't believe his words now. There's no way in hell I'm getting out of this.

I pull away from my dad, still refusing to look at Beck, who is standing no more than two feet from us. When my dad looks down at me, I say in a shaky voice, "Can we go home?"

My dad looks hesitantly at Beck, and even though I'm not looking his way, I can feel the irritation vibrating off him.

"For fuck's sake, Sela," Beck grits out, and his hand is then on my arm, turning me to face him. "Your home is with me."

"But—"

"You're coming back to the condo with me," he rolls right over me.

I pull my arm away, take a step back. Beck looks pissed and hurt at the same time. I notice my father turns from us and walks a few feet away to give us privacy. This tells me immediately that he is siding with Beck on this. By the mere fact that my father isn't pulling me down the street to his car right this minute tells me that he thinks I belong with Beck.

I just can't believe that.

Turning back to Beck, I nervously tuck my hair behind my ears with both hands and tell him with a raised chin, "Beck, don't you think this is over between us? I got you caught up in my crime, and I'm now trying to make things right. But to do that, you've got to let me go."

"You seriously can't be that naïve," he says curtly with narrowed eyes. And damn . . . he looks so beautiful even in his complete disgruntlement with me. Nothing would make me happier than to just walk right into him, snuggle in tight, and hang on.

Never let go.

But that's a pipe dream now.

My dad turns around quickly on us and puts an arm around my shoulder. "Honey, why don't we all go to the condo and talk this through. Beck and I have some thoughts, and frankly, you two need each other more than ever."

"How can you even say that?" I ask him in astonishment. "I've ruined our lives by my actions."

Beck makes a scoffing noise, but when I risk a glance at him, he's still glowering, his hands now shoved deep in his pockets.

"Sela," my dad says calmly. "Let's go to the condo. We've got things to discuss, and when we're done, if you want to come home with me, I'll take you there. Okay?"

What I really want to do is stick my head in the sand, my ass in the air, and become the proverbial ostrich. I want to ignore all of this, go to my childhood bed and stay in with the covers pulled over my head until they come to cart me away forever.

But one more hard look at Beck, past the anger in his eyes, I still see a deep and abiding love within them. No matter how mad he is at me, I don't think I killed the good stuff.

At least I hope.

I look at my dad and nod. "Okay. Let's go."

I rode in the backseat of Beck's car, my dad in the front. I really wanted to ask my dad where his car was, but the silence was so heavy I was afraid my words would sound like a thunderclap. Besides, I have to assume it's at Beck's place and they rode to the courthouse together as a means of solidarity.

Once we get to the condo, Beck goes straight to the kitchen to make coffee and some tea, while I mumble about wanting a quick shower. I didn't get one at the sheriff's department today, although I was given a bar of soap to wash my face, as well as a small toothbrush with what felt like bamboo stakes for bristles and a flat-tasting toothpaste. I felt the grunge of crime sticking to me and needed to wash it off.

I come back into the living room, my long hair wet and wrapped up in a bun, but otherwise fully dressed and ready to hightail it out of here when we're done. I sit on the couch beside my dad and see a cup of tea cooling before me on the coffee table. Beck is standing near the window-wall with his hands in his pockets.

He appears ready for a difficult conversation, much like he did when I told him all the details of my rape. He doesn't look as uncomfortable, but still a bit angry and wary of me.

Yes . . . of me.

There's something about me and my presence in his life at this moment that is making him wary.

I'm totally going home with my dad tonight.

No doubt.

With a regretful sigh, I look at Beck and say, "I'm sorry I went behind your back to the police station. But I don't regret my actions."

"Of course you wouldn't," he says bitterly. "If you did, you'd have to admit how stupid that was."

This pisses me off, and even though my dad says "Sela" on a low note of warning, I stand from the couch, pin him with my death glare, and say, "You should be thanking me, Beck."

"Oh yeah . . . how's that?" he snaps back at me.

"Because I'm taking responsibility for my crime. I'm freeing you so you can go on with your life, and I'm doing that because I love you."

In three long steps, Beck crosses the room toward me, coming to stand on the opposite side of the coffee table. "I hate to be the one to break this to you, babe, because clearly you're in the dark, but your confessing to this crime didn't free me at all. It just ensured we're going to be tried together as coconspirators in JT's death."

"What?" I gasp, actually falling back down to the couch in a defeated slump.

"The ADA isn't going to drop the charges against me," he says, and his words slice into me like a million paper cuts. "She has no reason to. Nothing you've told them disproves that I did it."

"But it's a confession," I mutter, glancing down at my tea

because I can't stand to see the look of reproach in Beck's eyes. "They should accept it and be done with this."

"Oh grow up, Sela," Beck says in frustration with his hands out. "This isn't all about you, you know."

"Okay, that's enough," my dad says, and levels Beck with a look that says *shut the fuck up*. Then he turns that same look on me. "What's done is done. Now it's time to figure out what to do about it."

Beck turns away, walks over to the windows again, and stares out, his arms crossed over his chest. I have no clue what to say. I mean, I just assumed that when I met with Kerry next week, we'd prepare and hope for the best at the preliminary hearing. I also assumed the judge would find enough evidence to hold me over for trial. Then I assumed that the ADA would come to Kerry and offer some sort of plea deal so that this could all go away and she'd get a mark in her win column.

That was how it worked.

Right?

"We need to run," Beck says quietly, and I'm quite sure I heard that wrong.

My head snaps up to look at him, but he doesn't turn around. I then turn to look at my dad beside me and he looks at me with raised eyebrows and hopeful eyes for my future.

And it's at this point that I realize Beck and my dad have this all figured out.

"You want us to run?" I ask Beck.

He doesn't respond, so I stand up from the couch, round the coffee table, and walk up to him. I come to stand beside him but still keep a bit of distance between us and look at his profile. His jaw is set, his eyes are determined as they stare out over the bay.

"You want us to run?" I repeat.

Beck's head turns slowly my way and he looks down at me.

His arms remain crossed over his chest and there's still a little bit of anger in his eyes, but his voice is so very gentle . . . almost pleading. "I want us to have a life together. The only way we're assured of it is if we run."

"But . . . but . . . how?" I ask in disbelief that this is even an option.

"I've got a call into Dennis," Beck says as he turns to me, his arms falling to his sides. "I've got millions at my disposal. With his contacts and my fortune, you and I could disappear."

And finally, for the first time in over a day, Beck touches me. He takes my upper arms in his hands and holds on to me tightly, pulling me in a little closer. His voice is the most desperate I've ever heard from a man who never begs anyone for anything. "It's the only way, Sela. Going forward with the trial is too risky."

"Leave here forever?" I murmur, the idea not fully penetrating. My head swivels to look at my dad. "And you're okay with this? Never seeing me again?"

"I'd rather you be living free and with someone you love than in jail, baby girl," my dad says simply. "It's the best solution."

My head turns back to Beck. "So we run?"

His mouth curves upward to form a tiny smile, and the last dregs of bitterness drain from his face. "I love you, Sela, and I'm not going to lose you over this. So yes . . . we run."

I fall forward into Beck, my head dropping so my forehead rests in the middle of his chest. My hands come to his waist and I grip him hard. I blow out a long breath and whisper, "Then we run."

. . . .

CHAPTER 24

Beck

I'm already saying my goodbyes. It's not been twelve hours since Sela and I decided to run, and I'm already trying to cram a bucket list of things I want to do with my loved ones into a few days. I haven't heard from Dennis yet, but I'm expecting him to call at any moment now, and there's no doubt in my mind he's got the means and the method to let us disappear forever. I know he'll come through for us, and I want Sela and me prepared to run fast.

It didn't take me long at all to convince William that this was the best decision. We met at that Starbucks and sipped black coffee while I told him his daughter was arrested for murder and I wanted to leave the country with her forever. I had to give the man credit: he takes stoicism to a new level. While I know he was greatly disturbed by what I told him—and I told him everything—I knew that his love for his daughter would have him supporting my idea. William has seen Sela sunk into despair so brutal that he'd support whatever would give her the best chance at lifelong happiness.

And running was that best chance.

After William left last night, I expected a bit of awkwardness between Sela and me. I didn't have to rehash all the ways in which she'd pissed me off and left me feeling betrayed. She got it. She understood.

I also think she was regretful.

Well, maybe not regretful for the intention behind her actions, but she understands that she screwed things up for herself when I was the only one at risk. It was altruistic though, and I know she did it out of devotion to me, so I couldn't stay mad. Besides, once she agreed to disappear with me, she was essentially promising me a forever, and it would be hard to stay angry when I was getting something that was beyond extraordinary.

I did have to make sure she understood something though before we went to sleep last night. I was lodged deep inside of her, my cock straining for release and both of us on the brink of letting go. I was lying on top of her, our chests pressed tight and my hips doing most of the action, which brought our faces very close to each other.

My lips grazed against hers as I rocked against her. "Sela?"

"Mmmm?"

"We're partners," I told her quietly. She didn't respond, but I knew she was listening intently because her eyes opened up and glittered with awareness as they locked onto mine. "We figure things out together, okay?"

"Together," she affirmed, and that was all I needed to hear. We were right with each other, and while we may be leaving behind an entire life—a complete existence—it was forever tarnished and would be a part of a bittersweet past. Our future is where true happiness lay for both of us.

It was time to start putting our affairs in order.

So today I'm making the most of my time with Caroline and Ally. Sela's spending the day with her father, because she too knows time is waning.

While Sela chose to go hang out with her dad at their home, I decided to finally put my money to use in an extravagant way. I sent a limousine to pick up Caroline and Ally in Healdsburg, telling Caroline I needed a day to decompress from all that happened and I wanted my sister and my niece to help me do it. She readily agreed, thinking she was helping her big brother out. She had no clue I was saying goodbye.

The limo driver delivered them both to me at the airport and I then shuttled them onto a private jet I'd rented, and we flew to San Diego for the day.

Ally is obsessed with animals of all types. When she first started learning to talk, the words that always came first and easiest were the names of various animals.

Dog, pig, goat. Ask her what does a cow say, and she'd grin and say, "Mooooo." She also gave an adorable pig snort when prompted. She then got better with speech and left domestic animals behind, focusing on elephant, giraffe, and kangaroo, which were obviously harder to say as they had more syllables. Her love affair with all things furry, scaled, or leathery blossomed into something that you knew would be a lifelong passion. I'm betting she becomes a veterinarian. Or maybe even a wildlife scientist.

Regardless of where my sweet Ally will end up one day, and of which I will never have a clue how she turns out, I'm going to treat her to a day at the San Diego Zoo. I'm going to try to cram a lifetime of memories into a single day.

"Did you know that lemurs have stink fights?" Ally says with confidence as we walk along a shaded path through the lemur exhibit. I have to admit the furry little rodents—or primates as Ally officially explained—were cute as all get out.

"Stink fights?" I ask in disbelief.

"Yeah," she says as she walks beside me, holding my hand. "They take this stinky stuff from their wrists and then rub it on their tails. Then they wave their tails at each other and whoever is the stinkiest wins."

I burst out laughing and look over to my sister walking on the other side of Ally. "Where does she get this stuff from?"

"She's obsessed with these nature shows that Snoop Dogg narrates on YouTube," she says simply as we walk along.

"Snoop Dogg?" I ask dubiously.

"Weird, I know," she says. "But they're hilarious and all the bad words are bleeped out."

"And why do they have stink fights?" I ask Ally.

She shrugs, which pulls on my hand a little. I tighten my grip because I don't ever want to let her go. "I don't know. Snoop Dogg didn't say, but then I saw another video where—"

And so it continues for the next hour. We walk through the winding paths of the zoo, looking at various animals. I'm partial to the pandas and koalas, animals I know instinctively would appeal to Sela's soft side. Ally's favorite are the hippos, and we have to practically peel her away from the underwater viewing area so we can see more of the park before we have to leave.

We eat ice cream and burgers. Look at grizzlies and tigers and bright pink flamingos. Dusty elephants and long-necked giraffes. I take a million pictures of her on my iPhone, knowing it won't do me any good because my phone won't be traveling with me. I'll perhaps print a few, my favorites, but we'll be traveling light.

We laugh and I give her piggyback rides and as many hugs as I can muster without making her squirm away from me. And when Ally runs ahead to look at the polar bears, I take a moment to start my goodbyes to Caroline.

Looping an arm around her shoulder, she reciprocates with one around my waist. "Thank you for coming to the zoo with me today."

She squeezes me in response, and because she knows me so well, she says, "What is it you wanted to talk to me about?"

I don't even bother trying to act surprised or affronted by her assumption. I don't have time for wasted words.

"There's no good way out for both Sela and me," I tell her as I keep my eyes pinned on Ally.

"I know," she agrees sadly.

"We have to leave," I tell her, cutting through a huge buildup of reasoning I had planned to offer her.

And all she says is, "I know."

We're silent for a bit as we walk along, but there's no denying the heavy blanket of sadness that covers both of us. My little sister.

The one who I lived for for so many years.

My only true family, and the one who brought the amazing miracle of Ally into our lives.

I've had an extraordinary life. Many friends, terrific travels, wealth beyond imagining, and business successes. I had it all, but I won't miss any of it except for Caroline and Ally. Those two reasons are what had me up the entire night Sela got arrested, struggling with myself over what to do about the situation.

I'd be lying if I didn't admit I considered throwing Sela under the bus. It only crossed my mind briefly, and only because Doug had brought it up that day at the police station, but it was an option I'd be stupid not to at least consider. But it felt like a poisonous cancer within me . . . the thought of losing her . . . and I immediately quashed it.

It just wasn't an option.

I also considered confessing myself, calling Sela a deranged girlfriend who came up with a ludicrous lie to protect me. I'd have weight behind my confession, because unlike Sela, I had access to the murder weapon. I could get it, leaving her clothes behind, and offer the cops a deal. I'd confess and give them the murder weapon only if they agreed to drop all charges against Sela.

That was viable.

But it wasn't optimal.

It left me rotting in prison without my soul mate.

So I started to consider a life elsewhere. There were a ton of countries that didn't have extradition treaties with the U.S., some exotic, others that would ensure a hard life for us. Didn't really matter though. I was going to rely on Dennis getting us to the one where we had the best chance of never being found. Preferably a country with a good plastic surgeon who could make Sela and me look different.

We had options and that's all that mattered. By the next morning, I was convinced it was the right thing to do, so I laid my plan out to William when he arrived at my condo as we'd discussed the previous day. Our intention was to ride to the courthouse together in a show of solidarity and also so we could lean on each other. I was surprised he took very little convincing, and he only wanted to be assured it could be done cleanly without us getting caught and no blowback on family.

I assured him it could be done, even though I hadn't been able to talk to Dennis then. I was putting a lot of faith in his abilities to rescue us, and I wasn't about to let William know that I was flying by the seat of my pants for the time being.

"When will you leave?" she asks, determination in her voice, but it's not hiding the heavy sadness I know she's feeling. The fact that my sister didn't even bother to question my decision shows the love she has for me and her desire to see me happy.

"As soon as it can be arranged," I tell her, watching as Ally runs up to the overlook for the polar bear exhibit. "I'm waiting on Dennis to call me back."

More silence for a moment as we stop several feet from Ally so she can't hear us. Caroline disengages her arm from around my waist and turns to face me. "What do I tell Ally?"

I give her a helpless look and shrug. "I have no clue. Just that I love her and I'll miss her very much. And maybe, let her know her uncle was a good guy, huh?"

Tears well up in Caroline's eyes and her lower lip quivers. "I'll tell her he was the best. Better than any man alive."

She walks into me and my arms wrap around her tight. In order to prevent me breaking down in a public place, I tell her urgently, "Ally's college is funded. Papers in my office. I've also got my attorney setting up a trust today that will put ten million at your disposal."

"I don't want—" she sobs.

"It will make me feel better," I tell her with a gruff voice before kissing her on her head. "I need to know my girls are taken care of, okay?"

She nods against me, squeezes me tighter.

"Also," I continue quickly so I can get this out of the way. "I'm transferring ownership of The Sugar Bowl to you. I have no clue if it will be worth anything after this is over, but hire a good business attorney right away and listen to their advice."

She starts crying in earnest now, tears wetting my shirt as her fingers dig into my back. "I can't do this without you."

"You can do anything, Caroline," I tell her softly. "That's how much faith I have in you."

A tugging on my jeans at my thigh catches my attention and I look down to see Ally standing there. I give her a smile and blink my eyes to chase away my sorrow.

"Uncle Beck, did you know that polar bears' fur isn't white? It's actually hollow and just reflects light?" she asks with a bright smile on her face, but then it slides a little as she takes in my somber look and the fact her mom is clinging to me while crying.

"That's an amazing fact," I tell her with a shaky voice. "I didn't know that."

Caroline pulls away, and with her face turned from Ally's, tries to surreptitiously wipe the tears away. Ally, of course, is way too savvy for that.

"What's wrong with Mommy?" she asks, her own face starting to crumble at the thought of something terrible having happened.

"Nothing," I say quickly as I squat down in front of Ally. "Just your mommy and Uncle Beck being silly, sentimental fools."

I can tell that doesn't quite answer her question, so I go for redirection instead.

"Hey," I say as if I'm struck with sudden brilliance as I pull my phone out of my pocket. "Let's do a selfie with me, you, Mommy, and the polar bears."

"Okay," she says, her lips peeling into a grin. I look at her full set of little teeth and realize I won't see the cuteness of when she loses those front ones. A strong stab of misery and regret hits me deep, but I shuffle my brood over in front of the rail that looks over the enclosure. I squat down again and pull Ally in between my legs, turn her around to face away from me. Then Caroline squats down beside me, throwing her arm over my shoulder, and for a moment almost throwing me off balance. My legs tighten and I stay in place, looping an arm around Ally's waist to hold her tight. With my other arm extended out holding my iPhone, I position it until I see all three faces looking back at me. Ally with her big smile, Caroline with lost eyes, and me looking like a man who's getting ready to lose some of the most precious items in his life.

I make myself put a smile on my face, because this is definitely one I'm going to print. I just hope Ally will remember this day as a happy one when she no longer has me around.

I snap a few pictures and we all stand up. "What do you want to see next?"

"Can we have another ice cream?" Ally asks, and she knows I won't deny her.

"Of course you can," I tell her, and Caroline pulls the map out of her back pocket to find the nearest concession stand to us.

My phone starts ringing in my hand. I had it on vibrate and it startles me a moment, and when I look at the screen, my heart gives a jolt to see *Dennis Flaherty* on the screen.

"I'll be just a moment," I tell Caroline as I step away.

"Hey, man," I say into the phone as soon as I connect.

"I am so sorry I'm just now calling," he says, and I wince because the line is filled with static. "We've been offshore for two days and I didn't even have my phone on me. Now what the fuck is going on? I've got a few voice mails from the police wanting me to call them."

"Long story short," I say as I lower my voice and walk away until I find a relatively quiet spot near an overflowing garbage can. "JT lured Sela to his house. Went after her. She stabbed him and he's dead. The district attorney isn't buying self-defense, and both of us have been charged with murder. They're calling you to verify my alibi at lunch that day."

More static but no mistaking when he says, "What. In. The. Ever-loving. Fuck?"

"We need to run, Dennis, and it needs to be fast. I'll make it worth your while," I tell him desperately.

"Just hold on a second—" he says in an effort to slow me down.

"I don't have a second. It has to be fast."

"Beck, I'm going to help you," he says reassuringly. More static. "Let me get online, get up to speed on what's going on, and I'll get on the next flight out of here. I'll call you with my arrival details."

"I don't see any other options," I tell him, so he knows this isn't a whim.

"Just hang tight," he says, the phone crackling even more. "I'm on my way."

. . . .

CHAPTER 25

Sela

It's Friday, late afternoon. The courthouse is all but deserted, lending an almost eerie feeling to this meeting. Because there's no hustle and bustle of attorneys, court personnel, jurors, and accused, the silence of the building doesn't make this meeting seem real.

Doesn't seem legitimate.

And yet I hope.

There are five of us in here right now, sitting around a battered-looking conference room table that sits two doors down from ADA Hammond's office. I saw the nameplate on her door when we were ushered back here by a secretary.

Beck and I sit side by side on one side, our hands clenched under the table. We both dressed up, on the advice of our attorneys, and he looks beyond handsome in a dark charcoal suit with a summer-sky-blue tie with little fleurs-de-lis in yellow. I wore a simple black A-line skirt and a rayon long-sleeve blouse that had a slight cowl neck that exposed the barely visible bruises on my neck. Even though it had been eleven days, there was still some yellowing to my skin, and if the reminder that I was attacked that night by JT helps, then I was going to use it.

My attorney, Kerry, sits to my left, and Doug took the chair on the end, since he's going to be leading this discussion on behalf of our group. To Beck's right sits an attorney I just met early this morning. His name is Roger Nichols and he's from New York, and you only need to look at his expensive suit and four-hundred-dollar haircut to figure he's a big-city boy.

I pull my hand from Beck's, because it's sweating, and wipe it on my skirt. He grabs it back, locks his fingers around me tightly, and gives me a squeeze.

Doug appears to be casually comfortable, his bow tie spiffily tied. Kerry is vibrating with energy. I can feel it coming off of her. And the New York member of our crowd is busily working over his smartphone, his fingers flying as he no doubt bills out several hundred bucks an hour for whatever work he's doing. You know damn well by looking at him that the man is working and probably doesn't know the meaning of the words *rest and relaxation*.

The door to the conference room opens up and ADA Hammond walks in. She glances around the room with an irritated air and sits just to the right of Doug and opposite Kerry. She's got two manila files in her hands, which she smacks down on the table, causing me to jump slightly. My hands start sweating even more.

"It's a little bit late in the week to be calling a meeting on this case, isn't it Mr. Shriver?" she asks dryly as she pins Doug with a superior look. Like she's the one holding all the cards.

"It couldn't be avoided," he says smoothly. "With Miss Halstead's prelim set for next Tuesday and Monday being a holiday, we felt we needed to have this meeting today."

Her lips tip up and she has a "knowing" look in her eyes. She strokes a finger on the files in front of her—clearly one for me and one for Beck—and gives Doug a contemplative look before she says, "Mr. Shriver, I'm not sure I really want to entertain a plea offer from you or Miss Suttenson. The evidence is mounting. In fact, we got in some more DNA results just yesterday that places the defendants in Mr. Townsend's house."

My heart is pounding as I take in her smug look and her condescending tone. She holds all the power here and we are doing nothing more than making a play to take it from her. My entire world depends on this working, and that's a lot of stress to bear right now.

If it doesn't work, however, Beck and I are prepared to run. This weekend, as a matter of fact. Dennis assured us he could get us out of the country quickly and with good documents.

"Miss Hammond," Doug says gently. "We are not here to discuss a plea deal for either of the defendants."

"You're not?" Her eyes widen with surprise.

"No," he says matter-of-factly. "In fact, we're here to discuss you dropping charges against Miss Halstead and Mr. North."

It's an indication of the level of her ego when Hammond's head falls backward and her mouth opens to let out a deep laugh of delight. Her eyes are shining with amusement as she tilts her head back into position, carefully sweeping her gaze over all the occupants of the room. She doesn't even hesitate when she looks at Mr. Nichols, who I note has been steadily texting or emailing or whatever the hell he's doing on his smartphone while this conversation is being played out.

"Mr. Shriver," Hammond says as the smile slides off her face and her eyes glow with an iciness I've never seen before. "I will never drop these charges. I have sufficient evidence to make my case and I'm sorry, but your clients are just going to have to suffer the consequences of their rash acts."

"I think you might feel differently after you've seen something," he tells her calmly, refusing to get flustered by her bullish ways.

"And what could that possibly be?" she asks sarcastically.

Doug nods down the table toward Roger Nichols, who

doesn't even look up from his phone. He takes a few more seconds, his thumbs flying over the screen, and I hear Hammond make a sound of irritation in her throat. Finally, he taps the screen one final time and says, "There. That's taken care of."

Then his head lifts up and he pins Hammond with a challenging stare. "Miss Hammond. My name is Roger Nichols. I practice criminal law in New York—"

In a move that's beyond rude, Hammond turns to Doug and gives an amused chuckle. "Doug, tell me you didn't bring in some big gun all the way from New York to help out your case. You're more than adequate to represent Mr. North."

No one could take that statement from her as a compliment, as the derision in her voice conveys a distinct lack of respect for Beck's attorney.

Nichols answers instead. "I am indeed a big gun all the way from New York, Miss Hammond, but I'm not representing Mr. North or Miss Halstead."

"Then why are you in this room?" she snaps.

Nichols opens the laptop that has been sitting in front of him completely ignored until this moment. He punches a few of the keys and turns it to face Hammond as he says, "Because we have evidence that proves Miss Halstead acted in self-defense and Mr. North was not there when it happened."

And yup . . . that's a strangled noise she makes now, followed by a scoffing cough. "You can't expect me to believe—"

"Miss Hammond," Nichols interrupts with a feral flash in his eyes. "I strongly suggest you be quiet and watch this before you embarrass yourself further."

Seven hours earlier . . .

There's a knock on the door and Beck gets up from where he sits next to me at the dining room table to answer it. Kerry's on the other side, looking flustered. "Sorry I'm late, traffic was a bitch."

"No worries," I say from my seat as she walks in and looks around at the people assembled. She nods at Doug, who's sipping on coffee, but looks curiously at Dennis, who is sitting beside me.

Beck makes introductions.

"Kerry, this is Dennis Flaherty. He's an investigator who works for me. And that man over there"—pauses and points to Roger Nichols, who is standing in the living room texting on his phone—"is Dennis' attorney from New York."

He looks up from his phone, walks into the dining area, and extends a hand to Kerry. "Roger Nichols."

She shakes it as she asks Beck, "So what's going on? What's so urgent you asked us all here?"

Beck moves and pulls out a chair for Kerry, then comes to stand behind me. Neither Beck nor I have any clue why we're all here. We just did what Dennis asked, which was to gather our attorneys.

That's done and Dennis, interestingly enough, brought his own attorney in from New York. When we're all seated around the table, Dennis pulls his iPad out from his briefcase sitting on the couch and turns to us. "When Beck originally hired me to work for him, it was to investigate JT and see if the identifications of Sela's other attackers could be made. As part of my service, I set up surveillance on Mr. Townsend, which included tapping into his home security system. I was trying to see if he had any contact with the other attackers or use any of his conversations to find out more about them."

A jolt of surprise stiffens my spine and I tilt my head up and to the side to look at Beck standing behind me. His eyes are filled with shock and confusion as they return my stare.

Dennis taps on the screen of the iPad and a black-and-white

video starts to play. At first, I can't place what I'm looking at, but then I understand. It's the inside of JT's den taken from the southwest corner of the room. The couch and back wall of windows runs across the top of the screen, and the desk where we had our scuffle sits at the bottom right.

And holy shit, that's JT walking in from the left with me following.

I gasp as I realize what I'm looking at.

The actual events of that night.

I'm even more stunned when I hear JT say like a ghost from the past, "Want something to drink?"

My head snaps toward Dennis and he gives me a casual smile. "I was able to tap into video *and* audio. He had a state-of-the-art system set up but it wasn't activated. He wasn't paying any company to monitor his house. It was ridiculously easy to hijack the feed, which we routed straight to my office server."

We all watch in silence, but there's no mistaking the increasing buzz of energy as the video continues. Kerry gasps when I pull my gun on JT.

Doug cringes when JT walks up to me, lets the barrel push into his chest, and says, "I dare you to fucking do it, Sela."

And Beck's hands come to wrap around me from behind as he mutters, "Jesus fuck" when JT's hands wrap around my throat and he screams, "You goddamn filthy cunt!"

Beck curses again when JT admits to raping Caroline and Kerry mutters, "Unbelievable."

We all watch as JT tries to kill me and then I pull out a miracle of all miracles . . . the letter opener. I have to close my eyes as my arm swings and makes contact. I don't open them again until I hear his body hit the carpet with a *thump*.

Dennis taps a button on the screen and stops the video, and we all stare back at him in stunned silence. You'd think he'd be

gloating right now. You'd think we'd all be screaming and danc-
ing in victory.

But as stunned as I am by Dennis having this, I have no clue
how this can help.

"Well, someone say something," Dennis says lightly to the
group.

"Is that enough to get Sela and me off the hook?" Beck asks
to no one in particular as he straightens up from behind me but
keeps his hands on my shoulders.

"It definitely proves self-defense," Kerry says confidently. "No
jury will convict her after watching that."

"And it proves Beck wasn't there," Doug says with wonder in
his voice that he's watching evidence that completely exonerates
his client. But then his tone turns somber. "But the video would
have to be authenticated."

"What do you mean?" Beck asks. "There's no doubt that's JT
and Sela on that video. It's crystal clear."

Doug shakes his head. "Doesn't matter. Before it could come
into evidence, it would have to be authenticated by the person
responsible for the video."

All heads turn toward Dennis. He nods to Roger. "That's why
I asked my attorney here. He's already seen this, and obviously
there are certain repercussions for me."

Roger nods. "Invasion of privacy, which is a criminal offense.
It carries up to six months in jail and a thousand-dollar fine."

"Then we can't use it," I say as my heart sinks. "No way we're
putting Dennis out there like that."

"Well, Roger and I came up with an idea," Dennis says, and I
can't help the hope that swells up in my chest again. Beck's fingers dig into my shoulders. "We take this to the DA and let her
watch it. See if she'll do the moral thing and accept it. If she
doesn't, we then threaten her with a leak to the press. Worst-case

scenario, I'll testify and authenticate it. I'm not too worried about criminal charges against me anyway, but I'd rather avoid the possibility first by trying out this idea."

"No," I say at the same time Beck does. While we didn't mind Dennis helping us set up a bribery for VanZant or getting us out of the country, this is asking him to stick his neck out publicly for us.

"It could totally work," Kerry says with excitement.

"It's at least worth a try," Doug says.

Dennis turns his gaze on me and Beck. "Let's go for it, okay?"

Back in present time . . .

The video finishes but I'm not watching it. I'm on the same side of the table as Roger and he's got the screen pointed toward ADA Hammond, which is even better, because I get to observe her reactions. In fact, not a single person at this table other than Hammond is paying attention to the video. We're all watching her.

First confusion as she leans forward to get a better look, narrowing her eyes.

When JT walks into the picture, followed by me, still confusion.

Then I see awareness filter in when JT offers me the drink. Her brow furrows and then presses into disbelief as she watches him float his idea by me to convince Beck to keep him in The Sugar Bowl and my refusal.

She locks her jaw tight when he comes after me, and her eyes narrow further when I pull the gun out.

All exactly like I told the police it happened.

It's then with bitterness as she watches the rest of the video, her chest rising and falling more deeply than her smug state of egotistical confidence had her breathing before.

Roger plays it all the way to the aftermath of JT's death as I look down at him, then as I walk like a zombie to pick up my gun. My sobs of anguish are loud and I bet are piercing her ears as she watches. I then grab the letter opener and leave the room from bottom left before the screen goes black.

"Who do you represent?" Hammond grits out as she nods down at the computer then back to Roger.

"I'm not authorized to say," Roger says smoothly. "But it's the owner of this video."

"Why isn't he here?" she asks.

"Not relevant," Roger deflects. "But what is relevant is that you are now in possession of evidence that exonerates these two from the charges. We'd respectfully request that you dismiss them."

"I can't just accept a video from someone I don't know," she scoffs. "This is out of left field. It's shenanigans, and I'm thinking because your client isn't here, it's because this video was obtained illegally. In fact, I'm guessing you've got no way to truly authenticate this and that means it's not coming into evidence."

Doug gives a cough to clear his throat, and tries not to sound like a disappointed dad, but fails miserably. "Is your ego so precious to you, Miss Hammond, that you'd let two innocent people go to jail so you don't have to admit you made a mistake?"

Before she can answer, and I can see she was going to defend her position, Roger says, "Miss Hammond, I'm only offering this once. If you don't accept this video as authentic evidence right now, my client has authorized me to turn this over to the press."

Hammond's eyes go wide.

"Along with the video, I'm also going to hand over your financial records, which include campaign contributions for your bid for district attorney. I believe the primary is in less than two months, and it looks like Colin and Candace Townsend contributed the maximum amount to you not three days ago. Clearly you have a very serious conflict here."

Hammond makes a choking sound in her throat and her face flames red. "That contribution has nothing to do with my oath as an officer of the court, so—"

"Save it, Miss Hammond. I've got a red-eye flight to catch back to the East Coast. I'm only going to cancel that flight if you don't dismiss the charges, and in that case, I'm going to stay overnight and hit all the major news media outlets tomorrow. Your weight in this county won't equate to a feather pillow when I'm done with you."

"That's blackmail," she practically screeches.

Roger just looks back at her silently, letting her know the ball's in her court. He doesn't negotiate.

My heart pounds terribly and Beck and I squeeze each other's hands brutally.

"But what about obstruction of justice?" she throws out. "Miss Halstead didn't report the crime; she took the murder evidence . . . someone needs to pay for something here."

"She's already paid," Beck says quietly beside me, and I jump in surprise that he's spoken. We were specifically advised to keep our mouths shut. "She paid with her innocence when that monster raped her and then got his buddies to rape her again and again. She's paid in blood and tears and semen and sweat. You are not taking anything else from her."

Hammond's eyes lock with Beck's, and I know this is the final showdown.

. . . .

CHAPTER 26

Beck

"Be quiet everyone," William yells above the chattering around my living room and dining room. "It's on."

He's well on his way to being drunk, and fortunately, his girl-friend, Maria, is here to drive him home, although we'll try to insist they stay the night.

William grabs the remote from the coffee table and aims it at the flat-screen TV mounted above the fireplace where he increases the volume. It shows a picture of the Marin County Courthouse with a banner across the bottom that says BREAKING NEWS and below that TOWNSEND MURDER CHARGES.

Everyone falls silent and I move to stand beside Sela, who is talking to Kerry as they both sip on whiskey. All eyes focus on the TV and mine fall to Sela for just a minute. I haven't seen her look this carefree and easy in weeks. It transforms her into an angel beyond trite words of description.

The courthouse picture fades and is replaced by video with the word LIVE in the upper right-hand corner and a male reporter standing in front of the courthouse. His hair is perfectly coiffed and his tan expensive. He looks soberly at the camera and says,

"There's breaking news out of Marin County this evening as Assistant District Attorney Suzette Hammond announced in a press conference that all charges are being dropped against Beck North and Sela Halstead. As you know, North and Halstead were charged with murder and conspiracy to commit murder . . ."

William gives out a drunken whoop as the reporter drones on but none of us cheer. This isn't surprising news to us, as before we left that conference room a few hours ago, we had Hammond's agreement to drop the charges in exchange for us turning over the video so she could show it to Colin and Candace. I didn't like the bitch one bit, but I did have a certain grudging respect for the fact that she wanted to make sure they got some closure.

And probably keep her campaign contribution intact.

But whatever.

The point being, we all came to the condo and cracked open the liquor to celebrate. Sela followed Kerry's suit and had whiskey, Dennis and I beer, Doug sipped on red wine, while William alternated between shots of whiskey chased by beer. Maria was the only one not drinking since she was planning on driving a drunk William home, and Roger wasn't kidding . . . he caught the red-eye flight out of San Francisco.

Doug found out that Hammond was going to give a press conference, and had in fact been fielding a few calls from reporters wanting a statement from the defendants, so we'd all been waiting for this news segment as we celebrated.

". . . said that evidence came to light—a video apparently—that supported Miss Halstead's claim of self-defense and that Mr. North was not involved at all. ADA Hammond has said that video will be released once the victim's family has been able to view it. In a call to North's attorney, Doug Shriver, a statement was issued on behalf of both defendants where they stated, 'We're just happy to have this ordeal over and look forward to moving on with our lives.' "

The reporter signs off and everyone starts the happy buzz of chatter again, but Sela and I lock eyes on each other.

Yes, we are ready to move on with our lives, although I have no clue what that will even look like.

It doesn't matter though. Just yesterday, I thought it might involve living in a dusty village in southern Mexico where Sela and I would raise goats or something.

She smiles at me, and I would have loved her there as much as here, regardless if we smelled like goat shit.

I look around at the people in my home. Some people I've known forever—namely Caroline and Ally, who came over as soon as I called them from the courthouse. Most of the others are recent additions to my life and I'm not sure what I ever did to deserve this type of support. I've done bad things and screwed up a few times over the past few months. I've contemplated killing someone, bribed another, and eventually covered up a murder.

Because I did it all in the name of love doesn't make me a good man.

It merely makes me clichéd.

Regardless, I can't castigate myself anymore tonight, as I'm merely too happy and satisfied that Sela's safe and she's not leaving my side. We've come out the winners in this frightful game of cat and mouse, and I'm going to relish the victory.

Selfish?

Absolutely.

Can I atone for these sins?

God I hope so.

CHAPTER 27

. . . .

Sela

"More whiskey?" I hear from behind me and turn with a smile to see Dennis walking into the kitchen. Just over his shoulder, I can see the rest of our motley gang standing around, talking about our victory. Beck gives me a quick glance, smiles, and goes back to talking to Caroline, who has her arm around his waist and her other grasping a glass of wine.

"Well, we are celebrating, right?" I ask with a laugh, and set the glasses on the counter while I reach for the bottle of Jack.

"That we are," he agrees as he goes to the fridge to pull out another beer.

As I pour the amber liquid into the glasses, already feeling an impending hangover, Dennis walks over to me and leans a hip against the counter. "You holding up okay?"

I give him a quick look and then back to the pour. "Of course. Why wouldn't I be?"

His voice lowers and he says, "It's just . . . have you even processed what happened with JT? Things moved so fast and you and Beck got all tied up in not getting caught."

Slick, icy fingers grab ahold of my spine, sending shivers upward until my neck prickles. Dennis is surprisingly adept at reading people, and honestly, I hadn't realized I hadn't processed what I did until I watched that video this morning. Or rather, I watched until the moment I swung that letter opener. I didn't need that grisly moment stamped upon my memory.

Having lived through the actual horror, I just didn't need the reminder.

I set the bottle down and recap it, turning to face him and resting my opposite hip against the counter. I have no problem admitting to him, "I'm horrified by what I did. I didn't realize taking a human life, even of a human being I detested beyond anything in this world, would feel so—so—"

"Burdensome?" he guesses.

Yes.

Burdensome. That's exactly it.

"I feel like I'll have a reckoning one day because it was wrong," I tell him truthfully. "Because I did something that wasn't within my right to do. I'm not sure if I believe in a higher power or what, but I have this feeling—just deep in my gut—that says I've been tainted by it. And I haven't really understood that feeling until just now. Because I didn't have time to think about it before."

Dennis nods, his eyes soulful and full of grave understanding. "I think the guilt is a common feeling, Sela. Anytime you do harm, a good person is going to feel it."

"Will it go away?" I ask him, wondering if perhaps my penance is to always feel it.

He shrugs. "I don't know. It's not an emotion I'm all that used to feeling."

I blink at him in surprise. "You say that as if you're implying you're not a good person. Look at everything you've done for Beck and me. You were going to put yourself at criminal risk for us by authenticating that video if the ADA didn't dismiss the charges."

Dennis gives a low laugh, his eyes shining with amusement. "You're adorable," he says with flashing teeth.

"I don't understand," I say, because I know he's gently mocking me for something.

"Sela, with my contacts, my former family . . . I wasn't going to get charged with anything," he says quietly. Not in an egotistical, *I'm-above-the law* way, but in a way that says simply *I'm the man who's sold his soul to the devil, and with that sacrifice also comes great rewards.*

Potentially evil rewards, but great nonetheless.

I shake my head at him. "Maybe so, but I refuse to think of you as anything less than a good man."

He smiles at me and pushes off from the counter. "Just remember one thing," he says before he heads back into the party. "Don't ever forget what that fuck did to you. The pain he caused. The innocence he destroyed. Go back to that anger and let it help fill part of that deep pit of guilt you're developing, because by my way of thinking, JT deserved what he got and I'm glad you did it."

My mouth hangs open silently as he walks past me, but I don't respond. I know he's talking about his wife and revenge and how good it must have felt to him when he exacted it. I want to argue with him, because that's not me.

But deep down I know there's some truth to what he's saying. I might feel horrible for taking another life, but I'm not sad JT is gone from this existence. My world is safer. Some other unsuspecting woman out there is safer.

I'll let that thought soothe my conscience and I'll keep that in reserve for when I get down on myself.

"That was a deep conversation," I hear from behind me and turn slowly to see Beck walking into the kitchen.

"Eavesdropping?" I ask with a cocked eyebrow.

He walks up to me, puts his hands to my waist, and pulls me

in close. "Couldn't help it. Wanted to make sure he wasn't hitting on my girlfriend."

I give a husky laugh because no way Beck even had that remote thought. There's few people he trusts in his life, and Dennis Flaherty is now unconditionally one of them.

I snuggle into his chest, feel his heartbeat, inhale his scent deep into my lungs and hold it there for a moment. When I let it out, I tell him, "I can't help being conflicted over what I did to JT. Is that disappointing to you?"

"No, baby," he says, squeezing me tight. "It makes you beautiful and kind and forgiving."

"I didn't forgive him," I argue.

"No, but you forgave what life handed you. You made peace with your pain long before you had to take his life and that's why you're conflicted," he says, and the man is wise beyond his years.

That makes perfect sense to me.

"Thank you for saying that," I whisper.

"Thank you for loving me," he says back so reverently I have to pull away and look into his face. I'm almost bowled over by the naked expression of devotion on his face.

"Beck?" I ask, my head tilted, because I can tell he's got something on his mind.

His hands come to my face. "Sela, there is no one in this world I love more than you. And I mean no one. I don't even bother questioning why you came into my life, or the crappy circumstances we were both handed. It was fucking destiny. Like there was this massive puzzle in front of me . . . of a life that was simple at times but still lacking. And I didn't know it was lacking, but there were these pieces missing. I didn't know what they were until you came along, and the pieces started falling into place."

I swallow against the emotion clogging my throat. "Pieces?"

"You gave me all the pieces that were missing," he says with a smile. His fingers stroke my cheeks. "Laughter, comfortable silence, a sounding board. Fucking amazing sex. Love. Devotion. Care. Did I mention amazing sex?"

I laugh and tuck my lower lip in, biting at it to keep from quivering with emotion.

"The point being, the puzzle is solved. You put all the missing pieces together and I'm so fucking complete and balanced right now, I feel like I could conquer the world with you at my side."

"Oh, Beck," I murmur, going up on tiptoes to kiss him lightly. I bring my hands to his face and hold him tight. "You gave me things I never dared hope for in this life. I never believed I would ever have true happiness. I just didn't believe it was possible, but you've proven me wrong on that."

"And I give you great orgasms," he says with a wink.

"Yes, that's what I love about you the most," I say dryly, but then go up to kiss him again. "You give me everything. You are my everything. And today our life starts brand new."

"What should we do?" he asks curiously, eyes bright and shining with beer, victory, and love.

"I think we should move to the beach," I throw out at him. "It's different. A major change. And besides, you can do your work from anywhere."

"I think we could do that," he says, looping his arm around my shoulder and turning me back toward the party. As we walk toward our friends, he reminds me, "But remember, you said it had to have whitewashed cabinets and a peeling linoleum floor that will need to be replaced but we'll never do so because it will be so charming."

"You remembered," I say with a laugh as my arm goes around his waist.

"I remember every smile you've brought to my face, Sela. And I can't wait for tomorrow because I know you'll do it again."

. . . .

Sela

My life is like a mental scrapbook, clips and images that I easily call forth into my mind that chronicle my journey of growth, salvation, and redemption. I try not to think about the past too much, but rather choose to start remembering them where the story left off, so you can judge the merits of how far I've come.

Three weeks after murder charges were dropped . . .

It's been three weeks since the charges were dropped against Beck and me, but it seems like a lifetime ago. We've already instituted so much change in our life that sometimes the past feels unreal to either of us. We're big believers of "clean slates" and we decided that we needed to simplify things so that we could start creating a new life.

We also need to leave California behind.

"The best feature by far," the Realtor says as she sweeps her arm across the narrow living room that leads out to a rickety-looking deck, "is the beach access and panoramic Gulf of Mexico view."

I watch as Beck walks to the sliding glass doors that lead out but I don't follow. I can see the view from where I'm standing in the kitchen, which sits behind the living room separated by an L-shaped counter, and it's breathtaking. A boardwalk picks up at the bottom of the deck stairs and extends out probably fifty yards over the dunes and down onto the beach. The sand is white, soft looking, and the gulf waters off the Florida Panhandle are shades of light blue to turquoise, which gets progressively darker as the water gets deeper. I turn my back on the Realtor and Beck, and take a slow walk around the kitchen, trying to envision what it would be like to live here. I've lived in California my whole life and it's very different here. Flat and hot. A moist hot. It will take some getting used to, but as Beck says, I can walk around in a bikini all the time and he's not opposed to that.

A hand on my hip and Beck is back with me briefly before he pushes past me into the kitchen. He looks at the Formica counters and veneer cabinets, running his hand over one of the doors. The three-story, narrow cottage is just 1,380 square feet and was built in the early eighties. It's very dated.

Very, very dated.

"The cabinets aren't whitewashed," he observes.

I nod down to our feet. "Linoleum."

"Curling in slightly at the edges," he adds.

The Realtor scurries over, fearing the loss of a sale on what is a lovely little beach house but definitely a fixer-upper. "I'm sure the owner would have the floors and cabinets redone if that's a sticking point."

Beck looks at me with his eyebrows raised, and I grin back at him a moment, needing no verbal communication to know we're on the same page.

I turn to the Realtor. "The floor's perfect as is and we can paint the cabinets. We'll take it."

Four months after murder charges were dropped . . .

Life on St. George Island is good. Beck and I moved as soon as I graduated from Golden Gate with my master's degree and we're acclimating. The hardest part is not seeing Caroline and Ally, but that's about to be remedied today. Beck is picking them up at the Tallahassee airport and I'm doing some tidying up of the place. Caroline is staying for a week and then she's going to leave Ally with us for another three weeks of fun in the Florida sun, most of which will be spent at the Disney theme parks.

Beck's work life has taken a decidedly different turn, and while he still has his fingers in some very important pies, his days are completely flexible. He prefers to sleep in late with me, then he usually wakes me up with his hand between my legs and we'll play in bed for an hour or so. We have a late breakfast and then he works from his home office, which is the third-floor loft.

The sale of The Sugar Bowl was finalized last month. Like our decision to leave California, Beck wanted nothing left that reminded him of JT. He worked out an ingenious deal with the owners of a start-up company called ET Technologies, who had apparently approached him and JT months ago about investing in their project to create software that could read facial expressions. Beck was highly interested in this and it got his computer engineering juices flowing. He proposed to sell The Sugar Bowl to them in exchange for 50 percent ownership in their start-up as well as full ownership rights to the patents to the software, since he'd be developing it. This was a good deal for them, as this venture was not without risk and there was no guarantee it could even be done, whereas The Sugar Bowl was a solid business that only needed maintenance. It would provide them with a flow of money to provide them a good life while Beck worked in his office creating this amazing software program.

I hear the front door open and then the stomping of feet as Ally comes flying into the kitchen.

"Sela," she yells out before throwing herself into my arms.

I pick her up, give her a quick hug, and then set her down, where I examine her carefully. "I swear you've grown two inches since I last saw you."

She beams at me and says, "Mommy says I'm going to be tall like a willow tree, which is weird, because Mommy's on the short side."

My eyes flick over to Caroline as she walks in and she gives me a sad smile. JT was tall, and clearly Ally is going to get her height from him. Beck comes trudging in behind with two large suitcases in his hands. Caroline and I hug it out with a little bit of tight clutching and rocking back and forth, because it's so good to see each other.

This week is going to be amazing. We've got so many things planned because the great but extremely hot state of Florida has an abundance of activities, attractions, and beautiful coastline to explore. But we also have business to get down to.

Beck and I are going to work on Caroline hard to get her to leave California and move here. She has nothing left back there except Dennis, who's been keeping a close eye on her for us.

Caroline pulls away from me and looks around. "I love this place," she says, taking in the decor. Beck and I furnished it with a coastal theme like seashell lamps, prints of sailing ships, and miniature indoor palm trees.

"But you need to do some serious updating," she says as she looks down at the linoleum floor. I believe it probably started out as a creamy white color with a design of mocha brown etchings done in four-inch squares and running on a diagonal. Over time the mocha brown has faded to a tan color and the creamy white has yellowed.

It's pretty hideous, but still I tell her, "We'll get to it . . . one day. But we did update the cabinets. I stripped them and then whitewashed them. It was a fun little project."

"You need to get a job," Caroline says with a laugh. "The Sela Halstead I know doesn't do home remodeling."

And she's not wrong about that. The cabinet project was fun, but I'm getting bored out of my mind. I finished my master's just before we moved and I'm trying to find a job as a counselor, but options are limited in this little community. Beck keeps pushing at me to just open my own practice and build it up slowly.

It's a good idea.

Maybe.

Eleven months after murder charges were dropped . . .

I fly up the deck stairs from the boardwalk, Beck hot on my heels. It's an unusually warm day for December, and when it's eighty-three degrees just two days before Christmas, you do what other Floridians do.

You put on your bathing suits and frolic on the beach.

I didn't have any appointments today, which isn't unusual. I only opened the doors to my counseling practice two months ago and I'm still building. I've also advertised as specializing in rape counseling, but in this small community there are—thankfully—precious few people who need those particular services. So I do general counseling too, and most of my clients are couples who are headed toward divorce and are struggling to keep the marriage alive.

"Better run faster than that, Sela," Beck calls out from behind me, and the pounding of his feet on the wood stairs is loud so I know he's really close. I dare not turn my head to look as I'll lose precious seconds on my lead.

The competition is to see who can get to the refrigerator first for a beer.

The prize?

The winner gets an oral orgasm from the loser.

And has to clean the kitchen all week. That's the bigger prize because Beck already spoils me with his mouth.

I fly through the sliding glass door, which we had left open, only fifteen feet from the kitchen when Beck's arms wrap around my waist. He lifts me up, spins me fast, and deposits me behind him, and I can't hold back my shriek of laughter.

"You're cheating," I scream.

"So what?" he laughs back, and then jets into the kitchen.

Except the minute he hits the line that delineates the kitchen from the living room—that line that goes from wooden laminate flooring to old linoleum—his foot catches a curled edge and he trips forward, completely off balance. His arms go flailing in a windmill pattern, trying to regain balance and ease off the trajectory. He's moderately successful in stopping his momentum by slamming into the refrigerator, which almost tips over.

"Jesus Christ," Beck grumbles as he turns to me, his face pale from the near disaster. "We need to get this fucking floor fixed."

I saunter into the kitchen laughing, step into him, and work at the drawstring of his board shorts. My voice is husky when I say, "Maybe. One day. But for right now, it appears I just lost the race."

Beck's face fills back up with color and I can feel his cock thickening when my hands brush against it as I untie his shorts. The look of anticipation and desire on his face fuels me to work faster.

The ringing of Beck's cell phone distracts both of us, and because we really haven't gotten started, Beck leans over and grabs it off the counter. "Beck North."

I watch as his eyes are open and curious as whoever is on the other line talks, and then they close briefly as he lets out a breath of regret. I immediately drop my hands away from his crotch area and rest them on his chest in a show of emotional support. His eyes open up and he looks down at me, as he tells the person, "Okay. Thank you for letting me know. I'll look for your email."

Beck hangs up and doesn't even bother to wait for me to ask what's happened. "My dad had a heart attack night before last. It was sudden and nothing could be done. He was dead when the EMS got to the house."

My hand goes to my mouth as I gasp, but I don't say anything. The words *I'm sorry* won't work, because I'm not sure if I am. I mean . . . I'm sorry anyone is dead, but I don't think his death is going to affect Beck very much. His parents haven't reached out once to their son after the charges were dropped against us, and likewise, Beck hasn't contacted them either.

"That was the estate attorney," he said thoughtfully. "Apparently my father had his will redone a few months ago. Provided for some money for both me and Caroline, with the rest to my mother."

"Really?" I say, stunned by this news. That's the first acknowledgment of Caroline as his daughter since before she was raped.

"Caroline won't take the money," Beck muses.

"Nope."

"I'll give my portion to a rape crisis center or something," he adds.

"I think that's a great idea."

"Now," he says, taking my hands and pushing them down from his chest to his stomach. "Where were we?"

I stop my hands and press my fingers into his abs. "Want to talk about this?"

"My dad dying?" he asks, eyes wide with surprise.

"Well, duh," I say with an eye roll.

"Baby . . . you know my parents were already dead to me,

right? I don't feel much of anything about it other than a general sorrow that someone I knew has died. He wasn't there for his kids when they needed him. My mother the same. So no, I don't want to talk about it."

I lean in and press a kiss to his chest, nodding my understanding. I'm sure this is affecting him more than he's letting on, but I'm going to let him process this a bit and we'll come back to it.

In the meantime, I drop my knees down to the yellowed linoleum and give my man his prize.

Fifteen months since the charges were dropped . . .

"They're here," Ally squeals from the kitchen window that looks down to the driveway. Being that this is a stilted cottage, the kitchen and living room level are actually one flight up. The three bedrooms on the next floor up, and the loft above. Our cottage is narrow and tall, and looks goofy from the beach, but I love it. It's been almost exactly a year since we moved in and I can say I am now an official Floridian.

"Come on, munchkin," my dad says as he walks to the front door and holds his hand out to Ally. "Let's go down and welcome them."

My dad's been here on vacation for nearly a week. He's almost ready to retire and he's contemplating a move here. Maria, he's told me, is not keen on the idea, and I think it's caused some friction between them. The few conversations I've heard them have on the phone while he's been here have been tense. I want my dad to be happy, but I want him to move to Florida more, so . . . sorry, Maria. I'm going to keep pushing at him.

Beck saunters out the door behind Ally and my dad, but I make it no farther than the entryway as I watch. Two vehicles are parked behind Beck and me: Caroline's little beat-up sedan that she drove and a large U-Haul trailer that Dennis drove across country to complete Caroline and Ally's move here. They're going to be living in a beach house about four blocks down.

Ally had flown out with my dad two days ago, as Caroline and Dennis had planned on driving hard and long hours to get here. I watch as Ally hugs her mom, and then Dennis, then Dennis and Beck are backslapping. My dad is already at the back of the U-Haul, opening it up and assessing the situation. It's late in the day and we won't go down to unload this stuff into Caroline's new house until tomorrow, but my dad's a planner.

They start making their way back up to the house, first Beck and Ally, followed by Caroline, and then Dennis. I don't miss the subtle move that Dennis makes, putting his hand on Caroline's hip as she moves in front of him to start up the stairs. It's intimate and I'd wondered if their friendship had turned into something more.

Later that night, we have a shrimp boil out on the back deck. Beck and I bought a copper fire pit and there's nothing like sitting under the stars with the rumble of the ocean and a glowing fire. We're all fat and happy from the good food and the several bottles of wine we'd opened.

Ally's laying on Caroline's lap, her head on her shoulder. Dennis is sitting in a lounge chair next to them, and not hiding in my opinion a genuine interest in Caroline. She seems a bit oblivious to me though. My dad balances his wineglass on his stomach and he looks like he's on the verge of going to sleep in his chair, while I sit on the love seat rocker and wait for Beck to come back with another bottle of wine.

When he steps out onto the deck, my breath catches.

It happens almost every time I'm away from him for more than a few minutes, and when he reappears, it's as if all my senses are on hyperdrive. In my opinion, he's gotten infinitely more handsome over the past year, and that's because his new life agrees with him tremendously. There's not a man who is more relaxed, happy, and content with his life.

"I'd like to make a toast," he says as he steps through the door onto the deck. My dad sort of jerks upward at the noise, blinking his eyes. All of us look at Beck expectantly. He takes the new bottle of wine and tops off everyone's glasses before setting it down on the deck railing.

He walks over to me and holds his hand out for me to stand up. I do as he urges, holding my wineglass as he rests a casual hand on my shoulder. "I'm just really happy to have everyone here in our home. Everyone seated here tonight is my family . . . Sela's family. A man would think he has everything right here that he could ever want, but sadly . . . there is one thing lacking in my life."

I turn my face to him quizzically, because I thought this was going to be a happy-go-lucky toast of friendship, but it turned very serious all of a sudden.

Beck turns to me, takes my wineglass from me, and sets it down on the deck rail near the bottle. His hands then take mine, where he squeezes them briefly before bending down on one knee.

I pull one hand away from him involuntarily and put it to my mouth on a gasp.

Holy shit.

Just . . . oh wow.

Beck reaches into his pocket and pulls out a gray velvet box, and it doesn't take a rocket scientist to figure out it contains a ring. He flips it open and holds it out for me to see in the glow of the firelight. It's beautiful, a simple round solitaire not too big and not too small. "Sela, you and I have been through hell and back, and those fires did nothing more than forge our bond as strong as steel. We've started a new life together and it's damn good. The only way to make it perfect is for you to be my wife."

He pulls the ring out in a suave move and has it on me before I can even take in a breath.

"Would you do me the honor?" he asks, so very formalized and traditional and even a little bit dorky, but it's one of the reasons I love him so much.

"You bet your ass I will," I tell him before I throw myself into his arms. "And no big ceremony either. Everyone we love is already here, so we should head to the county courthouse tomorrow and get it done."

Three and a half years since the charges were dropped . . .

"This has to be the longest two minutes in the history of the world," Beck says irritably as he paces back and forth.

"In the history of the universe," I retort tensely.

"Universe means space and time moves differently in space, right?" he asks, well, blabbers.

He's nervous and I get it.

The alarm goes off on his iPhone and we both rush over to the kitchen counter, shoulders touching as we bend down to peer at the pregnancy test we'd placed there after I'd peed on it in the bathroom.

A "positive" sign.

It's positive.

"We're going to have a baby," I whisper.

"We're going to have a baby," he yells as he picks me up and spins me around. My hand swings out and catches the pee stick, sending it flying across the counter and to the floor. I watch it skitter across the old, worn linoleum that we've walked across for what seems like ages and I think to myself, we should replace the flooring before the baby comes.

Eeep.

We're having a baby!

Seven years after the charges were dropped . . .

My back aches and I don't remember it hurting this much when I was pregnant with Sophie. I press my fingers down into the muscles and arch my spine trying to relieve the pain. I do this with a smile on my face as I watch Beck and my dad down on the beach with Sophie. Even from here I can make out the muscled definition of Beck's broad back, and the darkened form of this dragon tattoo that he'd had completed after we got settled into our new life in Florida.

I had thought Sophie, at four years of age, might be a little young to learn how to boogie board, but they think not. Maria watches them from under an umbrella that covers her in complete shade as she lounges back in a beach chair. Turns out, retirement to Florida wasn't such a bad thing for her, and I think that had something to do with my dad finally asking her to marry him.

I'm happy for them both.

I glance at my watch and note that Ally and Caroline should be here soon. They drove over to the mall on the mainland to shop for a dress, as Ally's attending a dance at her middle school in a few weeks. I'm glad they got out together, as I've been worried about Caroline. While her transition to becoming a Floridian went as well as could be expected, I think that had a lot to do with having Dennis by her side. Granted, he didn't live here permanently because his job took him all over the world now, but his visits had steadily become more infrequent until they only saw each other a handful of times a year.

It was no way to maintain a relationship, and Caroline finally called it quits two months ago.

I want to smack Dennis around and ask him what the hell he's doing, but Beck told me to stay out of it.

"Sela," he'd said somberly. "That man has too many demons and he doesn't want them resting on Caroline's shoulders. It's probably for the best."

What-the-fuck-ever.

Caroline and Dennis are made for each other, but he's too stubborn to give himself completely to a woman. I'd kill to get my psychotherapy hands on him. I'd make him let go of those demons with some hard work for sure.

But I'm staying out of it as requested.

Sighing, I turn from the sliding glass doors and pick up a box I'd set temporarily on the coffee table so I could rub my aching back. Little Sebastian is due in six weeks and I'm in my nesting mode. It happened with Sophie's pregnancy, where I ended up decluttering the house and purging all of our pack rat items. I'm not sure how in the four short years since her birth we accumulated more crap than I know what to do with.

I bring the box into the kitchen and set it on the counter before reaching in and pulling out a handful of items. Mostly papers of various sorts, a binder with recipes, and oddly, a Rubik's cube. I set that aside, as Sophie might want it, and start leafing through the paper items.

I make a stack for stuff to keep and a stack to purge, dropping the things into neat piles without getting emotionally attached to what I'm throwing away.

I do pause momentarily when I pull out a white piece of paper that has Sophie's handprint done in bright blue. I had had it hanging on the fridge for weeks and then somehow, it got taken down to make room for another piece of art and made it to this box.

It goes in the pile to save.

I discard mail flyers for various housing services we've received over the last few years, saving promo items for pressure washing and lawn care maintenance and the like. They all seemed like a good idea when I'd saved them, but now I put them in the purge pile. When I finally break down and get the house pressure-washed, I'll Google a company like other modern people do.

The next item I pick up causes my heart to flutter for a brief moment before it stills into calmness. It's a newspaper article from just about five months ago. The headline reads: PREVIOUSLY UNIDENTIFIED ASSAILANTS SENTENCED TO PRISON.

My eyes only skim the article because I know the details well. Almost seven months ago, two months before this article, I got a call from a detective in Los Angeles. He'd had a hit on the DNA from my rape case.

It had belonged to a man by the name of Boyd Martin, who had been arrested for raping a young woman he drugged in a nightclub. They sent a picture of him to me via email and I recognized him immediately, the way I had recognized JT on the TV all those years ago. Dark hair, tanned face . . . eyes with a slight Asian tilt. A tattoo of a red phoenix was on his wrist, which only further proved to me that this was one of my rapists from that night.

Things happened quickly thereafter. Because he was now up for two rapes, the DA had some room to offer him a reduced sentence on my case if he gave up the name of my third rapist. He jumped on the deal, gladly giving up the details of the crime, which included verification that JT had indeed raped me. I didn't need that little bit of vindication, as I knew in my heart he had. I'd merely had a few things confused in my memory thinking it was JT's DNA in my hair when it was Boyd Martin's.

Best of all, Boyd Martin identified the pale blond ghost who assaulted me and he was arrested. His name was Lyman Porter. It was confirmed that while Boyd Martin was a member of Beck and JT's fraternity, Lyman Porter was just a drunk college kid at that party who was easily roped in to committing a gang rape with JT and Boyd egging him on.

I never went back to California to face my attackers. They both pled guilty to my rape and were sentenced to fourteen years, with Martin's reduced by two years for turning on Porter.

The closure on that part of my life felt wonderful, and Beck and I celebrated that night after Sophie went down with a bottle of wine and some wild monkey sex. I'm pretty sure that's when we conceived Sebastian.

Who at this moment decides to give me a soccer kick, and I drop the article in surprise. Laughing at myself and putting a hand to the edge of the counter for balance, I stoop and pick it up from the floor.

The edges of it contrast starkly white against the yellowing of my linoleum floor. It makes me smile as I stand and scan the perimeter of our kitchen. Before Sophie was born, I had someone come in and finally fix the kitchen floor. But I couldn't bear to part with the old, yellowed vinyl that had borne so many new footsteps from my life.

That flooring was worn, cracked, and peeled. It was curled on the edges and was a hazard. But I had found over the years I had come to cherish every nick and scar that was cut into the patterned linoleum.

So I had the floor guy merely cut out the curled and peeling edges and put in a tiled border, therefore keeping most of the old vinyl covering throughout most of the kitchen.

Beck thought I was crazy but he didn't argue.

Because I was pregnant, and you don't argue with that type of crazy.

I think the reason I wanted to keep it was because I liken this old linoleum to my soul. It's been cracked and stained and hardened by years of rough use. It tells a story and it provides foundation. With care it's been fixed and polished to a soft glow. It's been revered and respected, because it held up to the toughest of times, and most important, it holds the memories of the footprints that have walked, trampled, and tiptoed across it.

It's held up.

It's persevered.

It's faced what life had to throw at it and it held steady.

Just. Like. Me.

ACKNOWLEDGMENTS

· ·

I'd like to dedicate this book to my best friend, Shelley. She's not a big reader, and chances are she'll never read this unless I shove it under her nose, but you know what . . . I love that. I love that she loves me for me and not because of what I do for a living.

Maybe one of our mutual friends will tell Shelley that I dedicated this book to her. I know she'll appreciate it and will call me up to tell me so. Then we'll do what best friends do, and we'll focus on the other important things in life.

Like trying to embarrass each other in public . . .

Or getting too tipsy at dinner so our husbands have to pick us up . . .

Or taking spontaneous girls' weekend trips . . .

Love you, Shelley!!!! So much!!!

Read on for an excerpt from

Max

A Cold Fury Hockey Novel

by Sawyer Bennett
Available from Loveswept

· ·

CHAPTER 1

Max

I stick the nozzle in my gas tank, depress the handle, and flip the catch down to hold it in place. Letting the gas flow on its own, I head across the nearly empty parking lot to the gas station, which is lit up like a bright beacon out here on Possum Track Road. I'm starved and I know my fridge is empty at home, so I'm going to break down and buy some junk food for my dinner. I just won't tell Vale about it, as I don't feel like listening to her bitch at me.

Vale Campbell . . . pretty as hell and nice to look at, but I dread having to hang out with her. That's because she's one of the assistant athletic trainers for the Cold Fury, and most important, working with me on my strength and conditioning. She would most certainly say Snickers, Cheez-Its, and root beer are not on my approved list, and then she'd have me doing burpees, mountain climbers, and box jumps until I puked.

Pulling the door open, I immediately see two guys at the cooler checking out the stock of beer. Both wearing wifebeaters stained with grease and faded ball caps. I, myself, pull my own hat down farther to hide my face, as I don't feel like getting recognized tonight. It's late, I want to get my junk food and get gone. We've got an early morning practice tomorrow.

I turn right down the first aisle, which houses the chips and other such snacks, slightly aware the other two customers are heading to the counter to check out. I keep my back to them just to be safe and peruse the options.

Funyuns.

Potato chips.

Doritos.

Corn Nuts.

Reaching for a bag of salt-and-vinegar potato chips, I hear one of the guys drawl in a typical North Carolina redneck accent, "Hey, sweet thang. How 'bout a pack of Marlboro Reds and how 'bout handing me that there box of condoms. The extra large size."

The redneck's companion snickers, and then snorts. I turn slightly to see them both shoot conspiratorial grins at each other, and one guy nudges the other guy to egg him on. While the clerk turns to get the condoms, the redneck leans across the counter and stares blatantly at the woman's ass. The other guy says loud enough that I hear, so I know the woman hears, "Mmmmm . . . that is a fine ass."

Turning my body full so I face the counter, I see the woman's back stiffen and she turns her face to the left to look at a closed doorway beside the rack that holds all of the cigarettes. I'm wondering if perhaps a manager or another employee is in there, and she's hoping for some help.

But she doesn't wait and turns to face the two assholes, squaring her shoulders.

And god damn . . . she's breathtaking. Looking past the red and gold polyester vest she wears with a name tag—clearly a uniform—I see her face is flawless. Creamy skin that glows, high cheekbones, a straight nose that tilts slightly at the end, and full lips that look sexily puffed even though they are flattened in a grimace. Her hair is not blond, but not brown. I'd describe it as caramel with honey streaks and it's pulled back from her face in a ponytail with a low fall of bangs falling from left to right across her forehead.

While she faces the two men resolutely, I can see wariness in her eyes as she sets the cigarettes and condoms on the counter in front of them. "Will that be all?"

Her voice has a southern accent but it's subtle. She looks back and forth between the two men, refusing to lower her gaze.

Redneck number one nods to the twelve-pack of beer he had placed on the counter and says, "That was the last of the Coors. You got any in your storage room?"

"Nope, that's it," she says firmly, and I can tell it's a lie.

"Are ya sure?" he asks, leaning his elbows on the counter and leering at her. "Maybe you could check . . . I could help you if you want, and we could make use of them condoms there."

I'd roll my eyes over the absurdity of that attempt to woo a girl who is way out of his league, but I'm too tense over the prospect that this could be more than just some harmless goofing by some drunk rednecks.

"What do you say, sweet thang?" he says in what he tries to pass as a suave voice but comes off as trailer trash.

"I say there's no more beer back there," she grits out, gives a look over her shoulder to the closed door, and then back to the men.

And that was a worried look.

A very worried look, so I decide that this isn't going any further. Grabbing the closest bag of chips my hand makes contact with, I stalk up the aisle toward the counter as I pull my hat off with my other hand. I tuck it in my back pocket, and when I'm just a few feet from the men, the woman's eyes flick to me, relief evident in her gaze. I smile at her reassuringly and flick my eyes down to her name tag.

Julianne.

Pretty name for a really pretty girl.

The sound of my footsteps finally penetrates and both men straighten to their full heights, which are still a few inches below mine, and turn my way. My eyes go to the first man, then move slowly to the other, leveling them both with an ice-cold glare. With the power of my gaze, I dare both of them to say something else to the beauty behind the counter.

Because I suspect the only sports these guys watch are bass fishing tournaments and NASCAR, I'm not surprised neither one recognizes me as the Carolina Cold Fury's starting goalie. Clearly the lovely Julianne doesn't either, but that's also fine by me.

The sound of Julianne's fingers tapping on the register catches everyone's attention and the two men turn back to her. "That will be $19.86."

One of the guys pulls a wallet from the back pocket of his saggy jeans and pulls out a twenty, handing it to her wordlessly. Now that they know there's an audience, neither one seems intent on continuing the crass game they were playing. At least I think that was a game, but I'm just glad I was here in case their intentions were more nefarious.

Julianne hands the guy his change and they gather their purchases and leave without a word.

As soon as the door closes, her shoulders drop and she lets out a sigh of relief. Giving me a weak smile, she looks at the bag in my hand and says, "Is that all?"

"Uh, no actually," I say as I give her a sheepish grin. "Got distracted by those assholes."

"Yeah," she agrees in a tired voice, brushing her long bangs back before turning away from me to an open cardboard box she has sitting on a stool to her left. She reaches in, pulls out a carton of cigarettes, which she efficiently opens, and starts stocking the rack of cigarettes behind the counter. I'm effectively dismissed and there's no doubt in my mind she doesn't know who I am.

I head back down the chip aisle, grab a bag of Corn Nuts, and continue straight back to the sodas. I grab a Mountain Dew, never once considering the diet option, because that would totally destroy the point of having a junk food night, and then head over to the candy aisle. I grab a Snickers and I'm set.

When I get to the counter, she must hear my approach, as she turns around with the same tired smile. Walking to the register, her eyes drop to the items I drop on the counter, robotically scanning the price of each. I watch her delicate fingers work the keys, taking in her slumped shoulders as she rings in the last item and raises those eyes back to me.

They're golden . . . well, a light brown actually, but so light as to appear like a burnished gold, maybe bronze.

A piercing shriek comes from behind the closed door, so sharp and high pitched that it actually makes my teeth hurt. I also practically jump out of my skin, the noise was so unexpected.

The woman—Julianne according to her name tag—does nothing more than close her eyes, lower her head, and let out a pained sigh. For a brief moment, I want to reach out and squeeze her shoulder in sympathy, but I have no clue what I'm empathizing with because I don't know what that unholy sound was. I open my mouth to ask if she's okay when the closed door beside the cigarette rack flies open and a tiny blur comes flying out.

No more than three feet high, followed by another blur of the same size.

Another piercing shriek from within that room, this time louder because the door is now opened, and for a terrible moment I think someone must have been murdered. I even take a step to the side, intent on rounding the counter.

Julianne moves lightning fast, reaching her hands out and snagging each tiny blur by the collar. When they're brought to a full halt, I see it's two little boys, both with light brown hair and equally light brown eyes. One holds a baby doll in his hands and the other holds what looks to be a truck made of Legos.

Looking at me with apology-filled eyes, she says, "I'm so sorry. This will only take a second."

With firm but gentle hands, she turns the little boys toward the room and pushes them inside, disappearing behind them. Immediately I hear a horrible crash, another shriek, and the woman I know to be named Julianne curses loudly, "Son of a bitch."

One more screech from what I'm thinking might be a psychotic pterodactyl and my feet are moving without thought. I round the edge of the counter, step behind it, and head toward the door. When I step over the threshold, I take in a small room set up to be a combo office/break room. Small desk along one wall covered with papers, another wall with a counter, sink, and minifridge, and a card table with rusty legs and four metal folding chairs.

It also suddenly becomes clear what manner of creature was making that noise that rivaled nails on chalkboard.

A little girl, smaller than the boys, is tied to one of the folding chairs with what looks like masking tape wrapped several times around her and the chair, coming across the middle of her stomach. Her arms and legs are free, and the crash was apparently a stack of toys she had managed to knock off the top of the table.

"Rocco . . . Levy . . . you promised you'd behave," Julianne says in a quavering voice as she kneels beside the little girl and starts pulling at the tape. The little boys stand there, heads hanging low as they watch their mom attempt to unwrap their sister.

I can't help myself. The tone of the woman's voice, the utter fatigue and frustration, and the mere fact that these little hellions taped their sister to a chair has me moving. I drop to my knees beside the woman, my hands going to the tape to pull it off.

Her head snaps my way and she says, "Don't."

My eyes slide from the tape to her, and I'm almost bowled over by the sheen of thick tears glistening but refusing to drop.

"Please, do you mind just waiting out there? If any customers come in, just tell them I'll be out in a moment," she pleads with me, a faint note of independence and need to handle this on her own shining through the defeat.

"Sure," I say immediately as I stand up, not willing to add further upset on this poor lady with the beautiful tear-soaked eyes. She clearly has enough on her plate without me adding to it.

Since the release of her debut contemporary romance novel, SAWYER BENNETT has written more than thirty books and has been featured on both the *New York Times* and *USA Today* bestseller lists on multiple occasions. A reformed trial lawyer from North Carolina, Sawyer uses real-life experience to create relatable, sexy stories that appeal to a wide array of readers. From new adult to erotic contemporary romance, Sawyer writes something for just about everyone. Sawyer likes her Bloody Marys strong, her martinis dirty, and her heroes a combination of the two. When not bringing fictional romance to life, Sawyer is a chauffeur, stylist, chef, maid, and personal assistant to a very active toddler, as well as full-time servant to two adorably naughty dogs. She believes in the good of others, and that a bad day can be cured with a great workout, cake, or a combination of the two.

sawyerbennett.com
Facebook.com/bennettbooks
@bennettbooks